Into the Desert

A Novel by Xuemo

A translation by
Howard Goldblatt and
Sylvia Li-chun Lin

LONG RIVER PRESS

San Francisco

Published in the United States of America by
Long River Press
360 Swift Avenue, Suite 48
South San Francisco, CA 94080

ISBN 978-1-59265-254-9

Printed in the USA

Contents

This is the story of two women in Western China, on the edge of the Gobi Desert, near the site of the Silk Road.

Bound together by poverty and tradition, they embark upon a perilous journey to change their lives.

Mountains of sand reached into the sky, dropping the sun closer to the ground than when they'd set out. As he began climbing one of the dunes, his daughter followed, stopping to look back at the path behind them. She could see their village, though not clearly, and the houses were like miniatures. It was freezing cold. Snow lay in the shaded side of the hollow. She didn't mind, she liked the sound of her feet crunching on snowy ground.

Seeing her face turning red from the cold, he took off his jacket to cover her and then hoisted her onto his back before walking on.

"You don't have to carry me," she said. "I can walk."

A gust of chilled wind carried her voice off. He kept wiping his eyes. She wondered why as she swayed on his shoulders, curiously scanning the peaked dunes, the blue sky, and specks of desert plants dotting the hills and hollows.

The setting sun painted father and daughter with blood-red streaks of light.

As they crested the dune, he stopped and put her down.

Where are we? she wondered as she rubbed her sore backside and cocked her head to look around. Sand dunes, sand hollows, sand shrubs, Artemisia, and many other things whose names she did not know.

Spring had just arrived, yet it was so cold she could hardly feel her fingers, which lay in the firm grip of her father's hand. She looked up as a crescent moon climbed unhurriedly into the darkening sky.

"Grandpa said foxes bow to a crescent moon, like kowtowing. He told me a fox will turn into a young girl after bowing for a hundred years, a pretty girl, like me."

He stared at her with such a strange look she had to avoid his gaze.

"It's her fate, it must be," he muttered to himself.

Night arrived.

Her teeth were clattering, her jaw had grown stiff. The moon now hung high in the sky, like a frozen disc, surrounded by starry chips of ice.

She gazed into the sky until the stars began to move and blurred her vision. Her thoughts, briefly occupied with the stars, soon returned to the cold air. Her feet were numb, so she jumped up and down. Don't worry, she told herself, Papa said he'll be right back.

The wind picked up, howling as it took her breath away. It swept across the desert floor, raining sand on her face, turning it numb and swallowing all sound. If she was crying, she could not hear it. She tightened the jacket around her, but that did not help.

Where is he?

The crescent moon vanished, leaving only sand and wind, darkness and bitter cold.

She sat down to wait for Papa.

Drowsiness slowly descended and enshrouded her like an enormous net.

1

Early in the morning, before the sun made an appearance, Ying'er and Lanlan left their village for the salt lakes in the heart of the Gobi. Ying'er was taking the family camel, one she had fed for years; Lanlan had to borrow her ride from a neighbor. They were traveling light—kitchen tools, a tent, bedrolls, essential items, water, food, and a couple of weapons they hoped not to have to use.

Lanlan had been taken along on a small caravan to the salt lakes near the Mongolian border when she was barely old enough to ride a camel. She still recalled how the sand hills rose and fell as she sat between the humps, where the rhythmic sway gently nudged her to sleep. Even now, in withered, yellow dreams, she could hear the sound of an erhu, played by a camel herder, his bow producing a forlorn melody that seemed weighted down by so much hardship. The sound carried suffering and yet nurtured hope for a better future, one that, though hidden behind a faint mist rising from the sand, unreal as a mirage, comforted her with its prospects.

They were planning to bring back a load of pure lake salt to sell to the salt-poor residents of their village. They would use the money earned to redeem Ying'er's freedom. Her mother would stop forcing her to remarry if she could get her brother another wife, now that Lanlan had broken the exchange marriage agreement and returned to her parents. They were sisters-in-law, married to one another's brother.

Lanlan's father, Laoshun, had opposed the trip, warning of coarse men, predatory animals, and the many unpredictable dangers they could encounter. Like all men of the village, he viewed the desert as a threat, one that was steadily encroaching on agricultural land and that brought wolves out to prey on their sheep; but it was also the source of desert rice, rabbits, and other desert animals that helped them through poor harvests.

"You can take your brother along," he had relented with a suggestion, when he realized that their options to earn money, even in nearby Liangzhou, were limited. What could they do in such an impoverished area, where even the men had trouble finding work? He could not force his daughter to go back to her husband, and he had no money to get out of the arrangement. All he could offer was a helpful gesture.

Lanlan knew that if her brother, Mengzi, joined them, whatever money they earned would belong to the family. "Don't worry," she'd said confidently, "we can fend for ourselves. And we'll have the camels. I know that worries you. If we lose the camels, we'll pay for them. I don't believe we can't make enough selling a load of salt to pay for a couple of animals."

Finding nothing more to say, he'd helped them plan the trip.

On the day they left, only Mengzi was there to see them off. Sorrowful events had brought the two women together in an exchange arranged by their mothers as the only way the poor could marry off sons without bankrupting their families. Their fates and lives were intertwined beyond their control, as they were expected to stay in their marriages for each other's benefit. Now Ying'er was a widow, her husband dead of liver cancer, her son still an infant, left in the care of her mother-in-law. Lanlan had suffered grievously over her inability to give her brutish husband a son. The desire to gain a bit of independence by earning money to ward off plans made by their elders was the motive behind venturing out of the village alone. In the backs of their minds, however, being free of ill-intentioned gossip and family pressures was a welcoming liberation, a much-deserved break, a desperately needed getaway. Without sharing their thoughts, they knew how happy and free they would be out in the desert. They could not have been more wrong.

After entering the desert, they walked for a couple of hours before making the camels kneel down for them to get up and ride awhile. Up on their perches, they saw ripples in the sand. Camel's hair is soothingly warm, like a mother's arms, creating a sense of security in a world filled with uncertainty.

Ridges of shifting sand twisted toward an unknown future, like a drawn-out night troubled by bad dreams. Bells on the camels' necks traveled into the distance in silky threads shredded by the wind. By feeding her camel, Ying'er had cemented an emotional bond between them. It was a docile animal that touched her hand with its lips each time she fed it. When it gazed at her, its clear eyes were filled with tenderness, but tinged with sadness. She liked to think the animal understood her somehow, and she loved the sound of its cushioned feet, a rustling as muted and indistinct as shadowy images in a dream.

Lanlan had volunteered to take the borrowed camel, suspecting that her less toughened sister-in-law would have trouble dealing with an unfamiliar animal. As expected, they were barely on the road when she had to scold her camel for shaking its head to free itself from the softened elm ring looped through its nose and tethered to her reins. A single tug brought pain enough to make it weep. She wanted the animal to understand what was expected of it without having to resort to the nose ring.

None of them, humans or animals, were aware that predators, their fangs bared, were hiding in a strange corner of their fate, watching with sinister green eyes.

A camel trail is a path connecting oases; it can be etched on roads traveled by carts and horse, or across sandy dunes, where human traces are easily erased. In the desert, established paths lead caravans mostly through shaded hollows. Wind blows clouds of loose sand into the sunny hollows, while shaded ones hold years of packed sand, accumulated over time and solid under the feet. Lanlan instinctively directed her camel toward shaded hollows, with Ying'er at her side. Sweat formed on the tip of her nose. She had once been quite pretty, which was why Ying'er's mother had agreed to the exchange. The girls were about the same in age and background, so neither family could claim it had suffered in the bargain. But time and events had changed her, eyes once set among soft folds were now ringed by crow's feet under a brow creased by suffering. I'll soon look like that too, Ying'er thought, which made her wistful. We've barely lived, and we're already getting old.

Lanlan dried the sweat on her face with a scarf and squinted into the distance.

"Don't worry," she said softly, seeing the wistful look on Ying'er's face. The concerns they shared were left unspoken. "We can make enough as long as we have two hands to work."

Ying'er silently joined her in gazing into the distance.

"See there," Lanlan said as she tilted her head back, "where those dunes connect to the sky? The salt lakes should come into sight after we cross a mountain range and a series of gullies. A few days, that's all."

Ying'er knew that reaching their objective, which sounded so easy the way Lanlan said it, would, for her, be like walking to the end of the sky. She had gathered desert rice in the past, but that had just been skirting the edge of the desert; they had yet to cross a single gully, and the thought of traveling to a strange place all the way to the horizon made her fearful.

Knowing what was on her sister-in-law's mind, Lanlan gestured toward the musket hanging down along the camel's side.

"No need for us to be afraid, Ying'er," she said. "I have this, two gourds filled with gunpowder, and a kilo of buckshot, plus a good many ball bearings. And, of course, my Tibetan knife. If we're unlucky enough to run into wolves, I'll feed them some steel."

2

On the night they reached the first gully, awaiting them was an oasis overgrown with weeds, but still with enough water and grass to sustain their animals for the next day or more. Lanlan could tell the oasis had shrunk. Water from the snow mass on the Qilian Mountains was a relative constant, though the amount could change by variations in the weather. Developments over thousands of years resulted in shifting locations of oases, but now that large tracts of land were being farmed, the oases were rapidly growing smaller—and drier. Like this one.

They unloaded the camels, removed the litters, and put up a makeshift tent, adequate to block the wind, but probably not to keep out the rain. It seldom rained in the desert, so no one worried about waterproofing. After driving in wooden stakes, Lanlan threw up a piece of coarse homespun cloth, tucked the edges into the sand, and spread out their bedrolls, while Ying'er tethered the camels to a spot with somewhat denser vegetation. Normally, they would loop the reins over the camels' neck so they could graze at will, but they did not want their rides to roam too far and delay their travel the next day. So, they decided to keep moving the animals to different spots to graze. Better to be cautious now that they were away from home.

They then gathered kindling for a fire and drank some water. Ying'er was too tired to cook, wanting to settle for a couple of dry buns for their meal.

"That won't do," Lanlan objected. "We have to eat well on

the road. If we skip a meal here and a meal there, that will sap our strength and drain our stamina." She told Ying'er to rest by the fire and add kindling while she retrieved a wash basin from one of the camel litters, scooped out some flour, and prepared a meal of hand-pinched noodles. Ying'er leaned back against the other litter, grateful for Lanlan's solicitude. It had been a tiring day. Lanlan was used to manual labor, but Ying'er knew that she too must be tired.

Darkness had taken over by the time they finished eating. Moonlit nights were Ying'er's favorite, a time for poetic sentiments, but the gods do not bring out the moon for romantic thoughts alone. She kept her feelings to herself as Lanlan lit the lantern, casting a yellow circle of light, small but bright enough. Just so long as long as there's light, Ying'er was thinking.

The deepening darkness also quieted Lanlan, who had not enjoyed a day without misery since her marriage. Ying'er was luckier, for her mind was visited by bits of happiness amid the pain. She was fortunate to have in-laws who treated her well, especially after giving birth to a son, Panpan. As for Lanlan, shattered by cruel reality, she had decided to leave her husband, greatly displeasing her parents, Ying'er's in-laws.

Back when the arrangement for both women was settled, Lanlan's mother and father could not have anticipated the sort of demeaned life they would be sending her into, and in truth she could not blame them, for how else would her brother, a simple, kind-hearted but dirt-poor young man get a wife? Now, years later, she could imagine how it must have pained her father when he realized the degree of abuse she'd suffered. She'd always been his favorite, so she knew he would have preferred for her to stay at home with them for good. And yet, an obligation to honor the marital contract and his old-fashioned sense of marriage had led him to pressure her to go back. "Divorce is such a disgrace," he had said. "People will laugh at us." Lanlan was angry over his concern more for what others might think of them than for her happiness.

Ying'er reached out to touch Lanlan's face, and was surprised by the wetness on her hand. Her sister-in-law was weeping silently.

"What's bothering you?"

"I must have broken Pa's heart," Lanlan said after a long silence. "I know he's never wished me ill, and yet I said those awful things to him. I'm a terrible daughter."

"Don't think like that. You know him, he's put it out of his mind already." Have you forgotten how he can fall asleep and start snoring immediately after a fight with your mother?"

They laughed softly at the image.

"Maybe," Lanlan said "but I still feel guilty. When I think about it, I know he's never enjoyed a truly restful day. He's worked hard and deserved a better life. And I should have been a better daughter."

"But that's what his life is like," Ying'er replied. "Isn't he always saying he can take whatever the gods dole out to him? Who doesn't suffer in life? You take what they give you and try to hold on to your dignity."

Lanlan dried her tears, tears she'd thought herself incapable of shedding after grieving over her daughter's death for so long.

Warming herself by the fire, Ying'er thought about her mother, whom she already began to miss, recalling only the good things about her, now that she was away from home, out in the wilderness. She picked up the lantern and walked out of the tent to move the camels after lengthening the tethering rope to give them a larger area to graze. Brilliant stars shone above. Perhaps because desert air is pure and clean, they seemed bigger and lower than they did back home, as if she could reach out and pluck one out of the sky.

Lanlan was sighing when Ying'er went back inside the tent to lie down. Afraid to make her even sadder, she refrained from asking more questions and said instead:

"Let's get some sleep. We have to be on the road early tomorrow."

She stuck a flashlight under her pillow before blowing out the lantern and silently reminded herself to sleep lightly so she could get up and move the camels to a different grazing spot. Before setting out, they'd been reminded to make sure the camels had a full stomach. To be sure, the reliable animals stored fat in their humps, but that was an emergency reserve that must not be squandered, not in the vastness of the desert.

Fatigue quickly overtook the travelers on their first night. Soon, Ying'er was dreaming; she was spending a night in the desert with her lover, who was staring at her coldly. Why is he looking like that? And there is Pockmark Xu, the man Mother sought out to find her widowed daughter a new husband. He leered at her as he touched her calf with his icy hand. She cried out, waking herself up from a dream that seemed too real. Something *was* touching her calf. After frantically nudging Lanlan, she turned on the flashlight.

Lanlan sat up quickly.

"Something got into my pants," Ying'er said.

Lanlan snatched away the flashlight, while Ying'er felt the thing squirm.

"Oh, no!" she cried out.

"Don't move," Lanlan said, "Good. That's good. All right, I've got it."

Lanlan caught her breath when she took the thing out, and smacked it on a tent stake, over and over.

"Don't do that, smack it on the ground," Ying'er cautioned, afraid the tent would fall over.

"Light the lantern." Lanlan panted, her voice quivering.

Ying'er groped and found the flashlight. She saw what Lanlan was holding. It was a snake, as big around as her arm. She feared snakes more than anything. Her legs gave out as she screamed:

"Throw it out, throw it out!"

"It's dead," Lanlan said, breathing heavily, as she spotted snake's blood on their bedrolls.

"Are you all right?" Ying'er asked. "Did it bite you?"

"I don't know," Lanlan said, trying to hide her fear. Her hand was covered in blood, but she could not tell if it was hers or the snake's. She wiped it on the blanket. When Ying'er shone the flashlight on Lanlan's arm, she noticed two tiny punctures on the wrist. It was bleeding.

"It's all right," Ying'er said, "I don't think it was poisonous."

Ying'er knew that a snake with a triangular head was poisonous, one with a rounded head wasn't. She swept the light over the dead snake, but the head was smashed out of shape. She was terrified that Lanlan might die. If she did, how would Ying'er survive in the desert alone? What a selfish thought, she realized. How could I be thinking only about myself?

As if finally coming to her senses, Lanlan tossed the snake out of the tent.

"What's going to happen to me?"

"You won't die, I promise. I won't let you." Ying'er grabbed Lanlan's arm and began sucking on the wound. When the sticky, putrid venom entered her mouth, she recalled her cold sores. Some were already festering. She could be poisoned too.

After a while, she figured she'd sucked out all the venom she could, so she stopped. Then she took a frantic look around the tent to make sure there were no more snakes inside. Tossing the blankets out, she did a thorough search. Nothing. That put her mind at ease, but only for a moment. "Does your arm tingle?" she asked. Lanlan said it was a little numb, but not really tingling. Ying'er, on the other hand, thought that her tongue felt tingly.

"It was my fault," Lanlan said, "Pa gave me a pouch of tobacco ash when we were leaving. I forgot to take it out when we got here."

11

Now she took the pouch out and spread ash on the sand to surround them with its special odor, which would keep snakes away. Still, they were worried, but there was nothing more they could do. They went out together and moved the camels to a grassy spot. When they returned, they slipped into their bedrolls, but neither felt sleepy, still keyed up over what had just happened. They dozed off only after dim light from the Eastern sky began to penetrate the darkness.

Ying'er woke up when the sun shone into the tent. She had a slight headache, but her mouth felt all right. Lanlan's arm, which lay outside the blanket, was puffy, but the skin had not turned black. That was a relief.

Ying'er walked out of the tent and saw the dead snake; its size and scaly skin almost made her heart stop. She shuddered with thoughts of what might have happened if she hadn't awoken. Stretched out on the ground, its dark blood had seeped into the sand. She was in awe of Lanlan. If it had been her, she'd have gone to pieces just touching it, let alone catching and killing it.

The camels were in a sand trough chewing their cud; there was still undisturbed grass around them, so they'd had enough to eat. As it had been dark out when they bedded down the night before, they hadn't noticed the burrow holes scattered all over the trough. They would have to pick a better place next time to be as far away from snakes' or rats' nests as possible.

Lanlan woke up.

"How does it feel?"

"It feels fine. Don't worry. The venom wasn't strong. My mind is clear. If it had been serious, it would have affected my thinking." Her skin had a sheen.

She gathered kindling to start a fire before picking up a thick Artemisia twig and using it as a spit to roast the snake over the fire. Even the thought made Ying'er queasy.

"You go ahead, I don't want any."

"It's a delicacy, a gift from the Yellow Dragon," Lanlan said with a smile. "Try it or he'll be upset."

She added more kindling to make the flame screech happily over the snake, which sizzled. Ying'er smelled the fragrance, but could not stop shuddering when she recalled how the fragrant creature had actually crawled into her pants.

"Snake has to be cooked the right way," Lanlan said. "Avoid contact with metal objects. A bamboo knife is best. Roasting produces delicious meat."

"Here's an offering to the Yellow Dragon King," she said, stripping the charred skin and tossing it into the fire. She tore off a piece and handed it to Ying'er.

"None for me."

"You'll regret it." Lanlan laughed. She sprinkled on salt she'd retrieved from the litter, tilted her head back, opened her mouth wide, and dropped it in. It looked tempting.

"You really ought to try it. When you think about it, so many of our ingrained habits need to be rethought. We can't change the world, but at least we can change ourselves."

Ying'er's resolve wavered. She's right, she told herself.

"All right, a small piece," she said, and got a large chunk instead.

She'd never tasted meat like that before, and it wasn't bad. They ate in the tent with steamed buns until they were both belching.

After dousing the fire, they got onto the camels and set off. Riding a camel takes practice. An experienced rider will sit to one side of the backbone. Being inexperienced, Ying'er sat right on top of it, and by noon her tailbone felt as if it were on fire. Lanlan handed her a blanket. "Don't worry," she consoled her, "it happens to everyone at first. It'll get better in a few days. Enjoy the ride now, because after we load the salt, your camel will not have the strength to carry you home."

So, Ying'er alternated between riding and walking, and while her tailbone felt better, for days, pain knifed through her calves.

Around noon, they ran into two old shepherds herding a flock of sheep that appeared enervated by the sun's blistering rays.

"What are you two doing out here all alone?"

"Looking for a couple of young men to help us on our way," Lanlan said with a grin.

"It's the young ones you have to watch out for. Maybe you should give us a try?"

"You're not going to take advantage of a couple of young widows, are you?"

"Not if you know how to use that musket you're carrying."

"We'll spare you if you'll tell us where the next oasis is."

"All I can say is, if it's the salt lakes you're on your way to, you're heading in the right direction. But be careful. This is a year for jackals. Many of the oases are filled with them. They'll go straight for your camel's guts."

Ying'er had heard of but never seen a jackal. The old shepherd's warning made her tremble. She'd heard they were sinister animals, worse than wolves.

"What's there to be afraid of? Jackals are flesh and blood too," Lanlan said as she patted her musket.

"It's good you have that," the old man said, "but it won't help you if they come in packs."

"What you need to fear is not jackals," the other one joined in. "With such a pretty face, just watch out for bad characters. Some of the herders are worse than their animals. It never hurts to be careful."

"He's right. They're out here all year round without ever seeing a female, so it's hard to say if they'll get ideas."

"Even if their minds don't get ideas, their bodies might."

Ying'er had enjoyed the banter until she recalled hearing stories about men out in the wild.

"I'm not afraid," Lanlan boasted. "I've sparred with petty thieves before. It doesn't take much to drive those ideas out of their minds *and* their bodies,"

"You look like you know how to defend yourself, so we won't waste our breath," one of them said with a laugh. They walked off with a friendly wave.

"What they said made sense," Ying'er said.

"You're right, but we wouldn't have come out here if we'd had a choice." Lanlan sighed. "At least this is peacetime, and I like to think that people are law-abiding."

Despite what she said, they stopped and smeared their faces with ashes. When she was done, Ying'er looked up to see Lanlan doubled over laughing. Ying'er could guess how ugly she must look. They pointed at each other's face and laughed until they could barely catch their breath. But then a wave of sadness stole into their hearts when they realized why they were doing this.

"We'll stay clear of any men we come across," Lanlan said. "If what the shepherds said is true, even looking like a couple of old hags might not be enough to avoid men with bad ideas."

Misgivings dogged them in spite of what they hoped awaited them when they reached their destination, and they walked on without further talk.

To settle their nerves, Lanlan stopped once to check her weapon and slung it over her back, while Ying'er took the Tibetan knife. That helped.

They entered the second gully after crossing a dune that rose halfway to the sky, and began to see more desert vegetation. Along the way they spotted camel carcasses, which made their own camels toss their heads. The sight unnerved Ying'er. Some of the blanched bones had turned gray, which meant they'd been there for years. Others were clearly fresh, with shreds of flesh still connected to them. She hated to think what this meant.

But since it was as good a spot to rest as any, they got down off their camels and took the animals to graze while they rested. After fetching their water jugs, they ate steamed buns. In the heat, moldy spots had begun to show on the buns. To prevent them from going completely bad, Lanlan divided them into two piles and wrapped them separately in a gauzy scarf for the desert breezes to pass through and carry away the dampness.

The sun was still up, so they could go a bit farther. It was a commonly traveled route, and they would spend the night in the next oasis. Ying'er, still reeling from the snakebite the night before, had a different idea. Oases were often swampy, a breeding ground for snakes. She wanted to find a relatively dry sand trough, where they could bed down near desert plants. They'd give the camels some of their water to make up for the moisture they'd miss from not eating grass.

"We have to tend to our camels first out here, they mean everything," Lanlan agreed. "Without them, we could cry to the heavens and not get a response." On the other hand, she understood how Ying'er felt. Anyone who'd had a snake slither into her pants would be wary of swampy areas.

The old shepherds were telling the truth about jackals. The women had barely left an oasis when they saw a dead camel on a sand ridge. Ying'er had heard about wild camels in the desert, but could not tell if this had been one of them. Wild camels were under government protection, but there weren't supposed to be any in the Gobi, she'd heard. Camels that were running loose were escapees, not truly wild.

This had probably been a sick or starving animal, its humps sagging on the sand. With no nose ring and no sign of a harness,

16

it had likely roamed the desert for years, though probably not a true wild camel.

Obviously killed recently, part of the animal's intestines had been dragged out onto the sand, presenting a scary, bloody sight. Frightened by the scene, Ying'er gripped the knife tightly. Lanlan got down off her camel and cried out, "Dear God of Fortune, thank you for this precious gift."

"Do you know how much a camel pelt is worth?" she said in answer to Ying'er's questioning look. "We got three hundred once for a single cowhide, and that was just a calf. This camel may be dead, but its pelt is still intact."

"That doesn't make it ours."

"It doesn't belong to anyone," said Lanlan. "Pa told me that many camels escaped from a farm many years ago. They bred and reproduced in the desert. Old Meng Baye roped one a while back. He did his best to tame it, but nothing worked. It bit and kicked, so in the end he let it go.

"If this had been a domestic camel," she added as she pointed at its nose, "this spot would be hairless."

"I guess you're right," Ying'er said.

"It was probably sick and couldn't run fast enough, so it was killed and gutted. But see how the pelt has hardly been damaged? If we don't skin it, wild animals will ruin it before the night's out. The gods have given us this pelt, but it's okay if you don't want it."

Lanlan tethered her camel to a desert rice plant.

"We'll let them graze while I skin this one. If they want it at the salt lakes, we'll sell it there. If not, we'll take it back and sell it at home." She asked for the Tibetan knife, but Ying'er knew it was too long for skinning, so she handed Lanlan a smaller knife from her bundle, a dagger her husband Hantou had bought for protection. It was almost dangerously sharp.

Maybe she's right, Ying'er was thinking. This pelt could fetch as much as a load of salt. Not bad. We'll get the money we need a lot faster if we have many sources. Then you'll have to stop forcing me into this marriage, Ma. Her eyes welled up when she thought about her mother, so she raised her head for the tears to flow back.

From what she'd seen back in the village, Ying'er knew how grueling a task it was to skin a camel, a job that normally required several men just to roll it over. That was the hard part. Lanlan read her mind.

"Don't worry," she said. "The meat doesn't interest us, so we'll have our camels turn it over. Two live camels ought to be able to handle a dead one."

She rolled up her sleeves and chased away flies as big as bees. Ying'er's stomach churned as she detected a foul smell, but she swallowed hard and kept everything down.

With a wrinkled brow, Lanlan searched for the best place to begin,

"We'll start on the belly," she said as she poked at soft spots. Ying'er covered her nose as a precaution, for fear that something foul would spurt out from a knife cut. Happily, only a few air bubbles appeared. Lanlan carefully slid the knife across, creating an opening like a skiff skimming across the water.

There was a screech, and before they could react, a black ball shot out of the opening. Lanlan tried to dodge but tripped over the camel's hind leg and fell onto the sand. Whatever it was spun around in midair and pounced on her. "Kill it!" Ying'er cried out. Lanlan screamed as she stabbed at the thing while Ying'er ran to pick up their musket, though she did not know how to use one. Even if she could, she might hit Lanlan. The thing was not big, about the size of a leopard cat, but frighteningly fast on its feet. Lanlan stabbed at it, but kept missing.

"Hit it with the musket!" she yelled.

Ying'er was terrified, but Lanlan was fighting for her life, so she put her fear aside. She swung the weapon, bringing it down hard. The thing leaped into the air with shrill yelps, and when it landed, it crouched and bared its teeth, though it was no longer brave enough to charge. That gave Lanlan the opportunity to roll over, grab the musket from Ying'er, and put the flint on; but before she could fire, the animal ran off, trailed by its yelps. The old man had warned them.

"A jackal," Lanlan said as she crumpled to the ground, as a couple more of them shot out of the opening and darted off to distant sand hills.

Ying'er stared wide-eyed.

"Glad we brought the musket." Lanlan was breathing hard. "They probably smelled the gunpowder and came out. They'd crawled inside the camel from the rear to get to more of its organs." She picked up the musket, aimed it at the opening she'd cut, and yelled. Nothing happened.

"Let's forget about skinning it," Ying'er said. "There could still be more inside."

"I don't think so, but get something to poke around in there. I'll shoot if anything comes out." Ying'er took a club from one of the camels' loads and stuck it into the dead camel's belly. She threw up after a few pokes.

"They're gone," Lanlan said. Her face was bathed in sweat, her energy drained from fright. But she smiled when she saw Ying'er's worried look.

"I'm glad I didn't have to shoot and ruin this pelt. No one would want it if it had a bunch of holes."

"You're still going to skin it?" Ying'er was incredulous. "Are you sure there aren't any more in there? There could be, you know."

"They surprised us, but now I'm prepared," Lanlan said, forcing a smile to mask her fear.

It could have killed her, Ying'er thought. "Let's forget the pelt," she said. Then she spotted blood on Lanlan's shoulder and rushed over.

"It's all right. Just a scratch from its claws. But if I hadn't fallen when it flew out, I'd be on the road to the Underworld by now."

Trickles of blood oozed from the shallow wound. Ying'er burned some camel hair to sprinkle over it. After-attack fright made her sob.

"Don't cry," Lanlan said. "Tears won't buy you your freedom." Her mouth was dry. She took a sip of water and slowly stood up. "Come on, let's keep at it. We can't suffer the fright for nothing. Don't be afraid, they're small."

Lanlan raised the musket and aimed at the hole, telling Ying'er to poke around some more to remove the rest of the intestines with the club. Ying'er tried, but was sick again. So they switched roles. "Here, pull the trigger if anything comes out."

Lanlan stuck the club inside the camel, wanting to drag out everything in there, so any remaining foragers would have no place to hide, But Ying'er could not stop dry-heaving, so Lanlan tossed the club aside and, keeping a watchful eye on the opening, began working on the pelt.

It was tough going, but the knife was sharp enough for the job. Nothing more happened inside, so Ying'er, finally reassured, forced back her disgust and came up to help. Tugging as they went, they tied a rope to the camel's legs and attached it to one of their camels, which made turning it over easy. After more than two hours of exhausting work, they had their camel pelt.

Dusk was descending, and the sun, suspended above a sand hill to the west, seemed to shower them with praise. Lanlan wiped her forehead; she was soaked in sweat. Ying'er hadn't worked as hard, but was sweaty from trepidation, if nothing else. As she dried Lanlan's face, she realized she really did not understand her sister-in-law. They hadn't known each other well until they were told about the exchange marriage. Then after going to live with the other's

20

family, they rarely had a chance to spend time together. Lanlan knew that Ying'er was the best folk-song singer within miles, while Ying'er heard from her husband about Lanlan's forceful personality and fierce love for her brothers. "She can be so pushy you want to tell her to get lost," Hantou once said. But at this moment Ying'er felt only admiration for her sister-in-law. She was also grateful that Lanlan showed no disdain over her timid and queasy nature. There was something extraordinary about her traveling companion. Too bad her brother wasn't smart enough to appreciate her.

The pelt was so heavy Ying'er could not lift it by herself. So, after taking a break to catch her breath, Lanlan came up to help. They tried hoisting it onto one of the camels, but failed after a few attempts.

"We've used up all our strength for today," Lanlan said. "Let's stop here. We'll find a clean spot to spend the night."

After locating a trough with desert rice, they unloaded the camels so they could graze the stalks. After many stops and starts, they managed to drag the pelt into the trough.

"We're too tired to cook tonight. Let's just have some steamed buns," Lanlan suggested.

"You get some rest. I'll make noodles," Ying'er said.

The trough was filled with kindling. She quickly gathered a pile.

She was cooking when they heard shrieks from somewhere nearby.

"Jackals!" Lanlan cried out.

Ying'er and Lingguan

Out in the family's yard, littered with corn stalks, Lingguan pushed open the pigpen door, startling the chickens into cackling noisily. The old sow grunted as she waddled over, looking for a handout.

Ying'er stopped and glanced his way when he walked in, but she did not greet him—no "So you're back" or anything like that. He was seeing her in a different light, now that he was aware of his brother's disease. Something in her eyes disturbed him.

"Has the manure turned hard?" he asked. How stupid that sounded, it made his face burn.

She smiled but said nothing, just looked at him.

"Did he have his checkup?"

"Yes, he did. Nothing serious. A little discomfort around his ribcage, that's all. The doctor prescribed some medicine."

She turned her gaze away. Their rooster was chasing a hen, stirring up dust. Ying'er sighed and jammed her spade into the manure; soon she was breathing hard.

Lingguan slowly regained his composure, but was angry at himself for being so flustered. He knew his face showed it, an annoying trait of his. Their village was overrun with coarse men and women who did not blush easily, which was why women liked to tease him. Ying'er never did. They seldom talked, but sometimes, when they were out working together, village kids would taunt, "Hei, hei—a young man diddling his sister-in-law." That always made her blush, and she would race ahead.

Lingguan's throat was dry. To cover up his unease, he worked fast with his spade. A moment later, Ling'er wiped her sweaty face with a corner of her headscarf and said,

"Women are born to suffer, don't you think? Take your sister,

22

for example. A wonderful girl like her forced to marry a hothead like my brother. There was nothing she could do about it. Your parents wanted her to marry my brother so your brother could marry me. Could she refuse? No, she was born a girl, she had no choice."

There was nothing he could say about the deal struck between the two families. Without it, his shy brother, Hantou, might have remained a bachelor all his life. Lingguan's heart softened at the thought of his brother, who had actually opposed the arrangement. Sometimes, when he had a bit too much to drink, he could weep like an old cow, saying his sister suffered because of him.

"I guess you're right," Lingguan said. It's fate, I guess." What else could he say?

"Fate. Fate. It's so easy to say, but it's a lifetime for someone, don't you know that?" She clenched her teeth. "In a way, Lanlan has done better than me, because she at least has her daughter. I know what Mother is thinking. I really do, even though she never says anything. She won't scold the hen that doesn't lay eggs, because she doesn't want to hurt my feelings." Her voice cracked and her face was soon streaked with sparkling tears.

That sent Lingguan into a panic. How would he explain himself if someone saw his sister-in-law crying like that around him? He didn't know how to comfort her, afraid that anything he said might make her cry even harder. So, he threw himself into the work, grunting loudly to draw her out of her sadness.

It worked. She dried her tears and went back to work, keeping her head down. "You men are all the same," she said after a moment. "Your hearts are filled with holes big enough to drive a camel through. I thought you were smart and sensitive, but you're as dumb as all the others."

His mind drifted. He sensed there was more to what she said, but he couldn't grasp the floating thought, like a silk thread gliding on a breeze. Her voice, soft and serene as still water, usually washed away the troubles in his heart. But the mellow voice seemed almost oppressive now.

"Don't you agree?" A smile danced around her lips. "Well, do you?" Obviously, she'd sensed his unease. "Have you heard the ballad about Liang Shanbo? He's as dense as a pine pole trying to carry a willow bucket. I think that's the perfect description of you."

Was she hinting at something else? Feeling pressure build in his chest, he was getting breathless. He forced himself to calm down and breathe more evenly, but that only made it worse.

He felt lightheaded, his face was hot. Ying'er was like the sun, drying up all the moisture in him and creating an unusual thirst. "I don't know, maybe, I forget." He turned to walk out of the yard.

"You're too young to have an old man's memory," she said with a laugh, and then,

"Want to hear a tune? I'll sing one for you." Without waiting for a reply, she started singing.

Drops of rain fall on the rocks,
Flakes of snow fall on the water,
Love sickness falls on the heart,
A bloody scab falls on the mouth.

At midnight I watch the moon take over the sky,
The door to my boudoir is opened a crack.
Elder Brother, you're like an elixir,
Little Sister is in need of treatment.

A cow drinks on the bank of the Yellow River,
The water does not reach the tip of its nose.

When I pick up my bowl I think of you,
The noodles cannot reach my lips.

A cymbal sounded in his head; his eardrums swelled and his mouth went dry again. Even the sun raised a dizzying clamor, like chirping cicadas. His brain all but stopped functioning. He thought he heard what she sang, but could not bring himself to believe his ears. Did she really say all that? Really?

"Want to hear more?" she asked in a soft voice.

A white peony falls into the water gray,
Fish it out quickly or it will float away.
Make sure to enjoy life in this world,
Hurry up, before you grow old one day.

The little chicks are chirping away,
Fighting over kernels of rice in a tray.
Do not be fooled by my silence among others,
I think of you no matter what they say.

Reputation is nothing but an empty word,
It all depends on how you wish.
Would you come to my little room?
We'll talk to our hearts' content, free as fish.

"Would you?" she whispered with a petulant glance. He knew what she meant with that look: You call yourself a man? When a woman broaches a subject like this, do you not have the boldness to accept?

An unnatural thirst assaulted him again, worsening as his heart pounded wildly. He strained to say something, but could not utter a word.

The light in her eyes went out as a hint of shame and resentment emerged on her lowered face. He was sensitive enough to catch the change.

I've hurt her feelings, he thought.

"Of course, I would," he managed to mutter.

They set out for home when the sun was directly overhead. It was a windless, stifling day; the sky felt suffused with sticky goo. A patch of something flashed in a distant field, so shiny that Ying'er felt she was dreaming. How could those words have come so easily, so naturally, when she would normally have blushed if she'd even thought them? It did not feel forced at the time, more like driven by a supernatural power. She was lightheaded, but not the dizzy feeling that accompanies an illness; rather it was a euphoric sensation stirred by happiness. Her face was hot and her heartbeat quickened, as if she'd done something roguish. That is exactly how she felt, and she recalled the term the villagers used to revile women: "man-thief." The term had always disgusted her, but now it embodied a wicked elation. In all fairness, she longed for something "wicked." Hantou was too nice, so good he might as well be an idol on an altar. She could not find any fault with him; he was just boring beyond words. She envied those women who could flirt with their own husbands in public. Women abhorred loose women, and yet they would all like to be naughty at least once, if they had the chance. That included her, regardless of what others might think. To be sure, what she'd just said was nowhere near the sort of behavior she had in mind; it was enough, however, to bring out a myriad of emotional reactions—unusual bliss, fear, shyness, and a sense of novelty. She wasn't sure if this was how it felt to be in love. In the dictionary of her life, love was a word covered in dust, hiding in a corner. Marriage had barged in before she'd had a chance to brush off the dust, and she'd become Hantou's wife, missing out on the one chapter that should never be passed up in the book of life—love.

"How could I have sung those words?" Covering her face, she stared at Lingguan's back. He walked with the carefree flair unique to those who have been to school. The sun disappeared, as did the cooling breeze and the flow of water in the ditch; nothing but his back existed in her universe at that moment, and that brought her waves of happiness. Everything about him, his steps, his posture, even his dust-covered sneakers, seemed well balanced and perfect, wonderful beyond words. "If—" A thought occurred to her. If it were him, and not "him," how wonderful the world would be. A fragmented dark shadow flitted across her mind at the thought of the other "him," but she forced herself to halt the thought, so as not to ruin her mood of the moment.

As they neared the village, people were returning from work, creating chaos on the road. The villagers' noise, the dust, and the livestock being brought back from the pasture enlivened the stifling, gloomy noontime. A baby mule was having the time of its life, tossing its head and flicking its ears, kicking its hooves and breaking for the village before affectionately turning back to its mother. It captivated her. Pretending to watch the mules, mother and offspring, Ying'er slowed down to put some distance between her and Lingguan, while making a point of not looking at him; yet she had a second pair of eyes—invisible eyes—that were trained on his back, as she continued to bathe in the swell of happiness emanating from his direction.

3

Indistinct black figures dotted the sand dune, some racing toward the dead camel they'd skinned, while others remained where they were. Ying'er's tongue went dry as she looked over at Lanlan, her expression a mix of shock and fear. Musket at the ready, Lanlan studied the scene.

"It's all right. They came for the food. That camel is big enough to feast on, and they won't attack with no regard for their own safety."

Lanlan had meant to calm Ying'er's nerves, though she was less than confident that the jackals wouldn't treat them as food as well. There were so many of them. The sight and the image of the animals that had poured out of the camel only hours before turned Ying'er's legs weak.

With their eyes on the distant dune, their camels grunted and made loud chuffing noises to scare off the jackals. Camel spittle can ward off wolves, they'd been told, but jackals are a different breed. Nonetheless, Ying'er was pleased by the camels' reaction, for they looked ready to protect them. That helped dispel her fears, yet she could not help recalling how her father-in-law had warned them of the dangers they might face. Such as now.

After chuffing a while, her camel turned to look at her as if to say, "Don't be scared. You can count on me."

She was energized by the gaze. Everything will be all right, she said to herself, keeping her eyes on the swarming predators. I may die before the day is over, but I won't be a lonely ghost, thanks to the camels.

"Don't be afraid," she said to Lanlan, "I'm not. Even if they come after us, so what? The worst they can do is kill us."

"You're right." Lanlan smiled as she lowered the musket. "When you think about it, what's there to be afraid of? Life is overrated. I just can't stand the idea of being eaten alive. We didn't come out here to feed a bunch of jackals."

Ying'er set up a pot, poured in water, lit the fire, and started making noodle dough. "If we have to die out here, we'll go with a full stomach."

Lanlan smiled as she retrieved a chopper from her litter to cut down some nearby shrubs. Ying'er is starting to toughen up, she reflected with a bit of surprise and a lot of pleasure. After her brother died and turned Ying'er into a widow before she was even thirty, she worried that her sister-in-law might not have the strength to keep going.

Her thoughts were interrupted by a commotion that broke out among the jackals when they heard the sound of the chopper hitting wood. Not sufficiently intimidated, they went back to the carcass, growling and fighting over the meat.

Lanlan had collected enough firewood to last through the night. Instead of putting up their tent, they spread their bedrolls out by the fire. Fearing that the jackals might come for their camels, Lanlan did not let them out to graze in the shrubs, but had them lie close to the fire facing out. That should keep the temporarily sated jackals from trying to get at them for yet another camel feast. Sensing what the humans had in mind, the camels lay down docilely by the fire, while Ying'er brought over some tender branches for them gnaw on.

Lanlan spread the newly skinned camel pelt on the ground, furry side up so the sand would soak up some of the moisture on the underside overnight, reducing its weight. Once they reached the salt lakes, they'd sprinkle on salt to keep worms from ruining it.

Shortly after nightfall, they heard the sounds of biting and tearing around the skinned camel. The jackals' deep, angry voices rippled in the evening sky and echoed back. Their camels twitched their ears and made chuffing sounds. Among the calmest of animals, they do not often do that, which could have meant they too feared the ferocious predators. Despite her bravado about not being afraid to die, Ying'er shuddered when she recalled the sight of jackals scrambling out of the belly of the dead camel.

The sounds of biting and tearing grew in intensity, meaning the fight over food was getting fierce, and one camel might no longer be enough for them. If the dead camel could sate the jackals' greedy appetite, they would be relatively safe; if there were more jackals than meat, then the beasts would remember them once they finished off the dead animal. Suddenly and absurdly, Ying'er flashed back to the village and her mother, a scene that at that moment seemed impossibly distant and hazy, as if it were a lifetime ago. She wished she hadn't fought with her mother the night before she left, but she could not abide the thought of marrying that repulsive butcher. Sacrificing her happiness a second time for a brother who had destroyed his marriage kept mother and daughter at odds. Lingguan, she had said silently, I'm waiting for you. Once I make enough money for my brother to marry again, Mother will stop pressuring me. But first, she had to survive the danger they were facing so soon after entering the desert.

Lanlan brought out her gunpowder pouch and the buckshot and lay them down a little distance away from the fire. Ying'er tossed wood onto the fire. Having heard that wolves feared fire, she suspected the same was true with jackals. If not, they had little hope of surviving the night.

The frenzied sound of jackals tearing into the rapidly disappearing camel were getting increasingly violent, with pitiful yelps and angry roars as they threatened one another. The pandemonium spread like an explosion, even cowering the stars into disappearing. The noise seemed to form a giant whirlwind that raged in the sand trough, rushing this way and that.

Lanlan reached out and squeezed Ying'er's hand. Ying'er squeezed it back. "Should we try to run?" she whispered.

"It's too late. You can't outrun an animal like this, no matter how fast you move. Let's gather more firewood to make it through the night." Lanlan asked Ying'er to hold the flashlight while she cut down all the branches in the sand trough, dry or not. She gave wet ones to the camels and tossed some of the others into the fire, producing a loud sizzle.

Lanlan tended the fire with great care, so it would neither die out nor flare up. Like the musket beside her, it was something they could count on. Before they left, her father had added two cigarette lighters, one with gas, the other with lighter fluid, to supplement their supply of matches. In the desert, fire bestows hope. He had put the lighters in two different bags. Now Lanlan understood why; he was afraid they might lose one or use it up. She recalled how she'd laughed at her father's "foolish" caution.

She moved the camel litters closer to the fire. The wind carried over the stink from the pelt spread out on the sand.

"They're too busy to bother us now, so you can get some sleep," Lanlan said, keeping the musket safely away from the fire.

"You first. I'll keep watch. You must be dead tired from skinning the camel."

"All right. Just take care not to let the fire die out, and don't use too much firewood. I've armed the musket, so be careful."

Lanlan leaned against her litter and soon was snoring lightly.

She is so coolheaded, Ying'er was thinking. She can actually sleep in the middle of all this. Lanlan had been a devout Buddhist for some time, and Ying'er wondered if that was where she

31

got her strength.

As she added more wood, the fire grew brighter. Sometimes, she too dwelt on the Buddhist concept that everyone is born to suffer, so dying without experiencing danger at all amounts to not having lived. That's that, then, she thought with a bitter smile.

The sounds of jackals fighting had died down a bit, but not completely, which meant there was still food left, and Ying'er had time to think about herself. But what purpose did that serve? She could not change her fate simply by wanting to, and too much thinking brought only exasperation, especially her bittersweet thoughts of her lover.

Lingguan

The yard was oppressively quiet. Gently folding back the blanket, he was alarmed by how it rustled, sounding in his ears like a raging torrent; his heart was pounding so hard his parents were sure to hear him. He took a deep breath and held it for as long as he could as he groped for his sandals, and then stepped gingerly forward, the soles scraping against the floor. His heartbeat seemed to fill the evening sky. Losing his nerve, he sat back down on the edge of his bed, discouraged. But those bewitching eyes summoned him, and crystalline laughter continued to ring in his ears. Holding his breath, he took a few steps and opened the door, making a thin sound like tearing a piece of silk, but, undaunted, he walked into the yard.

The moon was dim, yet bright enough to see blurry outlines. He noticed a faint light in his parents' room, and wondered if his mother was watching him through the window. He sucked in cold air.

She was in the habit of spying on people. As a child, back when they lived in a large compound, he'd often spotted her listening in on neighbors' conversations. She was a light sleeper. Has she heard me? Is she at the window? He could almost "hear" her say under her breath, Oh, no, is my boy really doing something like this? Is he throwing away all his schooling?

His fervor cooling, he backed up to his doorway, leaning against it to be out of her sight line, yet still able to survey his surroundings. He perceived nothing out of the ordinary after a long wait.

Mother must be asleep.

He tiptoed up to Ying'er's door. His footsteps continued to pound in his ears, no matter how softly he walked. Taking off his sandals, he held them in his hand as he inched toward his goal.

33

He took a deep breath at her door to steady his racing heart, but that did little good. Before pushing it open, he lay down his sandals, rubbed his feet on top of them, and then put them back on so he would not soil her bed sheet when he took them off inside.

The door was not bolted.

He pushed it open—there's no turning back—slipped inside and shut the door behind him.

It was dark in the room, the drawn curtain blocking out moonlight. That suited him, for he would have been embarrassed to do anything had there been light inside. With his hand pressed against his chest, he looked around to see more clearly. A rustle told him that Ying'er was sitting up. He could almost see the autumn ripples in her eyes.

"What are you doing here?" she asked softly.

He had not expected that. He had hoped she'd ask, "What took you so long?" and let her voice draw him to her. He would take her in his arms and kiss her under the cover of darkness, a daring act he believed he could carry out on a night like this.

What should he say? He could not say it openly. They were off to an awkward start. Frozen in the darkness, he had no idea what to do next.

"Come up here if you want to talk." Ying'er said lightly. "The floor is cold."

That simple comment erased his unease. With a smile, he took the sweaty hand reaching for him. He kicked off his sandals and climbed onto the bed, where he was enveloped in comforting warmth.

She held his hand so tightly it hurt, but it was a pleasurable pain. He was quiet because he still did not know what to say. Ying'er sighed softly. "What took you so long?" Holding her in his arms, he felt the two mounds of soft flesh through her thin chemise, and that set his body on fire.

She held him tight and began to murmur. Soon the murmur turned to sobs. Lingguan did not know how to comfort the lovely body in his arms.

"I've waited so long," she said. "Kiss me."

Taking her face in his hands, he kissed her over and over, but clumsily, for he did not know if lips should be tender or wild. All he knew was to lay his lips on hers, heavily, over and over. A dizzy happiness overwhelmed him, and he was rendered defenseless. "This is how I want to die," he heard her say, as she bit his lip painfully.

"Your clothes are so cold."

She was breathing hard and fast as she undid his buttons, slowly, as if to savor the act, while he stroked her hair. Suddenly he thought of Hantou, and reached out to stop her hand. "Will he be back soon?" Her hand trembled in his.

"No. And please don't say his name." She sighed. Some time passed before the hand resumed its movements. She struggled with the buttons, so he took off his shirt. With a moan, she hugged him; taut breasts that had yet to suckle a child quivered against his chest, while her hand moved from his shoulder to his chest and abdomen, where it lingered before moving down.

"Why are you so tense?" she murmured.

He did not know what he should be doing. With no prior experience in sex, he was rendered useless as he basked in surprise and happiness. He felt her hand slide down, drawing an involuntary groan from him.

She smiled. But then, afraid she might have hurt him, she stopped and kissed his chest, nibbling him occasionally with careful, focused bites.

"Are you made of wood?"

Lingguan was pulled into an eddy of bliss, and then waves crashed against the shore. He touched her breast, followed by an exploration; he was entering unfamiliar territory. His hands felt

35

the soft skin of her abdomen; an odd agitation swept over him when his hand reached the mound that seemed so full of life. Heaven help me! He felt himself sliding into an unknown world.

"Ah, so much . . ." he mumbled.

She was moaning. Afraid she might wake up his parents, he put his mouth over hers and felt her lips greet his with violent abandonment.

"I don't know how. You'll have to teach me." He was breathing hard.

"I don't know either," she said softly.

4

All sounds of fighting over the camel had ceased.

An immense silence rolled over. Ying'er could feel the texture of the oppressive quiet and thought she saw green eyes in the dark. She hadn't yet had a chance to study jackals' eyes, but she'd seen the eyes of rabid dogs in the village, and that must have been the way jackals looked at humans. Their eyes were tinged with avarice and ferocity, like the gaze the matchmaker Pockmark Xu cast on her. The mere thought of that odious man made her gag, and she gave her head a fierce shake.

Suddenly, the camels began spitting violently. That could only mean they sensed pressing danger. After nudging Lanlan, she turned on the flashlight and hurled its beam toward the dune, which was blanketed with green lights. They presented a powerful reality as they roamed like will-o'-the-wisps, drifting here and there. Ying'er shuddered as she added dry kindling and blew on the fire to make the flame shoot up.

"Don't worry, they're afraid of fire, all those animals are," Lanlan whispered, as she picked up the musket and pointed it into the sky.

"Are you planning to scare them off?"

"Not yet. We'd be doomed if they got used to the sound of a gun." She brought over the lantern and lit it.

To prepare for the possibility of a sneak attack, they pointed the bedrolls and camel litters in a different direction; instead of facing the camels, they now had their backs to them. Since camels can see well in the dark, the change added two more pairs of eyes

37

to watch the jackals' movements. Their backs clear, they could focus on what was in front of them.

Lanlan wished she'd cut more firewood, though she did not know how big the fire had to be to hold back predatory animals. If the firelight failed to curb them, and they kept pressing forward, then they would definitely need to make it bigger. The little wood they'd gathered would not likely last till dawn.

The jackals were as still as death. Clearly, they too were sizing up their enemy. Now that their bellies were filled, they were in no hurry. The camels had stopped chewing, but they weren't spitting either. All was quiet except for the crackling of the fire. The silence had turned into a confining wall. It was a strange sensation. Ying'er had always preferred quiet, heated noise, never expecting that silence could make her heart thump violently against her chest. The sand dune seemed filled with other racing heartbeats. In her mind, she heard many of them, from Lanlan, from the camels, and from those beasts. Lanlan's heartbeats were like feet pounding on the ground, the camels' heartbeats were rumbling millstones, and the jackals' were pebbles grating as they rolled in a cracked wok. They set her teeth on edge. Steadily, the grating grew louder, and her nerves were tormented as if by knives. She clenched her teeth, shook her head, and held her breath, but the noise did not go away. The jackals were grinding their teeth. She'd heard her father-in-law talk of seeing rats do that, a noise that nearly drove him crazy. That's what she was hearing. Her heart was beating so fast she was afraid it might burst.

Lanlan added more dry wood and the fire grew, but only enough to illuminate a small circle around them, not enough to see much. Distant dunes were hazy under the light. If the jackals stole up on them, Ying'er knew they would not be able to react in time. So she turned on her flashlight, sending its beam to the nearest dune, where the black dots erupted in commotion, mistaking the burst of light as a lightning strike. She'd heard that animals are afraid of lightning, which can be lethal in the desert. It made sense that this pack of predators would be afraid of their light, at least for a while.

Ying'er doused the light. They were able to see the blurred outlines of the dune, barely. The green lights in the surrounding darkness were only visible when the fire died down, which presented a critical dilemma. If they kept the fire low, the jackals might attack, but if it burned brighter, they could not see clearly. It felt as if the jackals were the audience to a human drama, fraught with danger, training their eyes on the stage, where the actors and their animal companions looked into darkness broken only by flickering dots and an undercurrent of ominous sound.

Lanlan had an idea. She told Ying'er to tend to the fire, while she went to lie a bit away from it, hidden from its glow, with her musket, gunpowder, and the flashlight. The firelight would not affect her eyesight, and if any jackals sneaked up on them, she would greet them with buckshot.

Once she was away from the fire, she saw green lights all around. They drifted and grew larger as they came closer and closer together, which meant that the sinister animals were pushing forward. Choosing a spot with several densely packed lights, she aimed and pulled the trigger, spewing flames like a broom. Yelps erupted and the lights retreated.

"That'll show you!" Lanlan said with a laugh.

The crack from her weapon had an immediate effect. The nearest attackers now looked to be two or three hundred feet away. Buckshot could only reach those in the front, hitting some but probably not killing any. So, she switched to ball bearings, which easily reached a far greater distance and could take down a gazelle. The next shot, if well aimed, would claim a life.

"We'll get some peace if I kill one of them. That'll show them what we're capable of while they fight over the dead one, buying us some time. Things will get easier after daybreak. Jackals are probably

39

like foxes, which are used to nighttime activities. At least I hope so. Legend has it that their heads ache under a blazing sun."

The human heart is a strange thing, for, in time, it can grow numb, no matter how terrifying the situation. They weren't as fearful now, though they were still surrounded by menacing predators, and their lives were in terrible jeopardy. To see their enemy more clearly, Lanlan went over to dim the fire, leaving only embers, immediately bringing the oppressive darkness down on them.

"Shepherds in the desert usually travel with muskets or rifles, so the jackals must be wary," Lanlan said.

"But they wouldn't have run off if they'd gotten used to being shot at."

Lanlan agreed. She swept the flashlight beam, noting that their enemy had gathered mostly to the east, with no green lights on the dune to the west. Following the custom when pitching a tent, they'd selected a dry spot with the wind at their backs. They faced the relatively open sand trough, against the western dune.

"This is no good," Lanlan said. "From up there they could roll right down into our midst before I had time to pull the trigger. We have to move into the trough. That way they'd have to run a long distance to reach us, which would give us enough time to prepare."

While the jackals had yet to recover from the musket fire, Lanlan lit a torch and found a wider spot in the trough to build a fire, so they could move their litters, bedding, firewood, and camels. Half an hour later, as expected, tiny black figures covered the western dune. Ying'er was thinking that if they hadn't moved their camp site, the jackals might not have dared go up onto the dune, since they'd have been within range of her musket. Their new position faced attacks from the front and the back.

The cold desert wind felt so much stronger now that they'd left the shelter of the dunes. Feeling a chill on her back, Ying'er fetched two coats, draping one over Lanlan and one over herself. At their backs, the camels were agitated, having spotted the jackals on the dune.

"We shouldn't have moved," she said, despite her reluctance to contradict Lanlan, who was more adept at surviving in the desert.

"There's an upside to moving and an upside to staying put. I was afraid of a sneak attack if we stayed put. I thought they'd simply roll down the dune. Now we're out in the open, and so are they. We're within sight of each other. We can fight with everything we've got, and the worst case is we end up in their bellies." She continued, "In this life of ours, the earlier we die, the sooner we'll be released from suffering. We all have to die sometime. So, we can cower and waste away, or we can fight bravely to the end. Meditation has taught me what life is about. Of course, I'm a long way from meeting my guru's demands. Shakyamuni Buddha could offer his body to a tiger and cut a piece of himself to feed a vulture. If I followed the same standard, I should strip naked and lie down to feed the jackals. But I'm not about to do that. I wouldn't mind if they were as docile as lambs, but they're not, they're savage wild animals that will drink an enemy's blood and rip out their guts.

"But don't be afraid," she continued with a tight laugh. "If you really have to die, it'll happen whether you're afraid or not. You can live your life in laughter or in tears, so why not be happy and enjoy it? I really have seen through it all. Mood is what matters most in life. What we call happiness and suffering are moods, nothing more. We're happy when we're in a good mood and sad when we aren't. We can't change the world, but we can change our moods, don't you think?"

Ying'er remained quiet as she tried to comprehend what Lanlan had said about moods. She realized they viewed life differently. Hopefully, they could learn something from each other.

Lanlan took advantage of the silence to sweep the flashlight beam across the sand, stirring up the black figures. She handed the light to Ying'er and told her to focus on one spot while she lay down, aimed, and fired. A plume of fire leapt out. They did not hear any yelps, but a commotion broke out.

"Damn, I missed. Bullets have distance, but less accuracy. Buckshot is better."

"Maybe you shouldn't keep shooting," Ying'er said. "They might keep their distance from us if you don't, but if you keep it up, they won't be afraid for long. Remember what they say, if you threaten a wolf with a stalk of hemp, it thinks you're holding a club and will stay away. But hit it once, and it'll know you're bluffing."

"I just want to show them what we've got," Lanlan said while reloading and suppressing her annoyance at Ying'er's comment. "I didn't expect to miss after taking such careful aim."

As before, the shot produced chaos among the jackals, but they quickly recovered and advanced, edging closer and closer. They'd also figured out that the flashlight held no threat, and kept moving no matter how much Ying'er swept the beam over them.

"Hurry. Get to the fire. Throw a bunch of branches on it," Lanlan called out urgently, rousing Ying'er, who saw that only embers remained. She flicked her lighter over some small branches, but they were wet and only sizzled. Lanlan handed her some dry twigs to get a fire going. "It looks like they're getting ready to attack." She shone the light around them. Ying'er gasped when she saw how many there were. "Tend the fire. Don't let it die out. I'm going to fire a few shots. If I don't show them what they're up against, they'll climb all over us."

At that moment, the silent animals suddenly let out loud shrieks.

Lanlan fired, but failed to overcome the sound.

She fired again. This time there were howls and yelps, and they held back; but they did not disperse. They were getting accustomed to the sound of musket fire, and it was no longer such a threat. Lanlan repeatedly sent buckshot whizzing into them, but it had lost its menacing power. Terror crept into Ying'er's heart, Lanlan looked rattled.

"Don't use up all the gunpowder," Ying'er cautioned. She couldn't help exhorting Lanlan, even though she believed her sister-in-law knew what she was doing.

"We're okay. I brought plenty. Enough to make it to daybreak, at least I hope so," Lanlan assured Ying'er and herself, for her confidence had begun to slip.

"What if they're still here then, as menacing in the daylight as they are now?" Ying'er asked silently.

Each time Lanlan paused to reload, a few animals leaped forward. They were probing. It was only the fire that kept them from swarming over their enemy, human and animal.

Lanlan dealt with the probes by taking careful aim, but not firing immediately. Instead, she waited for the boldest ones to draw closer, until they were no more than a couple of dozen feet from the fire, before pulling the trigger. The targets shrieked and fell, making hair-raising yelps that seemed more from anger than pain. Apparently, they hadn't thought much of the two women until, to their surprise, they suffered at their hands.

One of the jackals limped off, while the others gradually went silent after a racket of yelps and howls. The buckshot was obviously on target.

But the camels were spitting again. Several jackals had appeared to their west, where they threatened with explosive jumps and leaps.

After reloading yet again, Lanlan held her breath and aimed. One attacker charged before she could reload. Ying'er shook in fear, but managed to shine the flashlight on the animal, which crouched and snarled, huffing like a bitch protecting her pups. Ying'er had seen how they ran on the sand, like streaked lightning. She wanted to get to her Tibetan knife, but would have had to lay down her flashlight, which would then give the jackal the opportunity to come at her. It snarled, its teeth ghostly white, and its eyes, no longer green, had a shifty, vicious glare.

"Get away from us, damn you!" Lanlan hissed.

The musket fired.

Buckshot spewed out of the barrel. The jackal's eyes widened the instant the buckshot pierced its body. It barely had time to twist a few times before its legs kicked out and its eyes stared blindly at the sky.

"Get your knife ready. It looks like some aren't intimidated by our fire," Lanlan said as she wiped sweat from her face. Ying'er turned the flashlight toward the east, where she saw black dots closing in.

Nothing, it seemed, could hold them back.

Lanlan did not have time to take a breather. She kept reloading and firing, infusing the air with the smell of gunpowder. Each time the firing stopped, the jackals inched forward. Ying'er retrieved the kerosene they'd brought for the lantern, ready to pour it on the branches around them if the jackals charged. If they managed to break through the ring of fire, she'd set all the kindling on fire, jump in and let that be the end of it. Oddly enough, the thought removed some of her fear. Death was no longer at the front of her mind; now she was determined to fight for her life. Her chest tightened from the smell of gunpowder.

The musket shots grew sparse. It was not an easy weapon to reload, requiring the tamping of gunpowder down the barrel with a ramrod before adding buckshot and more gunpowder. During the pause between shots, jackals bounded over and backed off only when another shot was fired.

The range of their retreat was growing smaller. Ying'er made the fire bigger. None had leaped over it yet, but if nothing changed, they would be doing that sooner or later. Then what?

Hantou

Hantou was beset by a welter of emotions as he watched his wife and his brother from a spot behind them. With a sigh, he lay down on the wheat stalks, holding his head as he thought about his affliction. In his mind, Ying'er was a fleeting shadow, not a real person, forever beyond his reach. He felt unworthy of her, and it wasn't just because of his problem. She was gentle, calm, and lovely, always gliding around quietly, as if she were free of worries, no temper, not even acquiring a concrete form. During the many embarrassing and shameful moments in his life with her, she comforted him in a voice so soft, so tender it seemed otherworldly. There was never a hint of complaint, but her soothing comfort often gave rise to sadness in him, for he knew he held no attraction for her. He was aware of how dumb and inarticulate he was; he even walked in a clumsy way, devoid of carefree grace. Hantou was envious of his younger brother, Lingguan, for the confident, airy way he walked, but he could not carry himself like that. Once, he'd secretly imitated Lingguan, but blushed after taking a few steps.

Hantou was convinced not only that Ying'er was too good for him, but that his sister Lanlan was too good for Bai Fu, a conviction that weighed heavily on him. He knew he'd let his sister down as a brother and was not much of a husband to his wife. He regretted not objecting strongly enough to his parents' proposal of exchanging daughters. Back then, he'd already sensed it wasn't a good match, but he was smitten by the girl with big eyes framed by long lashes and a lovely nose that seemed carved from jade. The mere thought of her took his breath away. On their wedding day, he kept asking himself if it was really happening. He wasn't

45

dreaming, was he? Enveloped in a faintly surreal sensation, he had ended up embarrassing himself.

During their first three nights together, he could not bring himself to touch his wife, who was wrapped in a blanket as they lay in bed. He simply couldn't, even after mustering all his strength and mental energy. When he heard her sigh on the first night, he suspected she was lamenting her marriage to such a poor excuse of a man. He couldn't blame her. Made even more cautious by his speculation, he held his breath and maintained the same punishing position in bed, afraid he'd frighten her if he rolled over.

Finally, on the fourth night, he touched her, but only after bantering jests from Beizhu and his friends during the day. Beizhu had asked him if his new wife had cried out at night. Hantou had no idea what he meant, so Beizhu told him a woman cried out in bed when she had a good time.

"Well, did she?" he asked crudely

"She didn't?" he said in response to the silence. "Then you didn't do your job."

That night Hantou found, to his surprise, that Ying'er had undressed without turning off the light. On previous nights, she had waited until the light was off to disrobe. On this night, she removed her blouse, pants, and undershirt, before getting into bed in only a sleeveless top and a pair of red panties. He thought she gave him a look, but decided he'd only imagined it. Then she turned off the light before breathing yet another emotional sigh.

He felt his heart pound against his chest, while all he could see before his eyes was red, the color of her panties. Oddly though, it was that color, not her nakedness, that excited him.

Again and again, he reached out, but always drew his hand back. His heart beat wildly, loud noises roared in his ears. He was suffocating. He backed away once, twice, detesting himself each time; inch by inch he reached out to her, the miniscule progress nearly exhausting him, until midnight, when he finally touched her blanket.

She neither moved away nor responded to his action. But now that he'd poked open the invisible paper curtain separating them, he slipped under her blanket. He was surprised but happy to feel her arms around him.

Hantou would never know when the disorder had taken hold of him. He nearly collapsed the moment he came into contact with her searing body. He crumbled, his passion and happiness, even his self-worth, gone. Covered in sweat, his mouth was dry, and he was so enervated he could not even move off her when he heard her breathing hard under his weight.

He had failed to take control of the territory that was his to occupy. He couldn't, despite the passion he felt. And little by little, even that deserted him.

Hantou kept probing the cause of his disorder, but to no avail. He wondered if he was too old or if he'd been in too much of a hurry that night. But the most plausible cause had to be the summer day ten years before when he'd saved a girl who'd fallen into the Dasha River. He recalled that it had been a hot, sweaty day, and that when he jumped into the cold water, it felt as if many things had suddenly entered his body. Since then, he'd been plagued by a sore back, had difficulty urinating, and was often cold. And then this.

The symptoms never completely left him.

5

The musket was no longer a threat to the circling jackals. Ying'er could see that Lanlan had blundered by moving their tent site, as they now faced the enemy on all sides. But pointing that out served no purpose, she knew.

Terrified by the frightful attackers, the camels continued to spit and chuff. But the jackals were unfazed. The camels shook their heads violently in an attempt to break free, tugging and rocking the branches they were tethered to, until they realized how futile it was. If they tried to flee, they would become the first targets of a pack of animals that was laying siege to both them and the humans. They quieted down, no longer tugging at the tethers, though they never stopped snorting. Ying'er knew they were trying to frighten the enemy. They won't be afraid of your spittle if they don't even fear the musket, she said silently to them.

The situation was dire. They were short on firewood, which at the time had looked to be enough. It felt like several hours had passed since then, but maybe not. Ying'er had a purse with a watch and money in one of the litters. She took the flashlight from Lanlan, walked over to her litter, picked up her purse, and draped it around her neck. I could die out here, she said to herself, so why am I worrying about money? She chided herself, but kept the purse on her anyway. I'll need it if we somehow manage to escape. She took out her watch and saw it was nearly four in the morning. "A little over an hour till daybreak," she said to Lanlan.

The jackals occupied all the spots with vegetation and the

net was tightening. There would be no more kindling. Ying'er pulled what they had together; it made a pile no larger than a grave mound. How unlucky to be thinking about graves, she mused. Tears sluiced down her face.

"Why is the fire dying out?" Lanlan demanded angrily.

Drying her tears, Ying'er tossed a few of the small branches onto the fire, blew on it, and got it going again. She was mortified by her inattentiveness. They were fighting for their survival. Shamefaced, she stole a glance at Lanlan, whose profile showed ferocity but no anger. Lanlan immediately regretted her harsh tone and told herself not to forget that she was the reason Ying'er had to come out to the desert in the first place.

A few of the jackals were almost at the fireside now. Lanlan reloaded and hit two of them. Instead of fleeing, the remaining two bared their fangs, and did not back off until Ying'er threw on some wood to make the fire crackle. Obviously, that was what they feared most, but unfortunately, there wasn't much wood left. Ying'er looked longingly into the sky. She wondered if this would be her last glance at the stars, which flickered in the firelight, like the hope in her heart.

The firewood was nearly gone.

The lethal circle tightened as the fire grew smaller. The jackals were waiting for it to die. The women could see their bloodthirsty looks, convinced that they could detect human weakness. They shrieked in unison, their cries shrill and terrifying. Lanlan remained calm as she fired and reloaded, trying not to look unsettled. The once bright fire, the light of life, the light of hope, the warmest object in the dark, was shrinking fast. Food was no longer the focus of the jackals' assault; it had transcended the material level. The firelight and musket shots had awakened a different instinct in them.

The fire went out.

Darkness pressed down and highlighted a circle of green lights. Just as a cup of water cannot douse a mountain fire, the women's flashlight and musket were powerless to intimidate an enemy that was sensing a dawning victory. Lanlan wondered if she should continue their pointless resistance. The jackals were in no hurry to pounce; maybe they were playing a game of cat and mouse. They just kept shrieking. Nightmarish sounds like rabid dogs barking, hungry wolves howling, shrews ranting, and butchers cursing, were seemingly squeezed out between teeth, not from the throat, and accompanied by salivating and sinister laughs.

A blast of wind rushed toward Ying'er.

To her surprise, the blast was followed by flames shooting into the night sky. She detected the pungent smell of gunpowder. The jackals shrieked and backed off. Before she recovered from her shock, she saw Lanlan raise her hand, as the flames shot up again. She was sprinkling gunpowder on the embers. No wonder the jackals were intimidated.

"Don't just stand there and wait to die," Lanlan said. "Tear up the bedding and pour kerosene on it."

Ying'er understood—they had other things to burn.

Knife in hand, Ying'er shredded their tent and a blanket. One blanket first, she said to herself. They'd need at least one blanket if they were to make it out alive. She sprinkled kerosene and camel hair on the pieces. They'd brought the kerosene for the lantern, without which they would not be able to travel at night. But first they had to survive. After dousing the blanket with kerosene, she touched it to the fire and flung it at the jackals. The glowing ring of fire glided in the air, landed on a jackal, and set its fur on fire. Terrified, it shrieked and ran around in circles, trying to put the fire out, and driving the other jackals in retreat. The immolated animal howled from the pain, like a baying wolf.

"Great idea!" Lanlan cheered. Laying down her gunpowder pouch, she lit balls of camel hair doused in kerosene and flung them at the jackals. It did the trick. The beasts ran off in all directions, but not too far, refusing to be driven off that easily. After retreating thirty or forty feet, they stopped, a hateful glare filling their green eyes.

Hantou

Hantou did not think much about the lump he found near his ribcage one day and forgot all about it once the pain subsided. But it flared up again the next day during mealtime. "This is strange. I've got a lump here," he said.

"Wipe it with your spit first thing in the morning," his father told him. "Spit can take care of any skin problem."

"It's not on the skin. It feels like it's growing underneath. And it hurts, a dull pain that comes and goes."

"Inside you?" his mother asked, looking worried.

"I think so. It hurts here, by my ribcage. Maybe I should just let the pus build up and wait till it bursts."

She told him to take off his shirt and show her the spot. She pressed down a few times, and so did Laoshun, causing Hantou enough pain that he cracked his lips and sucked in cold air.

"When did this start?" his mother asked.

"I felt it last night. I think it's ready to pop. I hear it hurts when pus is forming. It hurt really bad a while ago when I was out in the field."

Lingguan walked up and pressed down on the spot. It was a worrying development, but he forced himself not to draw any ominous conclusion. "You need to see a doctor, even if it's just an abscess."

"A waste of money," Hantou said.

"No, it's not. That's what money's for. We'll take the bus into the city tomorrow."

"No!" Hantou raised his voice. "That'd cost a fortune. Forget it. I'll go see a doctor at the county clinic."

"Those quacks at the county clinic know nothing," Laoshun said. "If money has to be spent, use it for the right reason."

The next morning, Lingguan and Hantou caught a bus after breakfast.

By the time they arrived, the sun was high in the sky. Lacking the clean brilliance it displayed when shining down on the village, it looked different in the city, an object that sprayed people's heads with grime and clamor. Vehicles, big and small, zigzagged like startled mules, and people on bicycles seemed to be riding almost on top of each other. Pedestrians formed a deranged mass, shouting and cursing and bumping into one another. All the moving heads and swaying hips made Hantou dizzy; he stood frozen at an intersection, afraid to cross the street.

"Careful. You'll lose your eyeballs from all that staring," his brother joked.

"Sure, it doesn't bother you, after your school years here." Hantou blushed. "Why do they rush around like that?"

"They're going to work."

"They look like they're on the way to a fire. Can't they slow down?"

"They'll have their wages docked if they're late."

"Then why don't they leave home earlier?"

"City folks don't have the easy life we have. We can sleep till the sun bakes our asses, but they can't. They're busy with things like taking their kids to school before going to work. Some don't even have time for breakfast."

"That's so sad. I feel sorry for them."

"They feel sorry for us," Lingguan said with a laugh.

They went to a district hospital, where an elderly doctor shook his head after touching Hantou's ribcage. He could offer nothing concrete when Lingguan pressed him.

"Don't hold back, tell us what's wrong," Hantou said to the doctor. "How bad could it be? You can die at eighty or in your first year. I've lived a long life already."

"That's a good attitude." The doctor smiled. "It might be nothing. It's hard to say without an ultrasound. You know what that is, don't you?"

Lingguan nodded, telling Hantou to go pay for an ultrasound.

"Who is he?"

"My brother."

"It could be serious." The doctor looked into Lingguan's eyes.

"Like what?" Lingguan was alarmed.

"There are three possibilities. One, liver cancer, two, cirrhosis of the liver, and three, liver parasites. Has he been out on a grassland?"

"No."

"Too bad. Parasites would be best, since that can be taken care of with simple surgery. If it's something else, it could be a lot worse. Is he a big drinker?"

"He hardly ever drinks."

The look on Lingguan's face spurred the doctor into adopting a more comforting tone. "Take him to get the ultrasound. We'll know what it is once we have an image."

"It looks like parasites to me," the doctor reported after studying the ultrasound image. "Lots of people have come down with that from eating infected pork." He touched Hantou's rib area again and continued in a firmer tone, "It has to be that. The lump would not be so regular and smooth if it were something worse. Besides, you're young and you don't drink, so cirrhosis is out. And cancer doesn't seem likely."

Lingguan's mind was finally put at ease, and Hantou smiled.

The doctor patted Hantou on the shoulder and said, "No one's developed a pharmaceutical cure for liver parasites, so you'll need an operation."

"Then—how much—how much will that cost?" Hantou asked with trembling lips.

"Three to four thousand, I think. You'll have to check."

"I might as well be dead," Hantou muttered once they were outside.

"What are you talking about? It's not that serious. I was scared at first. Even the gods can't help you if it's cancer, so you're lucky it's only parasites."

"I'd rather have cancer and just die. But now—think about it—so much money. Where are we going to get it?"

"Don't worry so much. We'll spend as much as we have to."

Hantou stopped to rest. Looking miserable, he was silent for a long moment before finally saying, "I'd just as soon get hit by a car and put an end to it. That way, Mother and Father won't have to worry about me. Death is better than this."

"How can you talk like that? Do you really think they'd be relieved to see you dead? It's been hard seeing you grow into an adult, and you haven't started paying them back yet by raising a family and things like that, so no more of that ridiculous talk."

"How can I face them? What terrible luck to have a worthless son like me."

"Come on. Stop with the nonsense, will you? It doesn't do any good."

Hantou sat there silently, looking wretched.

"Life or death, it doesn't bother me," Hantou said with a sigh. "What worries me is the money. Three or four thousand! They'll be sick when they hear that."

"They don't scare as easily as you do." Lingguan smiled again. "Not after all they've been through." He tried his best, but could not talk Hantou out of his gloom.

"My god, three or four thousand!" he kept saying.

6

"We can't wait any longer," Lanlan said. "We have to find a way to escape."

"All right," Ying'er replied, as she doused more blanket shreds and clumps of fur with kerosene, making sure to pour on just enough to set them on fire. She emptied two large plastic bags to carry the kerosene-doused pieces, their homemade grenades, which she hoped would break open the siege. They loaded the camels and secured the litters before gathering up their belongings. Ying'er looked longingly at the pelt, hating the idea of leaving it behind, not because of the money it could fetch, but because of the time and effort Lanlan had put into skinning the camel. Lanlan followed her gaze, but didn't say anything; they both knew they had no time to get it loaded. Their lives were more important.

Lanlan picked up her musket and hung the gunpowder pouch around her neck. Ying'er stowed the chopper and tucked away her knife. Each carrying a plastic bag with balls of camel hair and a lighter, they had their camels kneel so they could climb on and sit between the humps. Riding in front, Lanlan cleaved a path through the dark night with her flashlight. The jackals stared silently, as they had yet to recover from the fiery shock, and scampered to the side when they saw Lanlan approach. Expecting to have to open fire to make way, she was pleased to see them move off on their own.

"We'll take it slow and not run. If we did, they'd know we're afraid." Lanlan told Ying'er, who had the fur balls ready to light and toss. "We can't outrun them."

They wanted to go slow, but not their camels. Fearful of the teeth lying in wait, they snorted and released long, monotonous cries. Both women had to jerk hard at the reins to keep them from bolting forward.

Now that the jackals were quiet, Lanlan knew better than to provoke them. As they passed through the gap in the surrounding threat, Ying'er held her lighter tightly in one hand, a ball of camel hair in the other. She would light it and toss it as soon as the beasts made a move. The jackals took a few steps back, as if they knew what was coming.

The flashlight beam shone on the undulating desert, where a faint, morning glow appeared in the eastern sky. It was the light of hope. Ying'er breathed a sigh of relief, as exhaustion crept up on her. She hadn't sensed fatigue under the intense pressure, but now her bones seemed hollowed out and her eyelids drooped. For a moment, she even felt a loss of consciousness and wondered if she'd fallen asleep. Maybe that would be best, just shut her eyes and go to sleep, even if a jackal were right at her heels.

Lanlan shone the flashlight behind them, where the line of black dots had changed into a circle that froze in the sand trough. The embers of their rekindled fire continued to emit a dim, yellow glow. A cool desert wind that seemed to have risen from the camels' chiming bells blew over like water and sent a chill into them. It was a welcome breeze. Ying'er was thirsty, after sweating so much. So, putting the ball of fur back into her bag, she unhooked the jug from the camel litter and took a few drinks before handing it to Lanlan, who hung the musket strap around her neck, took the jug, and drank her fill. She had been careful with water up till now, but surviving the harrowing experience justified a reward.

The black circle grew smaller in the beam. Ying'er was relieved, though puzzled over how such fierce animals would be so frightened by a few flying balls of fire. Maybe they'd simply been caught by surprise.

Dawn was deepening in the east. The wind turned cold and brisk, a wind the villagers called a downhill breeze, for it swirled down from the Qilian Mountains nearly every morning. When the autumn harvest was over, the village old timers would rely on the wind to winnow the wheat. Ying'er felt it had taken some of her fatigue away. The camels snorted loudly, as if to celebrate the narrow escape, and began to speed up; Lanlan stopped jerking the reins. The more distance they put between them and the predatory pack behind them, the better, naturally, but Ying'er was afraid that too fast a pace would alert the jackals. Lanlan shone the flashlight behind them again, and they saw no black dots, as a sand hill had risen between them and their foes. Feeling reassured, Lanlan let loose the reins, tightened her legs, and sent the camels flying.

Camel humps are sturdy, but they do not provide a comfortable ride. When a horse takes off, its back rises and falls gently, while a running camel bucks its rider. Ying'er secured her plastic bag of fur to the litter so she could hold on to the hump with both hands. The last thing she wanted was to frighten her ride, for she would then lose control of it.

Sensing what might happen, Lanlan began to pace them. Her musket swung violently across her chest, so she held onto it with one hand while tugging at the reins with the other. The camel was obedient enough to slow down. Ying'er's camel, following from behind, did the same.

Then they heard the shrieks. Ying'er quickly retrieved a ball of fur. She flicked her lighter repeatedly, but each time it went out in the wind. After several tries, she finally lit the ball and tossed it behind her, but it failed to stop the pursuing jackals, which merely swerved to the side. The camels panicked and started to run.

When Lanlan raised her musket and fired behind her, she heard only a soft pop. The gunpowder must have spilled out during their bucking ride.

Ying'er clicked the lighter over and over, and still the wind blew the light out each time. She knew they could no longer stop the jackals even if she set a whole bag of fur on fire. The desert was vast, with many paths, and the pursing animals could avoid the fireball she'd struggled to light by simply making a slight detour. She put the lighter away and stuffed the fur back into the bag. With one hand on the camel's hump, she gripped her knife in the other. So, this was it, the final struggle. Lanlan tried loading the musket several times, but the gunpowder spilled out each time, so she had to give up. The camel was running like mad, with no prompting from her legs. Their only hope for survival hinged on the camels' ability to run, though they both knew that jackals are among the fastest creatures in the desert, and that running alone would not spare them from the beasts' sharp teeth.

Ying'er was fairly new to camelback riding; in her experience, they were mostly docile animals that moved at an even pace. This was her first time galloping like this, and she was nervous as her camel took off. She sprawled over the hump, the pain in her tailbone from bumping against the hump behind her intense, despite the blanket padding. Lanlan, after shredding her blanket, was sitting on a few thin sacks, and she too felt the pain, but it didn't bother her as much. Sometimes, she felt like her father, the man who toiled and stoically bore the hardships, because that was life. They were born to suffer. She was the one who had chosen to come out here, when so much of her life had been decided by someone else. With an odd sense of exhilaration, she turned to grin at her companion. It looked more like a grimace to Ying'er, who then unhooked her bag of fur, nudged the camel forward to catch up, and handed it to Lanlan to sit on. Since the fireballs could no longer stop the jackals, they might as well make the ride a bit more comfortable.

It had gotten light out before they'd noticed. The pursuing jackals hung back a little, apparently still wary of any secret weapons the women might have. The shrieks were now overpowered by the wind whipping past their ears and the clanking cooking utensils.

"Don't be afraid now." Lanlan said. "They should run off once the sun is up. Just be careful and don't fall."

Her well intentioned reminder made Ying'er nervous. If I fall, she thought, I'll be quickly reduced to bones. What she feared most was the camel losing control over its front feet. It would pitch forward if it stumbled on a rat's nest and could break a leg from the momentum. The nest holes were mostly in the shady dunes, and that was where Lanlan was headed, since the sunlit ones were covered in loose sand over which the jackals could run smoothly, while the camels could easily roll off.

Clearly, their foe was not ready to let a meal escape so easily. They continued their pursuit and grew bolder when they saw no more new tricks from their human targets. Speeding up as if engaged in a game, they got closer and closer, so unnerving the camels that their rhythmic pace faltered. If we keep running like this, Ying'er said to herself, it won't be long before my camel's legs give out. It was a terrifying thought, but the weariness in her heart overwhelmed her fear, so she gave the animal its lead. She could hear the jackals' panting.

Lanlan flung something into the air. Ying'er saw it was the bag of camel hair. The jackals stopped momentarily, but quickly swarmed up to tear it to pieces. It hadn't stopped them completely, but at least it had delayed the inevitable. Grabbing the hump with one hand, Ying'er tried to remove her sack of pots and pans, but could not undo the knot; meanwhile, a shrieking jackal was running alongside her camel. She sliced the sack open with her dagger, sending the contents—pots, bowls, and chopsticks—to the ground with a crash. Her pursuer was stunned into standing still, mistaking the clamorous objects as lethal weapons.

"That's it!" Lanlan exclaimed. "Toss things at them to save ourselves."

It was the break they needed to make their escape, at least they hoped so.

"Take out everything except the food and water," she shouted. "Throw something at them every time they get close. We'll worry about the rest later."

Ying'er groped around in the sack to retrieve the bundle of clothing when the shrieks again came upon her from behind.

Half the sun had risen into the sky, but the white disc emerging from the horizon made little difference to the jackals, which displayed more interest in the women's colorful clothing than the escaping humans. They ran up in great excitement when a piece drifted down, tugging and pulling and tearing, until shreds littered the ground like butterflies. One after another piece was flung off, piquing their interest again and again. Obviously sensing that their opponents had run out of options, they took their time to enjoy the game of shredding clothes. Each time they finished off one item, they leaped and bounded excitedly. Fully aware that the jettisoned clothing had only slowed the arrival of death, Ying'er was nevertheless sorry to see her clothes disappear. The last piece was a sky-blue blouse, a gift from Lingguan. *I won't throw this one away no matter what. I'll die with it.* On a whim, she pulled it on over her coat.

Lanlan had cast off almost everything, and that should have done what she had hoped. By then, the sun was up and the sky was clear, with no red glow, meaning a hot day to come. But the pursuing jackals did not appear to be suffering from head pains. Once they had exhausted their enthusiasm over the destruction of the clothing, they turned their attention back to the women, who had mocked them by hurling useless objects. They were shrieking loudly, menacingly, sounding as if they knew the enemy had no more tricks.

They started their final assault.

The sand trough was filled with their shrieks.

They swept up like a whirlwind.

Ying'er stopped tossing things away now that the jackals had lost interest. Death was imminent, she knew, but she refused to accept it. The jackals' shrieks felt unreal, as did the bumpy sand ridges and Lanlan, who kept turning to reassure her from the back of her hurtling camel. Ying'er cast a dazed backward glance, and saw the jackals leaping like fleas in a hot pan. They were coming for her life. The camel bucked violently as it ran up and down sand troughs, nearly throwing Ying'er off. Don't fall, she told herself. Of course, I'll die sooner or later anyway. And yet her body lay down low on its own and pressed tightly against the camel's hump.

The sounds behind her disappeared. It was hard to say if they were truly gone or if it just seemed so. Either way, they were gone, or so she thought. The camel had stopped panting, and the wind no longer whizzed by their ears. Everything seemed to freeze into a colossal piece of crystal. Ying'er could still feel the bumping sensation under her, though it, too, seemed fainter. She was so tired she felt she could sleep on the camel's back. Lanlan had slowed down, jerking her reins to maintain the right distance between them. Ying'er was grateful for Lanlan's action. She thanked her fate for giving her a sister-in-law who was willing to die with her.

She was roused by Lanlan's screams, either to frighten the jackals or to draw them to her. Ying'er laughed sadly. Would they fear her scream if even their weapons no longer frightened them?

"Don't worry about me, Lanlan." She called out. "Run. At least one of us can make it out alive."

"What nonsense." Lanlan glared at her. "Don't worry. Their

heads will start hurting once the sun rises higher.

Ying'er knew that was just a ploy to comfort her.

She turned to see them inching closer. The closest ones were no more than fifteen feet from her camel. She could even see the greed in their eyes and the bared fangs, as well as the yellow sand they kicked up. The glance brought back the terror that had been lessened by her earlier sensation of illusion. Loathing for the jackals rose up inside, which made her tighten her grip on the knife. I won't let you get me so easily, she said silently.

"Step carefully," she said to her ride, patting the camel's back. "I'll give the jackals a taste of my knife."

The camel made a noise as if to tell her she could count on it.

"Behind you!" Lanlan shouted. Ying'er turned and saw a black object leaping into her field of vision. Reflexively, she plunged the knife down. It barely touched something, but then she heard a shriek and saw the thing tumble down a sand trough.

"Great! One down." Lanlan cheered.

Surprised, Ying'er looked at her knife. There was blood. She was amazed at how easy it had been. Emboldened, she raised her weapon when she saw another jackal leap for her camel. This time several attempts came up empty, not even grazing the beast's hair.

More jackals caught up with them. Ying'er, bolder now, swung her knife and sliced at them; she missed, but they were frightened enough to stay back. They shrieked and bounded, obviously trying to shattered their opponents' nerves. She was afraid, but never let up stabbing. Her camel was the first to panic, as it began to twist and turn. She had to jerk the reins to keep it from running off; it was hard maintaining her place alongside Lanlan.

A jackal took the opportunity to pounce. It seemed focused on catching her knife-wielding hand, but miscalculated and landed near the camel's tail instead. She raised her weapon but accidently brought it down on the camel's backside. Blood ran from a large gash, and the camel panicked.

The smell of blood incited the animals' wild nature, as they bounded up front, intending to block the camels' way. Hers fell for their tactic and swerved. "Grab its neck. Hold tight!" Lanlan yelled. Before she understood what was going on, Ying'er was thrown off by a great force. She flew into the air and tumbled over and over, feeling sand pelt her face.

"Hurry! Hurry!"

Ying'er heard Lanlan's urgent shouts when she stopped rolling. She opened her eyes to see two camel legs, then Lanlan's hand reaching down for her. Ying'er got to her feet by grasping the hand.

"Come up!" Lanlan shouted.

With difficulty, Ying'er climbed onto the camel's back by grabbing hold of Lanlan's hand and stepping on her foot. Then she saw the fallen camel struggling on the ground, crying in pain, but by then it was already covered by jackals.

"It's hopeless," Lanlan said. "Its leg is broken. It probably stepped in a rats' hole."

Jackals continued to pounce on the bleating camel. One of them tried to get near the women, but Lanlan gnashed her teeth and put it down with one shot. She was in no hurry to flee, for she knew their fallen camel would provide enough food for the jackals for a while. She took her time reloading the musket.

Lingguan and Ying'er

Lingguan took a break from the hospital to go home. He was surprised to notice how gaunt his mother had become, almost like a different person.

It was village women's busiest time of year, weeding and pulling up oat stalks, sweating under a scorching sun. Unquestioned conventions dictated that these were women's jobs, so the men had free time to loaf and shoot the breeze. To be sure, some women talked or forced their men into coming to the field to pull oat stalks, turning these men into examples for other women. But other women's husbands always showed their contempt for their henpecked fellow villagers.

Lingguan's mother blanched when she saw him walk in, but could not find the courage to ask why he was home.

"Nothing's wrong," he assured her. "The surgery is set for Saturday."

"Why did they drag it out so long?" Laoshun asked.

"That's the day they operate on infectious cases," Lingguan replied. "We shouldn't complain. At least they've found a slot for us."

"How many times did you have to give them something?"

"Twice. Five hundred Yuan each time. They asked for more yesterday, but I haven't paid them yet."

"So much has been spent already," his mother said. "How much more will it cost us after the operation?"

"Most of the money is spent before the operation. They had to take three ultrasounds. But what can we do? The actual procedure doesn't cost much."

"It's not right to have to pay for all that, but we'll do it. We have no say where illness is concerned," Laoshun said.

"Where's his wife?" Lingguan asked.

"In the kitchen," his mother replied. "She's lost weight. She doesn't want to eat."

"I don't feel much like eating either," Lingguan said. "I feel a pressure in my chest that makes me restless. Hantou asked me to give her something." He went into the kitchen.

Ying'er was rolling out dough. She blushed when she saw him, but the color soon receded.

"The surgery is set for Saturday, and he'll be fine once it's over."

She cast him a wordless glance before lowering her head, sending teardrops falling onto the dough.

"It's nothing, really. It's minor surgery."

Ying'er dried her tears with her sleeve and, still not speaking, continued working. "Are you going back today?" she asked after a long pause.

"Yes."

"I'll go with you. He's my husband, after all."

"There's no place for you to sleep."

"It's just one night. I won't sleep. They must have a place to sit."

"It's not up to me. Go ask Mother. You can go if she says okay." He took out a bottle of lotion and handed it to her. "From him to you."

"That looks expensive. How much was it?"

"That's not important. He said it's been especially hard on you, and wanted you to know that all the city girls use this."

Ying'er's her eyes reddened as she turned to remove a pot lid.

"She wants to see Hantou," Lingguan said to his mother when she walked in.

"Me too. I worry about him all the time."

"So, is it all right if I go?" Ying'er asked her mother-in-law.

"Why not? I'd like to go, but I can't bring myself to spend the money. Besides, there's work to do in the field."

"It doesn't cost much," Lingguan said. "The bus fare is only a few yuan, and the food is cheap."

"I'll take food with me," Ying'er said.

Lingguan's mother tugged on his sleeve for him to go out with her. "Make sure to keep your eyes open," she whispered once they were outside. "Leave them alone when they're together, all right?"

He laughed. "There are other people in the room. I can leave them alone, but I can't ask the others to do the same."

"Just do as I say." His mother glared at him.

"All right."

After lunch, Ying'er packed up a change of clothes for Hantou and made a few of his favorite snacks before leaving with Lingguan. When they neared the village entrance, they saw Beizhu and his friends teasing Maodan, the village bachelor, who was too poor to marry.

"Nonsense." Maodan was giggling foolishly.

Lingguan laughed when he overheard what they were saying.

"What are you laughing about, Lingguan?" Maodan blurted out. "Run and catch up. Your sister-in-law won't wait for you."

With that, Maodan shifted the target of the teasing to Lingguan.

"Just look at how she walks. You can see she misses you already."

Ying'er kept walking; her face turned a bright red, as she knew she did not want to hear what they were saying.

"What are you waiting for, Lingguan?" Maodan was relentless. "Go on. Put your arms around her and give her a kiss."

"Oh, yes, you'd better hurry. Just look at those red, smooth lips and flirty eyes," another one taunted.

Lingguan quickened his steps to catch up to her, knowing it was useless to talk back.

The Dasha River and a sand hollow separated their village from the highway. Once they were in the hollow, Ying'er turned and asked Lingguan, "What did they say?"

"I didn't catch any of it."

He looked into her eyes. She held his gaze, but then she bit her lip and began to sob.

"Look at you." Lingguan was alarmed. "I didn't do anything. Why are you crying?"

She lowered her head to dry her tears, but they kept coming, until her face was wet. Lingguan worried about what people would accuse him of if anyone happened to walk by. He looked around, and was relieved to see that they were alone.

No longer just shedding silent tears, Ying'er was sobbing audibly by then. He tried to get her to keep moving, but she fell into his arms. He failed to nudge her away, while her lips were all over his face, streaking it with tears.

"What if someone sees us—?"

"I don't care," she said in mid sob.

"He gently kissed her on the cheek, before pushing her away. She let go and, drying her tears, stared into his eyes intently.

Emotionally stirred by the gaze, he made sure no one was around before lifting up her face and kissing her. She sighed contentedly, rousing him so much that he smothered her with more kisses.

"Will it be all right?" he whispered.

"Here?" she murmured. "Too many people."

He was breathing hard as he pointed to a nearby ridge. "It's secluded over there." Wordlessly she followed him up to the ridge and rolled down the slope behind him. "In broad daylight—" she said cautiously.

Suddenly, his brother's face thudded into his head. I'm no damned good! he said to himself, but he was too weak to suppress his surging desire. His mind and body had been steeped in anxiety and agitation for days, and now Ying'er had appeared like a cool breeze, turning him into a hungry beast with no self-control.

When they had finished, Lingguan's passion spent, he was

drowning in self-reproach. "I'm no damned good!" he said. She blanched, and her hands froze in mid movement of smoothing out her clothes.

She sat up. "It's my fault," she said quietly. "Don't blame yourself. Let me accept the retribution and punishment. Don't be hard on yourself."

"I knew—I shouldn't—" He kept berating himself. "But I can't—I couldn't help it—let's go."

The moment he saw Hantou, Lingguan was inundated with waves of self-reproach.

His older brother was rail thin. Lingguan hadn't realized until now how gaunt he'd gotten, almost skeletal, in fact, and with a frightening yellow pallor. His face was covered in spots, but not enough to hide the sallow tone. It was almost more than he could bear.

Hantou was delighted that his wife could be with him at a moment like this. With no intent to hide his excitement, he smiled to show how pleased he was and how lucky he felt.

Obviously unprepared, Ying'er was startled to see how he'd changed. At that instant, he was like a total stranger, as if she'd never shared a bed with him. But her sympathetic nature gave rise to tenderness and brought tears, as she condemned herself for what she'd done earlier with Lingguan.

Too moved by her tears to know what to do, Hantou rubbed his hands and looked at his brother, as if asking for help. Lingguan, his eyes downcast, was mired in self-reproof. Hantou turned anxious. "This place—I, I don't have anything for you to eat."

"I'll go buy some fruit," Lingguan said and walked out.

"Who's this?" one of the other patients asked Hantou.

"My wife."

"Ah! She's beautiful."

"I know. That's what everyone says." He was smiling. "They all say she's a pretty flower stuck in a pile of cow dung."

"Who says that?" she pouted, which made him laugh.

Lingguan walked in with some fruit. When Hantou took it out to wash it, she looked at Lingguan, who shook his head and gave her a bitter smile tinged with self-reproach. She smiled too, but with the implication that what had happened had happened, and there was no need to dwell on it. That did nothing to dispel his guilt feelings.

7

Ying'er's camel had been Laoshun's favorite animal, which he'd refused to sell for any amount of money. She'd have rather fed herself to the jackals. Staring blankly at her mount crying pitifully under the jackals' teeth, she wept. How were they ever going to face her father-in-law over this?

"I wish I could take its place," she said.

"I feel terrible too, but don't say that," Lanlan comforted her despite her own sadness. "Staying alive means everything. And with the two of us working, we'll be able to pay my father for the poor camel."

Feeling the effect of the desert wind blowing through her clothes and into her heart, Ying'er was cold inside and out. The doomed camel, quiet now, lay splayed on the sandy slope, only its feet showing, the rest of its body covered in hungry jackals. The beasts left the two women alone, absorbed with the dying animal over which they swarmed in a frenzy, fighting over food and beginning to snipe and bite at each other. It felt unreal to Ying'er when she thought about how a pack animal that was carrying her life on its back just moments before was now being eaten by bloodthirsty jackals.

"Let's go," Lanlan said with a sigh, after loading her musket.

She let loose the rein, and the camel, without prompting, turned and ran off. It must have been affected by its companion's fate, for it kept at a fast pace, even when sweat soaked its body. The threat from jackals' teeth was an intimidating whip.

Ying'er dried her tears. Crying is a waste of time, she told herself.

"We can do without everything else, I just hate losing that water," Lanlan said with a sigh. "But that's all right. We still have some left; we'll have to pace ourselves."

The mention of water seemed to have turned on a switch of thirst and hunger, which came with a vengeance. They drank some water and had part of a steamed bun as they rode along.

"Lucky for us Pa was experienced enough to tell us to divide up our provisions. If not, we'd die of thirst even after managing to escape the jackals," Lanlan said.

"I guess it means we haven't suffered enough," Ying'er said with a sad smile.

"Don't worry. We have gunpowder left. I'll get us a couple of unlucky rabbits. Good fortune awaits those who survive a calamity, people say. I hope they're right."

Sleepiness spread over them like a net when their nerves settled. They started to doze off, swaying back and forth on the camel's back. Lanlan tried to stay awake to make sure they hadn't strayed too far off their route, but she knew they'd be fine so long as they kept going east. At worst, they'd reach Mongolia, and civilization, which would be their salvation. With two people sharing one person's ration of food and water, they wouldn't last long if they traveled in circles.

The camel was breathing harder. It had run a great distance, carrying two people, and was using up the energy converted from the feed it had consumed the night before. They needed to find a grassy area, not just for the camel, but so they could rest too. Lanlan was exhausted. Ying'er was sprawled against her, fast asleep. If they didn't stop to rest soon, one or both of them could fall off their camel.

As they rounded a sand ridge, they saw some desert plants,

which looked old but were still edible, at least for a camel. The so-called ships of the desert have a broad food source and eat most of the vegetation in the desert. Lanlan shook Ying'er awake, and they got down off the camel, tethering it loosely to a shrub and not removing the litter. Without a word, they slumped onto the dry sand and were asleep before they even lay down flat.

A long time had passed when the scorching sun roused Lanlan. Her face was bathed in sweat and her throat was on fire. It was nearly noon, and there wasn't a hint of breeze in the sand trough.

Their camel was gone.

Stunned by what had happened, she nudged Ying'er awake.

"The camel's run off," Lanlan said. A woman who did not like to show weakness, she was nonetheless choking up. Ying'er, who had been fighting jackals in her dream, felt her tongue turn numb when she heard. That's it, we're done for, she figured. The camel had their water and their food.

Luckily, there was no wind, so they could easily follow the trail left by the runaway camel. Long rows of large prints, some shallow, some deeper, extended into the horizon. If the camel has set its mind on going it alone, Lanlan despaired silently, we'll never catch it. Camels rarely run off. They somehow know it is wrong, no matter the reason. As she thought back to the night before, she lamented their decision to not remove the litter before they lay down to sleep. Now their food and water were gone. She was suddenly overwhelmed by her longing for the family camel; considered the best in the village, it was called the King of Camels, after it had swung two wolves to their death when they hung on to its hump. How sad that it ended up feeding a pack of wild animals. It's so true so often, she reflected, that the one that should have lived died and the one that should have died lived. But why must it be that way?

Their breathing grew labored after a while, for they hadn't

completely recovered from their exhaustion. Lanlan wondered if the camel had left in search of grass and water, or if it had simply taken off. If the latter, then it was pointless to keep up the pursuit. They slumped to the ground and gasped.

"Let's keep looking," Ying'er said, not willing to give up easily. "At least we have to try,".

So, they stumbled along, following a row of prints that swerved up a slope and down to a trough until they found a steamed bun that had rolled into an indention made by a two-toed foot. The camel was nowhere in sight.

"This is the camel that ought to have fed the jackals," Lanlan said as she wiped off her sweat. "But let's keep looking. The sack with the buns was obviously broken, so we'll at least recover some food even if we can't catch the camel."

Ying'er agreed, so they set off again. They came upon some more buns and, after that, nothing but camel prints.

"Maybe the damned camel ate the rest of them," Lanlan said

Sure enough, they found bits of steamed buns on a sandy spot.

"That's it," she said. "Let's turn back."

The sisters-in-law were still in shock, first by seeing Ying'er's ride being torn apart by the pack of jackals after stepping in a hole and nearly killing her in the process, and next by the flight of Lanlan's ride. Losing the food was tolerable, since there were desert rice plants to stave off starvation. But no water was a death sentence. It would not take long for the blood to congeal and stop flowing, with the sun's pulsating rays licking at the skin. Prolonged exposure will dry a person up completely. Ying'er already felt dehydrated after sweating during their search for the vanished camel. No wonder it left, she said to herself. All creatures cherish life. She and Lanlan hadn't been the only ones terrified by the savage predators, so had been the camel. None of them had known what dangers lay ahead, so naturally the animal had decided to strike out on its own.

Back in the trough where they'd slept, they sat on the sand as the sun beat down on them, neither of them feeling like talking. The fleeing camel had taken with it all chances of survival for them. They could not travel far, and each step would deplete their bodily fluids, helped by the sun, which would want its share. It was hopeless.

They'd been able to bear the thirst before the flight of the camel and had wet their lips with tiny sips to help relieve the craving. Now their bodies felt tormented by thirst, each cell crying out for water. Ying'er's throat itched, as if scratched by the paws of those frenzied jackals. She tried not to think about it. Fighting the jackals had been perilous, but she could at least see the enemy and deal an occasional blow. Now there was no enemy. Maybe the glaring white sun above them could count as one, but nothing good could come out of going to war with the sun. Her body was the only opponent she could see and touch. As her thoughts continued, she believed that her struggle had all been for the sake of her body, which she had worked hard to feed and clothe. Now, it appeared, the end had come.

Hantou and Lingguan

The days leading up to his surgery were the worst Hantou had ever experienced.

One of the causes was the frightening cost—more than forty yuan a day—for the hospital. Doctors annoyed him, for they were always prescribing drips of one sort or another. In his view they, the medications and the shots, were a waste of money, since they could not rid his liver of the parasites. Each IV drip amounted to drinking his parents' blood.

The other cause was that the date for the operation had yet to be scheduled. The doctors kept saying they needed to observe him carefully. Observe? What was there to observe? In addition to three ultrasounds, he'd also had a chest X-ray, a liver function test, and an EKG, all of which he considered doctors' tricks to make more money. His problem was with the growing lump in his liver, not with his head or his chest. Why did they have to perform all those other tests on a poor man like him?

There was one other patient in his hospital ward with the same problem as Hantou—liver parasites. One end of a tube had been inserted into the man's rib area, the other end connected to a bottle containing red liquid. He walked with a bent back, baring his teeth and holding the IV bottle in one hand. People said that whoever came into contact with the liquid in the bottle would be afflicted with the same disease, which was why the man was treated like the carrier of plague. Hantou felt terrible at the thought that he would end up like the man, and yet he couldn't wait for that to happen, for every day in the hospital meant more money spent.

"Be careful not to touch the liquid in the bottle," Hantou said to Lingguan, just about the only topic that let him pretend to be cheerful.

"Are you afraid?" Lingguan asked.

"I have to go through with it, afraid or not." Hantou did his best to look unconcerned, but gloom soon overtook him again.

Finding the smell in the room unbearable, he dragged Lingguan outside after he finished a bag of IV fluid. But he wanted to go back inside once they were on the street, as he thought of the empty bed they'd paid for; he wanted to spend as much time on that bed as possible in order to get his money's worth.

"Let's walk around some more. That will cheer you up," Lingguan said. "Even a healthy person would get sick being cooped up in that room all day. Besides, you'll have to stay in for a while once you've had your operation."

"But when will that be?" Hantou sighed. "More than forty yuan a day. It scares me just thinking about it. They're going to operate sooner or later, so why waste money sitting around waiting? Can't you talk to anyone about moving it up?"

"I've talked to them more times than I can count, but it's no use. They have their procedures, and everyone has to be put under observation for several days. Besides, they schedule operations for Saturdays, so we'll have to wait. But I'll go talk to them again in a day or two."

"Wait? How much longer?" Hantou scowled. "Why did they have to run all those tests? Open me up and take those parasites out. They make it so complicated. And I'm told you have to give them gifts. Without them they won't even schedule the surgery."

"Don't worry about that." Lingguan said. "Leave everything to me. Just take care of yourself and don't worry about anything else."

"Take care? I take care and the lump gets bigger every day."

They reached a busy street. All the vehicles and pedestrians made Hantou's head swim. The sun was hazy, not bright and clear like it was in the countryside. Feeling like a sleepwalker, Hantou would have preferred to return to the hospital for a nap, but he did not want to disappoint his brother, so he tagged along dreamily. When they reached a square with a bronze statue, Hantou gazed at the horse rearing up over him.

"That horse looks like it's falling over."

"I know. But the city has spent too much on it to let it do that."

"Then it can't fall," Hantou said.

"That's right." They laughed at how they were talking as if they had a say in such important matters.

Hantou said he wanted to have his picture taken. "It'll be my first ever. It could come in handy one day."

"Sure, let's do it." Lingguan studied his brother, who smiled back at him. "But no bad thoughts."

"I know." Hantou wondered if his brother was hiding something from him. Fighting the suspicion, he managed a forced smile as he entered a photo studio with his brother to have his picture taken.

"Since we're here, we may as well have one taken together." Hantou stole a glance at his brother. He was relieved to note nothing unusual on Lingguan's face.

Hantou's surgery twenty-one days into his hospital stay resulted in a diagnosis of cancer. The lump in around his ribcage was smooth because of the membrane around it. Stupefied by the news, Lingguan felt numb.

"What?" he asked in disbelief.

"A malignant tumor in his liver, about the size of a small melon."

"How long—does he have?"

"Hard to say, but not long. He's bleeding internally."

"Does he know?"

"Not yet."

"Did you remove it?" Lingguan felt his strength leave him.

"I couldn't. I just sewed him back up. You need to pay five yuan for the tissue sample." The doctor pointed at a lump of flesh bobbing in a jar.

The need to pay blunted Lingguan's shock, but he was overwhelmed by the absurdity of the situation. He felt like screaming at the doctor, "My brother is dying and you want five yuan for a damned tissue sample? What's the point?" But he wasn't brought up that way, so, instead, he rummaged through his pockets and brought out a handful of small bills. His hands shook so badly he couldn't be sure he had the right amount after counting it several times. The doctor took the bills and counted them quickly before they disappeared into his pocket.

"Please, don't tell—the others—especially my parents—I'm the only one to know. Please?"

"Of course. You can go get your folks. They'll be bringing him down soon."

Lingguan walked back to the hallway, where he leaned against the wall, feeling himself go limp. One thought stood out amid the buzz in his head, What if Mother finds out? She had endured so much already, her wrinkled face marked by years of pain and suffering.

Then another thought: he wished Hantou would die quickly. Liver cancer was the king of all cancers. Someone in their village had it and his screams from the pain, like a lowing cow, had sliced at the villagers' hearts for months. Instant death would be better than suffering like that. Moreover, Lingguan shuddered at the thought of the despair Hantou would feel once he knew; that would be worse than death.

Everything felt like a bad dream—if only it were.

Could the diagnosis be wrong? Lingguan thought hopefully. It was possible. How wonderful that would be. He mustered up the energy to walk back to the hall and wait for the doctor to come out.

With great effort, Lingguan managed to ask, "Could it have

been misdiagnosed, Doctor?"

"Unlikely." The doctor looked at him and continued in a firm voice, "There's always the tissue sample. We'll know when we get the test result."

"Could he have another operation if the result comes out negative?"

"We'll wait and see." The doctor smiled faintly.

Lingguan felt a bud of hope sprout in his heart.

He went downstairs, where he was greeted by his father.

"Did he have the operation?"

"Yes, he did." Lingguan could hardly look into his father's murky eyes, but he forced a smile.

"Good, that's good." Laoshun exhaled. "I'm glad it's over."

Lingguan's throat was parched. He wanted to swallow to smooth the itchiness, but his tongue was numb and dry. He sighed when he thought of his mother.

"Tell me the truth." Laoshun blanched. "Is it really bad?"

"Not really." Lingguan kept up his smile. He knew he'd put on a convincing performance when he saw the color slowly return to his father's face.

"Good, as long as it's not bad." Laoshun mumbled.

The door to the operating theater opened.

Hantou was lying on a gurney, his chest exposed above the dressing. He was awake; his eyes were sunken and his lips colorless on a face that was frighteningly yellow. What Lingguan found most shocking was how such drastic changes could occur in only a couple of hours. My dear brother. Do you know what you have? Lingguan cried out silently.

Hantou groaned.

Laoshun rushed up to him.

"Step back." The doctor tried to wave Laoshun back.

"Get back, I said," the doctor repeated impatiently. They

pushed the gurney into an elevator. Lingguan and his father raced down the stairs.

Hantou was moaning when they walked into his room. "They operated on me without a shot. When the knife first went in, it hurt like hell."

"Didn't you give him a gift? The guy in charge of anesthesia?" A ward mate asked.

"We had to give him one, too?" Lingguan asked.

"Of course. No wonder—no wonder." The man shook his head and sighed.

Looking at Hantou's bandaged and tubed belly and then at his sallow face, Lingguan was overcome by sadness. Hantou would not have had to suffer through the operation if they'd known what he had. Someone once told Lingguan that an ultrasound can tell the difference between an infected liver and cancer. In other words, the doctors had lied to them, for money, most likely. But deep down, he knew that Hantou would have had the operation even if they had known; his family would be appeased, giving up only after that. He shuddered when he thought about how the doctor had made a seven-inch incision on Hantou's belly without anesthesia.

"Aren't they afraid patients will sue?" Lingguan asked.

"The doctor would never admit it. He'd say the patient had reacted slowly. I hear there's some scientific basis for that; anesthesia has little effect on heavy drinkers."

"My brother doesn't drink." Lingguan said lamely.

"That's terrible." Laoshun sighed and looked at Lingguan, who knew his father was reproaching him for his incompetence, which, as he saw it, had led to Hantou's suffering.

First the doctor's incontrovertible diagnosis and then the brutal way his brother had his operation. It was all too much, and Lingguan felt he was on the verge of a nervous breakdown.

Hantou's moans were like a knife cutting through his heart;

it pained him to see sweat ooze onto his brother's gaunt, pallid face, and he wished he could take his place.

Does he know what he has? Lingguan examined Hantou's face, but failed to detect any sign. Probably not, but he'll realize that the lump is still there. Lingguan tensed at the thought. If— the earlier thought reared its head—if he'd died on the operating table, it would have been so much better. He'd have died without being aware of it.

Laoshun kept his eyes fixed on his oldest son, the corners of his mouth twitching, as if he were trying to transfer the pain from his son to himself. Lingguan looked at his father, who wore the hint of smile, as if to say, "I'm glad the surgery is over."

If he only knew— Lingguan could not bear to finish the thought.

A nurse came in with a syringe. With great effort, Lingguan and his father managed to get Hantou to lie on his side. Lingguan followed the nurse out after she finished.

"Please keep it a secret. No one must know what he has."

"So I've been told," she said.

That night Lingguan spread out bedding on a borrowed army cot and placed a blanket in the middle for him and his father to sit on. The room had a terrible smell, but what Lingguan found truly unbearable were his brother's moans, which scraped against every nerve in his body. He was barely able to hold himself together. Afraid he might break down in front of his father and brother, he went out to sit on a heating vent in the hallway, the window open to bathe his head in a cool night breeze.

Laoshun, obviously also unable to stand the torment in the room, came out into the hallway to smoke his pipe. That was, of course, not allowed in the hospital, but he managed to sneak in a few puffs. Knowing that the acrid tobacco smoke could irritate his son's throat, making him cough and pull at his wound, he shut the door and opened a window in the staircase to blow away the harsh smell.

Lingguan could see that his father had lost weight. He was not used to studying the old man's face, deeply tanned with wrinkles and a few scraggly whiskers that gave him a coarse appearance. It was a common face, the kind Lingguan would have trouble picking out in a crowd. He'd always been gaunt, burdened with the look of someone who'd been through many hardships. His once healthy glow was gone, replaced by a wizened, steely gray.

"As if being poor isn't enough, someone has to be sick in the family." Laoshun said with a sigh.

8

Lanlan rushed up. "Reed roots!" she shouted.

Noting the puzzled look on Ying'er's face, she said, "You know what they are, don't you? Well, I'm telling you, they're more than just the roots of reed plants. They say that Daoist masters in ancient times called them beards of the dragon's vein."

Her enthusiasm lifted Ying'er's mood a bit, knowing that her sister-in-law was not the type to get excited over nothing.

Seeing some of the gloom lift from Ying'er's face, Lanlan said no more about the dragon's vein. People in Liangzhou knew it meant a waterway, though it carried much more significance than that. A dragon's vein, as she'd learned since childhood, was a place that produced important people. But that was meaningless at the moment. To her, reed roots meant only food, water, and life. She bent over to pull up a section of the root, tucked it under her arm, and scraped off the sand before breaking it in two. She gave the longer section to Ying'er.

"Chew on it. It has lots of moisture. Don't spit out the pulp. Just keep chewing and then swallow everything."

Ying'er took a bite and felt a coolness spread in her mouth. What a wonderful sensation. It was her first taste of the woody but juicy reed roots.

Holding her piece in her mouth, Lanlan followed the complex root system, slowly digging farther and farther, creating a pit and tossing out roots as she went.

"Save some for later; this will be our lifesaver," she said to Ying'er.

The enticing roots, snowy white, plump, and watery, were piling up. Like licorice roots, once a root is spotted, you can pull out more by following the root system. Folklore had it that the reed roots under the imperial tombs could spread thousands of miles, and that an emperor would be born to anyone whose ancestral tomb came into contact with the dragon's aura. There had once been a dragon's vein in Shawan, their village, but it had been severed by an emperor to preemptively ward off competition. So Shawan residents considered reed roots to be lucky, and a celebration was called for anyone who had a root growing in their ancestral grave.

Lanlan's breathing grew labored from tossing out sand one handful at a time, as the pile of roots grew and the pit deepened.

"You need to rest," Ying'er said. "I'll take over."

"I'm fine. I'm not tired." Lanlan wiped her sweaty forehead. She flung out her head scarf, which she'd worn to prevent sunburn.

Ying'er was about to change places with Lanlan when she saw sand slipping down the wall.

"Get out of there, Lanlan, hurry. The pit's going to collapse."

Lanlan got to her feet but before she could climb out, the sand had already risen to her chest with no sign of stopping.

Sick with fear, Ying'er reached down to drag her sister-in-law up by her arm, but the more she pulled, the faster the sand fell. Soon it had reached Lanlan's shoulders, forcing her to gasp for air. Ying'er did not dare pull again, and Lanlan kept still. Finally, the sand stopped flowing.

As the specter of death descended, they both knew that if the sand started down again, it would bury Lanlan, slipping into her ears, nose and mouth, every opening it found. Even if she could still be dug out, all that sand in her would be fatal.

Afraid that struggling would only increase the sand slide, Ying'er told Lanlan not to move. The desert's Yellow Dragon would envelop her at the slightest provocation. Shawan villagers all believed in the Yellow Dragon, which was in charge of sand, with water in the domain of the Green Dragon. In earlier times, the villagers had offered sacrifices to the Yellow Dragon at his temple. If they missed even once, they drew his ire, and there would be severe sandstorms. Times were different now. The earliest sacrifices required virgin boys and girls, who were later replaced by domestic animals, until the temple was destroyed by the Red Guards. The elders said that sand began to inch toward their village after that, and had already claimed a large section of their land. Ying'er had always considered that to be nonsense, but at this moment, she'd believe in anything that could save Lanlan. She pleaded with the Yellow Dragon not to take her sister-in-law, who in turn was praying to the Tibetan Vajravārāhī, silently, looking calm on the surface. The sand had pressed against her so much she had trouble breathing, but she strained to keep her composure, for she knew that panic would not help her. The sand could start falling at any moment, and she wanted to take the opportunity to settle some things that had been on her mind. She did not want to die with regrets.

Ying'er had an idea. While still praying to the Yellow Dragon, she began digging another pit to the side of Lanlan, who might then be able to slowly pull herself out.

Lanlan gave Ying'er a sad smile, but did not stop her; she knew it was the only possible solution, not whether it would work or not.

"There are some things I want to say to you, Ying'er."

"Don't talk, just stay motionless."

"No, these are things I need to say. I feel bad about two people in my life. You're one of them. I know I caused you heaps of trouble by leaving your family. I know that, Ying'er. I know the harm I've done to you. Only a woman can understand what goes on in another woman's mind. I did all this, Ying'er, for one reason only—I couldn't take any more of your brother's beatings.

I simply couldn't. I just wanted to live, even if I had to live like an animal. I mean it, like an animal. Like a cow or a pig. I envy pigs. You know the kind of life someone leads if she envies a pig. Did you know I had to get up at the crack of dawn to sweep the yard, clean the house, cook, work in the field, until it was dark? It went on like that every day of the year. Weeding the field, digging and harvesting. I did it all. A cow works hard, but there's always a slack period for them. Not for me. Just look at me. No one who sees me believes I'm not even thirty years old. I'm like an old coin, worn thin. But that's all right. I was born into a peasant's family, to a life of hardship, and I accept my fate.

"But I couldn't take the beatings. I just couldn't. He slapped me, he hit me with his fist and his elbow, and he kicked me. Those I could handle, they were bad, but not the worst. What I feared most was the whip. He went at it for what seemed like an hour. An hour, sixty minutes, three thousand and six hundred seconds. When he was done each time, the whip had turned my body into a mat of bloody welts. And what did he do next? He sprinkled salt on the wounds, saying to prevent infection, because treating it would cost his family money. It hurt a hundred times worse than the lashing. I remember how I couldn't get away from the whip even when I was asleep. I'd be startled awake when I dreamed about it. Once, that time when you picked thorns off me, well, you know he'd gambled and lost. I said something, which made him so angry he went and got thorny branches, and ripped my clothes off.

"You came to visit your parents the day after he'd lashed me with the branches. Do you remember picking out the thorns? You didn't count them, but I did. There were four hundred and fifty-one of them. I vowed at the time that in our next life, I'd spear him the same number of times or shoot four hundred and fifty-one arrows into him. Don't be mad at me. It's what I was thinking at the time.

"Don't cry. Please don't. I'll stop if you keep crying. I've kept this inside all this time and it's festered. I did not dare tell anyone, because you know, some people, instead of showing sympathy, will actually laugh at you. I remember there was a woman in the village. Every time she railed at her daughter-in-law, she'd say, 'Don't talk back to me, or you'll end up like Lanlan.' I felt I'd been lashed in the face when I heard that. So how could I tell anyone? I had to do what the proverb says, swallow my teeth when they come loose. I suffered so much silently. Ma and Pa knew he beat me, but they had no idea how badly. Ma would be heartbroken if she knew. They've had a hard life and I couldn't make it even worse, you know.

"I'd better stop. Hearing you cry tears me apart. See, how sad I've made you? All right, let's not talk about this. I just want you to know I couldn't stand the beating any longer. I remember once I tied a rope to the rafter, but your father stopped me when I'd barely stuck my neck through the noose. I thought of drinking pesticide, the kind that rots your guts. The pain's unbearable, I hear, but that's just short-term pain, while there would be no end to my life of suffering if I didn't do anything.

"Then my brother, your husband, died, and I knew I had to live. Ma and Pa nearly cried their eyes out when he died, and if I died too, that would be the end for them. So, I had to ask for a divorce. Please don't cry. I'm not talking to make you feel bad, I just want you to know I couldn't live like that any longer. If I could have, I'd have gritted my teeth and suffered through it. It's only one lifetime, isn't it? We all have to die. I realized that I'd die whether I fought back or put up with it, but we aren't born to be whipped."

Lanlan thought back to her days at her parents' house after leaving Bai Fu. She'd spent a little time alone with Ying'er, talking about everything except the subject of divorce. She'd nearly blurted it out a few times, but in the end had swallowed the word. Bai Fu was, after all, Ying'er's older brother, she reminded herself.

Nonetheless, she knew that Ying'er was the only one to whom she could open up, the one person who might know what went on in her heart, who could understand and empathize over the pain inside her, and who, more than anyone else, could grasp the traumatic blow to her spirit brought on by the death of her daughter.

"You know," Lanlan continued, "I'm not an ambitious woman, I never had high aspirations and felt no need to rise above anyone else. I just wanted to live a stable, safe life, quietly muddle through."

"Of course, I was heartbroken over Yindi's death. I felt my world had fallen apart during those days, and I could understand the pain Ma and Pa felt over the death of their son. Ying'er, I have to tell you, I know he did it, he took her out into the desert and he left her there."

"You can't be serious! He couldn't do that to his own daughter," a shocked Ying'er cried out, forgetting for the moment that a shift in the sand could bury Lanlan before she reached her. She recalled her niece's face and her unique way of saying how much she missed her Auntie. Anyone who saw her immediately took to her. How could her own father be so cruel as to let a loving daughter die in the desert on a cold night? How could he?

"He claimed that a fortuneteller said that in her previous life Yindi had been the white fox Bai Fu had killed, and she was the cause of all my miscarriages and the reasons he had no sons. At the time, I couldn't bring myself to even think about her, but you know, pain and hatred dull at some point. No matter how great the pain, it begins to fade after a while, and eventually I got over it. They thought that was why I wanted a divorce, and that's what I told them, but actually I just didn't want to be hit anymore."

Ying'er by then was awash in tears.

"Don't cry."

"After my little girl died, I cried my eyes out, but I couldn't cry her back to life. She was dead, and there was nothing I could do about it, so I decided to consider it her fate. But I knew he'd do anything he had to do for me to give him a son, including listening to the crazy ideas of a fortuneteller. He killed her, Ying'er, I know it, I'm sure of it. She would never have gone out into the desert on her own. She was such a sweet, clever little girl, and it feels like a knife slicing through my heart every time I think about her and what he did."

Ying'er's tears flowed unchecked.

"You can stop digging, Ying'er. Look, your fingers are bleeding. It's useless. You could scoop a thousand handfuls, but one swipe by the Yellow Dragon's tail would wipe that out. Besides, why should I go on living? Go up to the slope and kick the sand down to bury me. I thought I wanted to live, but all these thoughts have taken the desire away. The sooner I die, the faster I'm free of suffering.

"Sometimes, I really do feel I have nothing to show for my life. But what can I do? Look at the women in the village. Every one of them has a tough life. I admire Pa when he says he can take whatever Heaven doles out to him. You can think until your head hurts, but you still have to put up with whatever you're fated to take. It's better to accept it calmly from the start, don't you think? Especially if you're a woman." Lanlan paused for a few gulps of air before continuing,

"Don't cry if the sand buries me. Tears are water too. You'll have to conserve. You don't know the area, so just keep going east and don't stray. Forget about the salt lakes for now and make sure you survive first. The desert here is narrow east to west and wide north to south. You'd never make it out if you took the wrong route. And don't walk when the sun is blistering hot, or you'll turn into a mummy before long. Best to travel at night. Follow the Big Dipper, make sure it's to your left, and keep going. Don't use the flashlight too often, and keep the musket with you. Sometimes a doomed rabbit will run right into your muzzle. If you're lucky, one shot will get you a rabbit. Remember, not too close.

"Stop scooping now. See that? The sand is falling faster than you can scoop.

"Remember not to let fear get the better of you, no matter what. You know what fear is? It's a knife. Once you sense it's there, it will cut deep. You might start out slightly afraid, but little by little it will take root, sprout, bloom, and produce fruit. In the end, fear turns into a fog that blots out the sky and blankets you. When that happens, you'll accept your doom. You won't want to walk and you'll stop fighting. You'll say to yourself, time to give up, it must be my fate. Then you're dead, because your heart has died. Once the heart dies, you die.

"At moments like that, your greatest enemy isn't the desert, it's you, because you'll tell yourself to give up and accept your fate. You'll say, I can't get out of here. Ideas to keep you from moving will sprout and mess with your determination. This is what I learned from my Master Guru. He's the Living Buddha who taught the Vajravārāhī Doctrine.

"I don't think there's any better guidance in the world.

"Now stop scooping the sand around my chest and help me get my arms out. Look at me. I was so busy telling you not to lose heart I almost succumbed to my own fate. I'll give it a try. I may cause more sand to fall, but I'll just pretend I'm already buried. The worst outcome is, well, you know.

"Right. Like that. Let's try to get my arms out."

Ying'er's fingers were bleeding, but she kept at it. She was shocked and heartbroken by what Lanlan was saying. They'd been sisters-in-law for years, and she hadn't really known Lanlan until this day. The beatings, the death of her daughter, the cruelty of her brother. But no need to talk about that now, for she had to get her out first. If Lanlan were buried there, Ying'er vowed, she'd do the same to keep her company. She would not leave her sister-in-law behind in the desert.

"Don't dig too fast. Take your time. Use both hands to cup the sand, right, like that. That's it."

A gust of wind blew sand in Lanlan's face. She shut her mouth to keep from breathing in grains and coughing, since moving could be disastrous. She sputtered and blinked to clear her eyes, but still couldn't stop saying what was on her mind.

"You can guess the other person I feel bad about. I don't have to tell you. Yes, it's Huaqiu's wife. Nothing happened between him and me, honestly, not a thing.

"I guess you could say we were childhood sweethearts. Before I was married, we were like two kids playing house, and after I got married, I was no longer in the mood. I have to admit that we kissed and he touched me. There's no reason to hide that from you now. That time when I went in for the seven-day meditation, we did spend a day and night together. Yes, that's true. We were together for seven days and eight nights, but we were meditating, in Vajravārāhī's mandala. How could I have done anything seedy? Besides, there were others meditating there too. So much hoopla was created over Huaqiu and me, but nothing bad happened.

"I was stunned when I heard she'd try to kill herself. I really was. How could she be so foolish? She heard a rumor and believed it. She thought Huaqiu and I had done it, so she carried out her own foolish act. It was his fault, if you ask me. Some women like to nag. He should have let her complain and pretend he didn't know what she was saying. He could have left the house when he couldn't take it any longer. Why did he have to hit her? She was already fuming before that, and once he hit her, she naturally felt she had nothing to live for. If it had been me, I'd have wanted to hang myself too.

"You know, she came to see me the day after Huaqiu and

91

I met one night, and he had tried to talk me into finally being lovers. When I refused, he went home, and I haven't seen him since. But she obviously thought otherwise. Why does she want to see me? I wondered. Could she have detected something? Or had Huaqiu said something to her? She led me over to a spot near the Vajravārāhī Cave. She looked sickly, rail thin, she wore a sad, gloomy look. When she stopped walking, she turned and stared at me blankly. I wanted to say something, but nothing appropriate came to mind. What do you say to a woman who thinks you're having an affair with her husband? Suddenly, she fell to her knees. I tried to pull her up, but she refused. 'I saw you last night,' she said flatly, so I knew she'd followed us.

"I told her not to listen to gossip about Huaqiu and me. She had nothing to worry about. But she made me swear I wouldn't keep seeing her husband. 'Actually,' she said to me, 'I don't care whether you swear or not. I'll just hang myself at your gate if I see you two together again.' Then she banged her head on the ground to show she meant what she said and drifted off like a sleepwalker.

"I want to ask one favor of you: if the Yellow Dragon takes me away and you make it out alive, would you help her if you can? Her neck is scarred, but I've heard that the rope-burn marks can be removed by cosmetic surgery in a Lanzhou hospital. You know, her neck is a mark of my shame. The villagers will denounce me for as long as the marks exist. Besides, Huaqiu is fickle, and a woman with a scarred neck isn't going to keep him around. Sooner or later he'll stray. She's suffered, so you help her out if you can.

"Listen to me, I'm putting so much pressure on you. You're not upset with me, are you? I have to say these things, it makes me feel better. If I don't, I'll feel worse. Now that I've told you, it's up to you whether you do it or not."

Lanlan was exhausted after pouring her heart out to Ying'er with the sand exerting painful pressure on her chest. She knew that now she needed to concentrate on trying to survive. "Take it slow," she said, "don't be in a hurry. It feels like it's loosening up. That's right, scoop away the sand on my chest first. That's right, there."

Ying'er's efforts were finally seeing results; a trough had been opened to the north of Lanlan. Loose sand continued to flow down, but her chest was freed. Ying'er would keep going until she scooped out the sand pressing down on Lanlan's upper body.

After getting her arms out, Lanlan began pushing the sand away. She had limited movement because sand was still sliding slowly behind her. Luckily, it was damp and stuck to her enough to hold up the wall around her. Even luckier, they were in a shaded hollow with packed sand, unlike the sunny hollows with loose sand that would have taken her life long before.

A dizzy spell came over Ying'er. She had sweated profusely from the hard work, which worsened her dehydration; now her eyes were blurry, and her throat was scratchy. But she was finally seeing the hope of saving Lanlan, even though they were a long way from leaving the desert alive. At least they were about to storm through one of fate's iron doors, something one had to face a few times in a lifetime. Each successful charge brought a level of maturity.

The sun was moving westward; they had been trapped for over two hours. Hunger and thirst surrounded them like a spider web, and Ying'er felt she was about to pass out. All she wanted was sleep. She continued to scoop, but her consciousness was about to enter a dormant state. How she wished she could sleep.

"That's enough," Lanlan said and Ying'er stopped scooping robotically. Lanlan told her to move back a bit. They could see there was less sand constricting her chest, and that she might be able to struggle her way out if the sand didn't immediately slide. After Ying'er had moved back a little, Lanlan took her hands; she had to move swiftly because the effort would touch off the sand along the wall of the pit. Otherwise, she'd be buried anew in the cascading sand; not only would their efforts have been in vain, but even more would fall, and the end would come when it reached the top of her head.

The women prayed to their individual gods, Lanlan to the Vajravārāhī and Ying'er the Yellow Dragon. Then Lanlan told Ying'er to steady herself before she called out, "One, two, three." Sand began to fall aggressively as they worked together pulling Lanlan up. Fortunately, she was able to extract her legs with the first surge. They depleted the last vestige of their strength with one final spurt of manic energy, pulling together and ending up rolling into the trough. Sand spilled down and, in the blink of an eye, filled the pit where Lanlan had been standing.

Stunned, they stared wide-eyed at the spot for a while before wrapping their arms around each other and crying.

They cried with abandonment, to which the sand trough responded by echoing the sounds that bounced back and forth in the void.

Hantou and Lingguan

After Hantou had been in the hospital several days recovering from what proved to be an unsuccessful and unnecessary operation, his treatment and medications were suspended. The nurse came in the morning to set up IV drips for every patient in the room except him. The doctor told the family that Hantou was being discharged and that they would have to settle the account. A scowling Lingguan walked out without a word and went to tell his brother that his wound had healed enough for him to go home.

The wound didn't look bad, with a fresh scab that looked like a red snake. Hantou appeared to believe the explanation.

"That's wonderful. I can't wait. I'll go crazy if I spend another day here." He tried to smile to show his eagerness to leave, but because of the pain, he managed only to move his lips.

Hantou had never asked about his condition. The only thing he'd said to Lingguan was that he wanted to leave the hospital in a new set of clothes. He needed to look his best, he said. By then, Lingguan was secretly preparing for his brother's funeral, and had already bought cloth shoes, a blue cotton shirt, and pants. He'd sought an excuse to make a jacket for his brother, whose request had given him what he needed. Lingguan wondered if Hantou knew how ill he was and that the request was meant to have his own funeral clothes ready.

Hantou put on the new clothes. His eyes had sunk deep into the sockets, his cheekbones protruded, and he was skin and bones. The lump, on the other hand, looked more prominent than ever, as if he'd hidden a basketball under his shirt, while the spots on his sallow face were conspicuous. The blue shirt helped his appearance, but the color only accentuated the pallor of his sickly face.

Mengzi, their third brother, hired a three-wheeler as Lingguan continued his search for pethidine. The head nurse had promised to give them two boxes of the painkiller, but now she indifferently offered an excuse: "The account is closed."

Lingguan was outraged. She laughed coldly,

"What do you expect? I wouldn't give him any even if I could. The rules say these shots can only be administered in the hospital."

His eyes clouded the moment he walked out of the nurse's office. What had happened to the world and the people in it? She had no compassion, no empathy. Hantou's illness was a huge catastrophe to his family, but meant nothing to the doctors. He was a medical specimen and a paying customer.

That was all.

An impossible task suddenly landed on Lingguan's shoulders—where to find more painkiller, now that the head nurse had broken her promise. Pain was worse than death, but control of the pethidine was tight.

Lingguan's head ached. His brother's life was beyond saving now, so relieving him of the pain was the only thing he could do. Don't worry, my dear brother. I'll do everything I can to get more painkiller, so you won't suffer so much.

Lingguan dried his tears when he saw Mengzi in the corridor. His younger brother could not know about the hospital's decision to force them to leave. Mengzi was a hothead, easily provoked into rash actions, and Hantou would suffer if Mengzi picked a fight with the medical staff.

The two brothers packed up everything to leave. The general surgery department had yet to send the bill to the accounting office for in-patients. "Come back in a few days," the bookkeeper had said icily.

Everything was so cold and impersonal. White walls, expres-

96

sionless people, trees with bare branches, leaves gnawed away by insects, and hard floors that hurt the feet. Good riddance to the lousy place, teeming with death and inhumanity, with its nauseating smells. Lingguan hoped he'd never have to come back ever again.

They followed the three-wheeler's slow progress in a headwind. Hantou had one hand on his abdomen and gripped the handrail with the other. A dazzling sun shone down. Lingguan wondered what his brother was thinking and feeling at that moment. Was he calm or just numb? Lingguan knew this would be Hantou's last time out on Liangzhou's streets, the thought of which nearly broke his heart.

The three-wheeler rolled along slowly in a world bustling with people and action. Noise rose all around them—shrieking car horns, listless shouts from vendors, eager calls from young men offering motor scooter rides. Everything was near and yet far, as if the world had abandoned them. The people out on the street all looked happy, while on this lonely vehicle sat a man who had been sentenced to death.

Lingguan walked along in a sort of daze; hearing Mengzi tell the rider to take it slow and seeing Hantou's face twisted in pain from the jolting motion felt like something out of a dreamscape. Sunlight was magnified and yet hazy. Nothing felt real to him, only his anguish, so deep it would be etched in his memory forever.

"I want to visit the Confucius Temple." Hantou said. "I've never been there."

The Confucius Temple? Lingguan studied his brother's sallow face, which was still twisted from pain. What for? Lingguan wondered. Maybe he was aware of his condition, but if so, how could he remain so calm? Why didn't he ask for details on what was wrong with him? Lingguan took another look at his brother, who was staring at the street with eyes as unfathomable as a deep well. He could be obstinately clinging to worldly desire or indifferently holding himself aloof from everything around him. Lingguan could not tell. Maybe his illness and hospitalization had transported Hantou onto a different realm.

"What's there to see?" asked Mengzi.

"I just want to stretch my legs," Hantou said casually. "I was bored sick in the hospital."

"All right, let's go." Lingguan told the driver to head over to the Confucius Temple, while asking himself why his poorly educated brother had chosen a temple dedicated to teachers to visit. He had never been there, which was a perfectly sound reason, but there were other places he had never visited, such as the Drum and Bell Towers and other interesting sites. Why the Confucius Temple? Maybe he wished he'd been a better student and stayed in school. But of course, as the eldest, his family responsibilities were the greatest. Better to help keep the family afloat and let his brother, who loved learning, attend school.

After leaving Mengzi at the gate to watch their belongings, Lingguan walked in with Hantou. It was a fine place to be. The bronze horse at the entrance held Hantou's attention for quite some time. Lingguan heard him sigh softly. Hantou stared at the pine and cypress trees for a while before going into a room whose walls were filled with calligraphy and paintings, where he stopped and gazed raptly at every scroll. Lingguan realized he was greedily savoring art works, his mouth hanging slack, like a child at a circus.

"So real," he mumbled as he pointed to a portrait of someone from the late Qing period; he swallowed two painkillers and slowly moved along.

They entered another display room. Lingguan decided not to offer any explanations, and his brother, looking at the works silently and diligently, asked no questions. The room showcased relics excavated in Liangzhou, a city rich with history and culture, and he knew they were all new to Hantou; carved figurines, wooden carts and horses, rusty knives, stone axes, porcelain vases, armor like bed springs, cloth paintings, and Buddhist statuary, all uniquely wonderful. He stood in front of giant bronze figures so long Lingguan thought his brother might be praying, mistaking them for Buddhist statues.

"Let's go," Hantou said.

He smiled when they got home, a genuine smile, though as brief as a meteor.

Their mother ran out from the kitchen and looked pleased when she saw her son. "Good." Her eyes were moist as she repeated, "Good." It was impossible to know whether she was saying it was good that he was home or that he'd been restored to a good condition. Lingguan felt his heart tighten. "How can I tell her? It could be the death of her." He gazed over at his father, who wore his usual stony look. Lingguan tried to decipher the look; numbness, despair, resignation? None of the above or all of the above?

They went inside. After folding a blanket in half to lay on the kang, their mother dragged over another blanket to prop against the wall. Laoshun and Hantou's brothers helped him up onto the kang. Lingguan had thought their mother would ask Hantou if he felt better, but she didn't. Instead she stared at her son, the tears coming so fast she couldn't keep her face dry.

To Lingguan, the nightmarish days after his brother came home felt frighteningly surreal. He did not recall ever seeing the sun during those days, as a dull gray pervaded the space everywhere he looked. Their mother hardly ever stopped crying, carrying on with the household chores tearfully, smiling only when she was with Hantou. Lingguan could not bear to see her smile like that, with teardrops swirling in her eyes as she smiled and rolling down her cheeks when she let down her guard. She would hurriedly wipe them off and put on a broader, yet awkward smile. It was a good thing Hantou rarely looked any of them in the face,

99

since he usually had his eyes shut, and when he opened them, he turned to the wall. He moaned when the pain was unbearable. Lingguan would give him a painkiller, after which Hantou would shut his eyes again or turn to face the wall.

Lingguan knew that his brother had only weeks, maybe only days, to live, according to the doctor. Everything lost its meaning, and life would burst like a bubble when death arrived. Days or weeks were but an instant in the river of life, and a man's life was nothing but a spray of water that passed fleetingly down the long river of history. When facing the inevitable end, decades were not all that different from weeks. Hantou had been given a death sentence, while the others in their family had received a stay of execution, a term that could not be reduced further. That was all.

Recalling Hantou's one and only fight, with Maodan, the village's perennial bachelor, Lingguan was convinced that his brother would have avoided it if he'd known his life would be over soon. The eternal concern of death rendered all old scores meaningless. A man would be able to see beyond many worldly matters and refuse to fight over petty profits if he could sense that death was never far ahead. He would not be obsessed with transient fame and wealth, since nothing was permanent. Only death was real.

In addition to giving Hantou shots, he continued his frantic search for pethidine. During that time, his days were filled with a benumbed despair, interrupted only by the temporary elation over finding another dose of the painkiller.

One night, when Hantou was moaning in agony, Lingguan had an appalling thought—stop his suffering, since the end would be the same. Relieving him of pain would be a compassionate act. What would they do when they ran out of painkillers? Lingguan knew he wouldn't be able to face that. He went to see his high school friend and pleaded with him until the friend told him to inject Hantou with several doses of pethidine at once if it came to that.

More than once the thought of ending it all for his brother occurred to him. Stop the nightmare then and there, for his brother, for his parents, and for everyone else. But the thought was always followed by self-inflicted condemnation for his lack of humanity.

Hantou was quiet, all but the moans and the occasional explanation to their mother that the protrusion was caused by infection in the surgical wound. He did not know that she had already guessed what he had. He did not talk about his illness with anyone, nor did he ask any questions. The doctor had said Hantou did not know the severity of his situation. Lingguan did not believe him, for his brother was too calm, unlike other cancer patients, who were usually restless, complaining and blaming others, sometimes even getting hysterical. Hantou was unperturbed, at least on the surface.

Lingguan gave him shots at regular intervals, one to ease the pain and one to reduce the swelling, though the latter was bogus. Then for two days in a row, he stopped the pointless shot for inflammation reduction, telling his brother that he was giving him a combined dose for both the pain and the swelling. "You're all lying to me," was how Hantou reacted. He did not talk to anyone for days after that.

Money flowed out like water. Their father sold his favorite black mule, though it pained him to do so. Lingguan gathered up what he'd bought for Hantou's funeral and handed them over to their mother. She wept when she laid her eyes on items usually reserved for old people. Then, tearfully, she put them away in the cleanest and safest spot in the house, fearing that someone might soil the best clothes her son would ever wear.

Everyone in the family was exhausted. Dispirited and seemingly ready to drop, their father began to snore the moment he leaned up against a wall, his mental and physical energy depleted. Their mother was cadaverous, walking on unsteady feet, as if braving a headwind. Mengzi was doing better, well behaved, like a changed man. As instructed by her mother-in-law, Ying'er stayed away from the room she shared with Hantou; she was expecting, and their mother did not want the aura of a pregnant woman to hex her son. Ying'er and Lingguan avoided each other the best they could without letting on, both too overwhelmed by the impending tragedy in the family to consider the ramifications of their relationship.

Lingguan could tell that their mother still harbored unrealistic hopes.

People in the village came to see Hantou, bringing gifts of refined sugar and canned goods. The visitors all did their best to console Laoshun's wife, who wept with every one of them.

"What are we going to do? Ai—" She was like a helpless child.

"It'll be all right." They offered the same words each time. "Heaven has eyes. A good man like Hantou will surely get better. He will."

She would sigh with relief, as if having received a promise from Heaven.

Hantou was discomfited by the string of visitors, seemingly angry at himself over the trouble he'd caused their neighbors. He would struggle to sit up when a visitor came, nearly out of breath, and lean against the blanket. The lump was getting bigger, spreading from his rib area up to his chest and down to his lower abdomen. His belly was now rock-hard, which for him became a second private area; he would cover his belly with a blanket or his clothes each time he sat up. But no one could spend more than a moment or two with him, not with him gasping for air. Unable to watch him suffer even more, they offered a few words of compassion before saying good-bye and going into the kitchen to comfort his mother, who continued her teary muttering:

"What are we going to do?"

Maodan's visit mattered most to Hantou, who smiled at his friend, a genuine, sincere smile. He waved for Maodan to come closer and held his friend's hands wordlessly. Maodan smiled foolishly, but said nothing. Lingguan knew they'd made up. He also saw Hantou heave a sigh and, racked by exhaustion, shut his eyes. A teardrop rolled out from the corner of each eye and down the cheek. He licked them off when they reached his lips.

That was the only time since leaving the hospital that Lingguan had seen his brother cry.

9

Lanlan and Ying'er ate half the roots in the bag, the food for which they'd traded sweat and nearly a life; it was delicious and energizing. The moist flesh produced an exquisite sensation, after they'd been parched from roasting in the sun all day. A gentle bite sent a unique succulence and fragrance deep into their bodies. It seemed to make their souls tremble. Lanlan considered it sweet dew from the land of Buddha, where a single drop on the tongue could wash away life's hardships.

All Ying'er's consciousness had been focused on Lanlan's safety, and there had been no room for hunger or thirst in her mind. That changed as the roots entered her stomach. She had to curse the fleeing camel again. It wasn't nearly as docile as her father-in-law's, but Lanlan had been able to control it, never imagining it to abandon its human riders when it needed to share hardships with them.

Now that Lanlan was safe, the sun's fiery rays felt more relentless than ever. And no wind.

"Let's scoop out a spot in a shaded hollow and wait till nightfall," Lanlan said.

Despite her lingering fear of digging in the sand, Ying'er nonetheless knew they'd fall victim to heatstroke if they stayed under the blistering sun. She followed Lanlan to pick out a spot. Experience taught them to dig a wider, shallower pit this time. They crawled in when damp sand came into view. Overcome by fatigue, Ying'er felt a disorienting sensation that grew increasingly dense as it enveloped her, and she fell asleep.

The sun was. hanging above a sand hill to the West when she awoke. Fiery red clouds decorated the western sky, portending another hot day. Oh, how she wished it would rain. She felt sticky and dirty, hungry and thirsty. The joy of stripping and letting rain wash over her would easily eclipse the brief and ultimately perilous pleasure she'd obtained from chewing the reed roots.

Lanlan was still asleep. The sight of the musket and gunpowder sack outside the pit gave Ying'er a sense of security. She fought the inclination to despair over their situation, for they weren't out of danger yet. She knew it was pointless to fret over what might have happened or to worry about what was yet to come. They had no food, and no water, and no amount of worry would bring them either. Best not to spend any mental energy on excessive concern, which could only result in low morale. We'll just have to go slow and see what happens, she thought. With what energy remained, they could only rely on the gods or on fate. Except for the impact of Lanlan's heartrending confessions and the happy tears shed after freeing her from her sandy imprisonment, she had tried not to cry, knowing it was useless; that alone felt like progress.

Suddenly something stirred beneath a shrub close by. A jackal, she thought, given what had happened only the day before, and her heart nearly stopped. She wanted to wake up Lanlan, but wasn't sure if her eyes were playing tricks on her. Slowly she reached for the musket and breathed only when her fingers wrapped around the stock. But the moving dot disappeared under the shrub. She laughed at her jumpy nerves. A careful survey of their surroundings had turned up no jackals. As she breathed a sigh of relief, the thing abruptly moved again and she tensed. She recalled that the musket was loaded, so she took out a flint and placed it on the firing pin, as she'd seen Lanlan do. Just in case. Then it showed itself: a mud-yellow rabbit.

She was elated. The gods had sent them food. Slowly, she

aimed at the shrub. Lanlan had told her that the buckshot, if fired from several feet away, would allow her to hit her target. The key, Lanlan had said, was to line up three points. Her heart was thumping. This was, after all, her first time firing a weapon.

Forget it, she thought. I'll wake Lanlan up and ask her to shoot. But a thought grew ever more powerful in her head: she'd really like to surprise Lanlan with a rabbit when she woke up. The idea began to overcome her fear of firing her first shot. Seeing how the yellow spot shifted whenever she inhaled and exhaled, she held her breath and worked hard to pull the trigger. After struggling for a moment, she realized she'd actually been pulling against the trigger guard. She laughed at herself. I'd better give up and have Lanlan do it.

Lanlan cut an inelegant figure in the pit with her sand-pocked face. Ying'er nudged her several times, but failed to interrupt her snoring. She was absolutely exhausted, and Ying'er reproached herself for even thinking about waking her up. Holding her breath, she aimed at the moving yellow dot and pulled the trigger. The butt recoiled violently against her shoulder, while her eardrums rang from the deafening noise. She hadn't seen flames or smoke, but she knew the musket had fired.

Lanlan jumped to her feet.

"What was that?"

"I shot a rabbit." Ying'er said, as she laid down the musket, climbed out of the pit, and ran toward the shrub. But before she reached the spot, the rabbit sprang out and bounded away up a sand hill.

Lanlan caught up.

"Look at you." She felt like laughing despite the situation. "You were way too close."

Ying'er was crestfallen, for she'd forgotten the distance. She could kick herself for not getting Lanlan to shoot. It would have been so satisfying to bite into roasted rabbit. But their meal had run off.

"Don't feel bad," Lanlan said, though she'd obviously wished for a different outcome. "Rabbits don't wait nicely for you to shoot them. It wasn't your fault. It ran off because you weren't supposed to get it."

I guess she's right, Ying'er told herself when she got over her self-reproach. There's no point in being upset over it, it's gone. No matter what, I fired the weapon. It wasn't all that hard.

"Watch me reload," Ying'er said. "See if I'm doing it right." She followed Lanlan's instruction and then asked her to teach her how to aim. Finally, she asked about firing distance and so on. The desert cooled at dusk. They finished off the rest of the roots, having no desire to touch the steamed buns they'd picked up from the fleeing camel. Without water, they couldn't possibly swallow buns that had been dried by the desert wind.

Lanlan reemphasized the necessity of traveling only at night, heading east. The salt lakes were located to the north, but now they needed to reach someplace closer, a place with human habitation, where they could find ways to survive, including work that would bring in enough to compensate for two lost camels. Lanlan would be ashamed to face her parents if she could not walk in the door at home with enough to pay for them. They had entered the desert in hopes that they could resolve their family problems, forgetting that human plans are no match for heaven's design. They knew that, with the current market value of a camel, at the very least they would have to come up with five to six thousand yuan, enough for two animals and the expense of finding a new wife for Lanlan's soon-to-be ex-husband, Bai Fu.

Seeing the downcast look on Ying'er's face, she said consolingly, "Let's not think about any of that now. One camel's dead and the other ran off, but that one might go home on its own.

107

Then we've only lost one."

"But if it went back on its own, they'd worry about us," she said.

"We won't think about the camels now. The important thing is to get on our way. We'll consider it the end of our lives if we run into jackals again. But if we make it to the salt lakes, we'll think of something."

Ying'er was encouraged, but still wary. So much had happened in only a few days, it would be hard not to wonder about their chances of survival.

When the sun sank behind the hills to the west, they set off, Lanlan carrying the musket and Ying'er holding a flashlight. The reed roots were long gone, and they remained trapped in a web of hunger and thirst. Thirst, in particular, came in waves. Lanlan's lips were purple, alarmingly swollen, and thickly scabbed. She'd licked them too much, despite her own caution to Ying'er to avoid licking lips when in the desert, no matter how thirsty you are. Ying'er had been careful, but this time Lanlan forgot, and now her lips were an inch thick. Moreover, her cheeks were sunken on a face with large, dull eyes. Ying'er knew she could not look any better. She touched her face; it felt dry and slack, obviously caused by a lack of water.

Water. The thought first brought coolness to her heart, then a wave of desperate thirst.

A breeze had started up, warm but with a slight chill. The stars were not out yet, and a red glow bled into the hills to the west, giving the inky black sand hills a lovely outline. But to Ying'er and Lanlan, who were fighting for their lives, the sight meant nothing. Ying'er glanced at the hills woodenly and swallowed with difficulty. To keep from sinking into despair, she tried to think of Lingguan. If he were with her, life would be worth living again, she thought, but her mood remained bleak. Gone was the stirring sensation she'd once held on to. He had been . . . love is just a feeling, he'd said.

They walked slowly, their feet having lost their spring. Every step was taking them closer, she reminded herself, and she wondered if Lanlan shared her thoughts. Her sister-in-law swayed as she walked, her body now seeming to have a mind of its own. It took them a surprisingly long time to scale a gentle slope, and once they reached the top, the silhouettes of endless soaring sand ridges in the distance hit them like a thunderbolt.

Lanlan slumped to the sand dejectedly, while Ying'er lay down and looked up into the sky. It was dark, and the wind was cool, the air growing damp around them. It was the best time to travel, but they both knew that their bodies no longer obeyed them. While resting in a pit with damp sand during the day and traveling at night sounded good, the lack of food and water would sap both their strength and their stamina. The little bit of reed roots had provided them with a pathetic amount of nutrients, barely enough to ensure that they would live for a day or two, little more. It would be impossible to cross the towering sand hills and traverse the vast desert without a source of food and water.

"We have to keep going," Lanlan said.

"Yes, we do," Ying'er echoed.

"We can't be stuck here."

"No, we can't."

"Let's go," Lanlan said.

"Yes, let's go."

They talked about going, but neither made a move. Ying'er let out a long sigh as she pillowed her head on Lanlan's abdomen.

She wished she could just go to sleep; her body felt like it was stripped of both marrow and blood.

"We have to go even if it means crawl. Heading east, the desert is only eighty li wide, and I think we've traveled more than half that. Once we're on the other side, we'll see herders."

"Yes, even if we have to crawl," Ying'er said.

They stood, arms out to help each other up, and walked along the ridge.

They talked to stay awake.

"Back there," Ying'er said, "you said you knew Bai Fu was responsible for Yindi's death. Did you mean it? How could you be sure?"

"Grannie Shaman tried a remedy she said worked for many women who could only have daughters. But it didn't work for me. She told us it would have worked if Yindi hadn't hexed it. Any girl who can sing and dance and is concerned only about how she looks at such a young age must have been a fox in her previous life, she said. Yindi was the white fox coming to exact revenge on Bai Fu. Otherwise, why had every boy died right after it was born? Did you know I had another miscarriage after Mengzi took a search party out into the desert and found her bluish corpse in a sand hollow? Bai Fu said he'd been out drinking and he thought Yindi probably went looking for him and got lost. His mother was standing there next to him when he said that. Neither of them even shedded a tear, and I knew it was a lie. I had to get even with him, so I ran across the room, threw myself at the table, and rammed my belly into one of its corners.

"I passed out and miscarried that night."

Ying'er could hardly believe what she heard, and had never felt so sorry for or so close to her sister-in-law. What kind of despair must a woman have to do something so drastic? Ying'er knew she could never have done it, but then again, she had never been put in a situation like that. She'd given birth to a boy, on whom the family doted. Lanlan wasn't sure if Ying'er believed her story. Sure, Ying'er knew what her brother was like, but could she believe him capable of leaving his own daughter to die in the desert? Probably not. Even Lanlan had wondered at first, but she reached the only plausible conclusion when she thought back on the day her little girl didn't come home. Bai Fu had sent her to buy something obscure that required going to several shops before she finally located it. He had even given her extra money and told her to buy something for herself! How could she have been so dense? She should have been suspicious when her brutish husband was suddenly acting nice. She told herself to stop thinking about it. She'd return with salt and release herself and Ying'er from the bondage of the exchange marriage. A gift from her little girl.

They walked on, neither feeling like talking any more. Their feet were sore, and they needed water. Thirst at first obscured the pain in Ying'er's legs, but after a while, her calves felt as if a knife were slicing into them. Not an experienced desert traveler, she had not learned the best way to walk on sand. Lanlan was little better in this regard, but she had been forced to do heavy work often enough at her in-law's that she had more stamina. On the other hand, the musket over her shoulder sapped her strength; not particularly heavy, it turned into an energy-depleting tiger when they had to travel a great distance. Even the flashlight in Ying'er's hand felt like it weighed a ton.

It was dark, but with the Big Dipper shining brightly above, they were not worried they'd walk in circles. Their thirst, however, was getting worse; they could neither see nor think straight. Their creaking joints crackled in the dark night. Shortly after midnight, Ying'er could hardly take another step, and climbing required help from Lanlan. She was barely conscious. Lanlan had turned the musket into a cane to help her along on sand. She wanted Ying'er to use it, but her even weaker sister-in-law lacked the strength to hold it. They moved forward by holding on to each other, with Ying'er supported by Lanlan, who was helped by her musket. They were able to travel a while like that, but collapsed after crossing a gentle slope, their will and determination destroyed by the brutal feelings of thirst and hunger.

"I may die, I don't care. I've done the best I could," Ying'er rasped, barely audibly, but Lanlan understood her. She did not respond, for she knew she mustn't agree, even though she felt the same. They might last a bit longer, if at least one of them continued to hold out. They'd be as good as dead if they both gave up. Deep down, however, Lanlan felt less optimistic after calculating their chance of survival. Even if they were spared the blistering sun the next day, the approaching thirst would end their lives. They'd gone without water for a very long time, subsisting on the miniscule amount of water from the reed roots. She recalled how excited she'd been when she first dug them up, hoping they would sustain them enough to leave the desert. To her disappointment, the roots she'd nearly paid for with her life were inadequate. She didn't dare contemplate what awaited them the next day, when the scorching sun again reached above their heads.

Ying'er was sure her life was like a candle flame in the wind, flickering, on the brink of going out. Her heart beat weakly, as if it would stop at any moment. Finally, she understood what people meant when they said that life existed between breathing in and breathing out. Once her feeble, thread-like breaths ceased, the desert would gain another lonely ghost. The old Daoist priest back in the village had once said that the King of Hell refused entry to those who died away from home, the wandering ghosts. They had to stay near their drying bones and cry, and their souls could finally gain peace only when the bones became part of the soil. The many rumors about death circulating in her village now came rushing back to her. She wondered what she would become after she died. It didn't matter what, as long as it wasn't another human, much less a woman, for that was too exhausting. She would prefer being a bird, the best being a lark that sang all day in the trees. Or a fox. Like Lanlan, Ying'er liked the clever creature with the air of a fairy, an immortal. It came and went like the wind, leaving only plum-flower footprints as evidence of its existence.

Reminded of the imminent passing of her life, she sensed she would not see another sunrise. Death had seemed momentous when she'd thought about it in the past, but now it was just like dozing off. Then her thoughts turned to Panpan, who, oddly, had not been on her mind in recent days. She had full confidence in her mother-in-law that her baby would not suffer, even if he were to become motherless. Of that she was certain. Was she an undeserving mother to think that way?

She strained to gaze at the evening sky. Her eyes were dry and scratchy. The stars sparkled noisily, as if engaged in heated arguments. She'd never expected stars to make such a din. How odd.

The darkness around them seemed to fade after the long, nighttime trek, and the shapes of dunes were dimly visible, their outline an enigmatic blur. Ying'er believed that if she fell asleep now, she would wake up to find herself turned into a wisp of gentle mist, and that her soul would drift above the desert like a wind.

She recalled her mother's stories about the *wuchang*, a demon sent by the King of Hell to seize people's souls. Hantou had wasted away at home, since the doctor had told him there was nothing more anyone could do. He had not been able to breath his last and let go of his soul as long as his younger brother was by his side. Their mother had said that a vibrant young man like Lingguan carried so much yang that, in the eyes of a *wuchang*, he made its approach impossible. Forced to stay away, it failed to take Hantou's soul. Hantou died as soon as Lingguan left the room. That young man, whose yang had prolonged the life of Ying'er's husband, was not there beside her now, and she wondered if a *wuchang* waited nearby to take her soul. Lanlan was snoring, making Ying'er feel more alone than ever, alone and scared. How strange; though death did not frighten her, ghosts did. She would become one when she died, and yet she was still afraid of them. She didn't dare even turn around, afraid she'd see a *wuchang*.

Fear took away the fatigue enveloping her, though in her semiconscious state, she imagined that she heard footfalls behind her. It could only be a ghost making a noise like that in this remote, forsaken spot. Her heart beat frantically. It had been about to stop, but now it was thumping wildly. One of those ground-pounding ghosts had resided in an old mill back in the village; it would start pounding the ground after nightfall until the roosters crowed. Could it be the same ghost that was making the noise behind her now? The sound was getting closer, and she could hear it breathing, heavy and laborious. She'd have cried out if she hadn't been afraid of scaring herself.

The noise was right behind her. Probably reaching out to claim her. Puffs of hot air blew down her neck. Get hold of yourself. What's there to fear? She thought, out of desperation. The worst that can happen is death, isn't it? If I have to die now, I must see what the ghost looks like. She groped in the sand to find her flashlight and spun around.

An immense dark, oddly shaped figure towered over her.

She turned on the flashlight and screamed.

Lanlan

Snow fell heavily on the third day of the lunar year, the first snowfall of winter, and the temperature dropped precipitously.

Naturally, the farmers preferred snowy days. As the world outside their windows was blanketed in white, they could sit or lie on their heated kangs, catching up on sleep or talking casually as they sipped tea and cracked watermelon seeds. Words can hardly describe the lazy, carefree pleasure.

But not Bai Fu, who had come to visit his in-laws the day before and had spent the night. He'd gotten up in the morning in a bad mood, after dreaming that his wife had given birth—to a boy. He even experienced the sensation of touching the baby's head, until a white fox ran up and snatched it away. He woke up screaming, even waking Lanlan. "What's wrong?" It took him a while to mutter, "A fox—"

"What fox?"

"A fox snatched our boy away —the one in your belly." His throat was parched.

He closed his eyes to think about the dream. Suddenly, he realized that the fox in his dream was the one he'd killed a few years earlier. He shuddered. "Do you remember the fox I killed that year?" he asked her.

"What about it?"

"It was a white fox. People say a white fox lives a thousand years and a black one ten thousand. I killed one, don't you think it would want to get back at me?"

"What do you mean?" Lanlan tensed.

"Grannie Shaman told me the two dead boys were hexed to death." He sighed.

115

"By who?" She asked, wide-eyed.

"Who else could it be?" He looked at Yindi, who was fast asleep, her face a bright red. "Someone in our house, so who do you think?" "Do you mean—Yindi?" She hesitated to say the name.

"Who else?" Bai Fu fumed. "Just think, since she came, both of the baby boys died at birth. And there's more. She was born after I killed the fox."

"What does that have to do with Yindi?" Lanlan said. "A sweet little girl like that. How could she be a fox? No. I don't believe it."

"Why not?" Bai Fu was getting angry. "Do you think I'd say anything bad about my own daughter, a clever little girl who can memorize all those songs after hearing them once. Can you think of a single child in the village who's as smart as her?"

"So that's your proof? Tell me then. My brother Lingguan is smart, so what was he in his previous life? I want you to stop this nonsense."

"Lingguan's brain is no damn good." He glared at her. "He couldn't learn how to yoke an ox to plow the field after three days. If he's so smart, why isn't he in college? Your parents wasted a decade supporting him, and he went through baskets of food in the process. Yindi isn't like him."

"What did I do?" Yindi awoke and sat up. "What did I do?"

"Go back to sleep," Bai Fu yelled, scaring the girl back under the blanket. Lanlan mumbled, her arm around her daughter, "My Yindi is such a sweet girl." She patted her daughter's backside and said to Bai Fu, "I don't want to hear any more of your ideas, so don't bring them up again."

Lanlan's mother walked in "What are you yelling and screaming like that for on the first day of the year? Sleep in if you want. If not, go watch people play cards. Do something besides argue."

Pulling a long face, Bai Fu shot Lanlan an angry look. He was sure his wife was carrying another boy.

Lanlan whispered something to Yindi, and they laughed. The sound bored into his ears. Pushing the blanket to the side, he shouted, "What's so damn funny? Go outside if you want to laugh."

"You can leave if you don't want to hear us laugh. No one's stopping you."

Bai Fu balled his fists and could barely stop from hitting her, but they were in her parents' house, so he had to hold back. All thoughts of sleep vanished; he got dressed, washed up, and walked out into a snowy world, suffused in a blinding light. Snowflakes hung on trees; an icy wind seemed to blow right through him.

Dark thoughts had begun to take hold in his head.

10

On that terrifying night in the desert, the monster came into view in the light of Ying'er's flashlight.

"The camel, it's our camel!" She shouted and nudged Lanlan, who snapped awake. "Our camel's come back to us!" The camel was snorting. What wonderful news. They'd thought they'd lost it for good, but, to their joyful surprise, it had returned on its own. Lanlan stumbled over to it and untied a rope to remove their water jug. They were in luck, it was still more than half full.

"Water!" Ying'er cried out, the word more refreshing than anything else.

Lanlan twisted open the plastic cap and handed her the jug, "Don't drink too much. Just a little for now, or your stomach will burst."

Ying'er took a pleasing sip and swallowed little by little. She'd expected a coolness to slide down her throat, but to her surprise, it was on fire. Maybe her throat was cracked. The thirst was even worse after she swallowed a few times.

Lanlan took the jug away from Ying'er so she wouldn't drink more. Her stomach had probably shrunk to the size of a fist.

After taking a small sip, Lanlan picked up the flashlight to shine on the camel. Quite a few items it carried had been lost. Their flour sack was in tatters, its contents gone; the goat pelt flask had cracked, so it held no more water. But at least the jug was undamaged and retained enough liquid for their survival. The gauzy scarf was there, still wrapped around two large steamed buns. There had been more than a dozen when the camel left, but obviously they'd fallen off as it ran.

Their bedding remained on the litter, as did a canvas sack with ball bearings, a pack of gunpowder, and a roll of twine. Ying'er naturally wished that the flask was undamaged, so she could drink to her heart's content, but that was a pipe dream that would only make her unhappy, so she put it out of her mind.

The reins had been trampled and broken and were now only ten feet long. Lanlan took a length of the twine and divided it into pieces that she attached to the reins, unable to suppress a happy smile over the surprise return of their companion. Laoshun had told them that camels had a great sense of smell and could detect an odor ten li away if the wind was blowing in their direction. Their camel would have had no trouble catching up with them. It had not lost much of its body fat, so obviously, it had found something to eat.

What had gone on in the animal's mind was a mystery. It wasn't hard coming up with reasons why it had fled, such as the threat of the jackals or the sweltering heat. They could also explain why it came back, perhaps feeling bad about abandoning the two women. She could not fathom the internal struggle it had experienced, though it must have been as violent as battling jackals. But it was back, and that's all that really mattered.

Having their hands on the reins once again, they felt better. Ying'er pitied the animal: after escaping human control and experiencing an internal struggle, it had returned, only to be rewarded with the gift of the reins. That could mean the humans didn't trust it, she thought, as she shone the flashlight into its eyes and saw only kindness and compliance. There was no sign of guilt over fleeing or happiness about its return; it was composed, as always.

Their hunger intensified after a few mouthfuls of the buns and water. Despite the urge, neither of them dared to have more, for they did not want to die of bloating. And, of course, there was still a long way to go. The return of the camel fortified their minds, but fatigue sneaked in to take over their bodies again. Lanlan made the camel lie down for them to lean against and dozed off. It was a brief respite, but the most peaceful sleep they'd had in days.

It was bright and light when they woke up. They nibbled more of the steamed buns and felt their strength returning.

"Let's not go east now that we have our camel back," Lanlan said. "We'll head north again, which will take us to the salt lakes. We'd have to turn north after we reached the herders in the east anyway, and that would cost us time."

She could not have imagined that her idea would cast them back into the boundless desert, where the sword of death would again hang over their heads.

The sun was visible in the east, where a faint red glow showed in the sky. A striking contrast formed between the shady, dim sand hollow and the luminous eastern sky, like a woodblock painting. Waves of sand rippled in undulating patterns, rising up to become sand hills. The texture of the nearby patterns looked like wavelets, so delicate they hated to trample on them.

Ying'er shivered in the cold desert wind, though her jacket blocked some of its force. Lanlan's face had a greenish hue and was covered in goose bumps. They'd been too tired to take down the bedding from the litter, so, not long after they'd fallen sleep, they were awakened by an early morning chill typical of the desert. That was fine with them, as they could take advantage of the coolness and get moving again.

They got settled behind the camel's humps, solid, warm spots that gave them the feeling of climbing back into a small boat after falling into the water. Now they had something to depend upon.

The camel's back rose and fell gently, slow but confident, making the sand ridge sway from their vantage point. The sun that had forced its way off the horizon was pitching, but it too appeared to be carrying a heavy load. Their faces warmed by the sunlight, they felt alive again. The sun would show its power in a few hours, but now that they had their camel, Ying'er felt assured. Pain still knifed through her feet and legs from traveling on foot for many nights. Without the camel, she could not have taken another step. She was too weak, too thin to muster the strength that would have taken her to the sea of sand's far shore. But the camel could.

From the way the camels had shaken their heads and flicked their ears when they first entered the desert, Ying'er assumed that was a sign of their reluctance. Camels obviously know their backs will be used either for humans or for cargo once they are in the desert. Their destiny is to be beasts of burden. No animal would suffer willingly, so the camel she was riding had now earned her respect, and her gratitude, for returning after its flight. If you'd decided not to come back, she said silently, you could be having an easy time now, either lying down in a sand trough to chew your cud, feasting on desert rice or, enjoying tender grass. Now you have to carry two women who have had a tough time of it, like you, and set off again for an unknown future.

How could I not admire and respect you, camel?

Lanlan looked around to get her bearings. She knew a route to the salt lakes, but the jackals had ruined her sense of direction.

"Have you figured out where we're headed?" Ying'er asked.

"I'm not sure. I'm kind of lost. But let's get going. If we're headed north and follow the stars, at some point we'll know for sure where we are."

The sun rose higher and the heat began to attack again. They had to conserve their water, since they neither knew when nor where nor even if they might find more of it. They took small sips only when they couldn't focus.

They got down off the camel after a couple of hours. Frothy saliva had formed at its mouth and it was panting like a bellows, clearly exhausted. Lanlan said they had to let it rest. They picked a spot with desert stalks and unloaded the litter. Lanlan was shocked to see the animal's back festering and emitting a stench, obviously

121

caused by the litter, which had rubbed it raw, bumping up and down when it ran. It looked horrible. Ying'er felt guilty that they'd sat on the camel's wound and made it travel for so long.

Lanlan took some salt from the canvas bag to mix with a small bit of water to wash the wound. "Why didn't you make a noise?" she said to the camel. "We wouldn't have ridden if we'd known you were hurt."

She asked Ying'er to hold the water jug between her legs while she made the solution. Fearing the jug could slip from her grasp and spill the life-saving liquid over the sand, Ying'er was on tenterhooks. Her arms ached from the effort and concentration to secure the jug. She was exhausted by the time Lanlan finished.

After rinsing the wound, Lanlan slowly poured the remaining solution into her palm and showed it to the camel, which lapped up the cool liquid. Camels love salt, and the saline water could be considered its reward even if the coolness had little effect. In the end, the camel actually had more water than they did, but they didn't mind. They did not want the wound to get infected, and hoped it would scab soon. They needed the camel as their ride, but, more importantly, they felt reassured by its presence.

The sun rose higher and the heat grew more intense.

"We'll have to keep doing the same thing, lie down in a damp pit when it's hot and get on the move at night and in the early morning," Lanlan said. "We should have enough water to last us to the salt lakes if we ration it."

Ying'er knew Lanlan was trying to make her feel better. The attack of the jackals had driven them off their planned route to the salt lakes. Now it was hard to say if they would ever get there, after heading east for so long before turning north. But she kept the thought to herself.

"We'll be all right now that we have our camel back," she said.

Lanlan was happily surprised to find in one of the bags on the litter a large glass container that was more than half filled with flaxseed oil. They'd packed it in a separate bag so it wouldn't break if it bumped against the pots, and it had been saved from being jettisoned. It wouldn't taste very good, but it would supply them with some nutrients "Let's not touch that yet," Lanlan said. "The buns are so dry we need to eat them with sips of water so they'll go down easily. We'll make do with that for a few meals and drink the flaxseed oil as a last resort."

They found a shaded hollow and scooped out pits until they reached damp sand; the larger one was for the camel. They made it lie down to take in moisture. Lanlan cut down some desert stalks and carried them into the pit for the camel to chew on while it stayed out of the sun.

Thirst and hunger continued to torment them, but they felt better than when the camel had gone off on its own. With a little food and water, their chances for survival were much improved.

Two more days passed as they traveled by night and rested by day. They thought they might have reached the salt lakes by then, judging by the progress they'd made. Instead, to their chagrin, they found themselves in a rock-strewn gobi. Lanlan panicked at the sight, as she did not recall seeing rocks on her earlier trip. They'd taken a wrong turn. The buns were long gone and they had little water left; they hadn't touched the oil, which would not last them long anyway. The camel's wounds were scabbing, but neither had the heart to get back on. When fatigue overtook them, one led the camel, the other held onto its tail to conserve energy. Their legs felt as if they belonged to someone else, so after a while they took turns riding, a couple of hours each.

The camel's humps had begun to cave in, a sign that it was losing its reserve energy. Lanlan tried to stop at grassy spots to rest for the day, for the camel's sake, but its humps sagged anyway. She recalled that several sites specially designated as camel supply stations had been established along the route to the salt lakes. Obviously, the animal had missed its chance when they took a wrong turn. Lanlan unloaded the litter and removed the grass padding under the saddle to feed to the camel. She replaced it with a blanket. The little bit of grass was of scant use to a hungry camel.

At least its wound was healing. Camels are used to carrying loads that rub their backs raw, and, as time passes, callouses form. The saline solution aided the scabbing process, and the camel would be able to carry them as long as it had the strength.

The rocky desert was actually dotted with grassy spots here and there for the camel to enjoy and keep from losing interest. Lanlan was convinced that its humps would swell again if it could eat like that for several days. But they hadn't come out into the desert to graze the camel. She mentally retraced their steps before concluding that they had missed a life-saving oasis, though not a very big one, by being slightly off course somewhere along the route.

Now what?

"We have to turn and travel west, back into the sand. We'll make it if we're lucky," Lanlan said.

They tied the camel to a desert shrub before retracing their steps and began climbing the highest sand hill in sight. Dragging their leaden legs, they slowly headed upward, taking a break every few steps. It took at least two hours, and they were spent when they reached the top, where they gasped for air before they could get up to look around. The hill had seemed to be the highest in the area, and they thought they'd see smaller ones down below. They were dismayed to see more soaring hills, each one higher than the next, all around them. Just looking at them drove any thoughts of more climbing out of them.

Ying'er slumped to the ground, where she remained silent for a long time.

Lanlan was quiet too, looking glum. They felt like crying, and their minds were a blank. They'd have crawled if they'd seen a patch of white—the salt lakes—even if it had been on the distant horizon. But there was only sand as far as they could see; maybe they would never reach their destination.

"Let's go back down," Lanlan said.

"I can't move," Ying'er said. "I'd rather die up here."

"Let's go. We have to keep going and see where it takes us.".

With her eyes on the camel, a yellow dot, down below, Ying'er knew she wouldn't have bothered climbing if she'd known what awaited. It not only drained them of energy, it was demoralizing.

Too tired to walk, even down a gentle slope, she found a steep spot, sat on the sand, and started sliding down. Surprisingly, it felt like she'd sprouted wings as she tobogganed down, the wind whipping past her ears, light as air. When she reached a slightly flat spot, she heard Lanlan call out, "Be careful. You'll tear a hole in your pants if you keep going like that."

Ying'er did not want that, but it felt too good. I don't even know if I'll live, she said silently, so why worry about a pair of pants? She jumped back onto the slope, where the sand carried her along like water. So exhilarating. She hadn't felt that relaxed in a long time. She shouted happily, enlivening the quiet trough. Infected by her excitement, Lanlan sat down on the sand, not worried about her pants either, and glided down. They yelled joyfully.

After a moment, Ying'er turned over, and began swimming in the sand. Every stroke propelled her a distance; sand drifted into her collar, ticklish but pleasant. Lanlan copied her, and they filled the sand trough with their cheerful shouts. The unanticipated delight erased their worries, at least for the moment.

When they reached the bottom, they spat out sand and laughed themselves silly. For years, they'd lived under the gaze of others; this was the first time they'd been able to let go, and they were surprised to rediscover their inner girlhood at a time and in a spot where they were about to abandon all hope.

They each took a sip of the flaxseed oil to celebrate their good mood.

Lanlan

Bai Fu came back for Lanlan. She wanted nothing to do with him. A failed relationship is worse than broken furniture. At least you can still make do with a broken chair, but she could not tolerate the notion of "make do" when the feelings are gone. How could she have slept in the same bed with someone like him for all those years? She was so disgusted with herself she thought she'd need to soak in water for three days to wash it off.

He looked as though he'd lost weight in only a matter of days. His clothes hung on him, which she noticed the moment he walked in, but not out of concern over his well-being. She just thought he looked different, like a stranger, and very strange, disgustingly strange. It went beyond her ability to tolerate, especially his bow legs, which made him waddle when he walked. She could not believe she'd given up Huaqiu to marry that man, part of the trade—her as a wife to a brutish man for her brother to marry. How had that become her fate?

Lanlan believed in fate, trusting that everyone had a preset track in life, one destiny. And yet she refused to accept this as her lot in life. She'd once heard a fortuneteller talk about changing one's destiny the way time and one's luck can change. He said he'd told many people's fortunes, and that most of what he'd predicted had come true. A few had not, because those were people who practiced Buddhism and followed its guidance, one building a bridge, one repairing a road, one setting free captured animals, and one doing other good deeds. They had ended with a better fate than they started with.

So Lanlan believed in fate, but she still refused to accept what lay in store for her.

The truth was: she'd considered divorcing Bai Fu even before learning of her brother's illness; the exchange marriage was no longer a consequential matter to her, and she refused to be controlled by fate. After going through so much, a girl grows up to be a woman and eventually opens her eyes to her destiny. She lives but once, and when it is over there is nothing left. Lanlan had often questioned herself whether the man before her was worth spending her life with. If he had been, she'd have stayed with him; if not, she needed to make a different choice. Otherwise, she'd have wasted her life. That happened to so many women she knew, and she refused to join their ranks. She wanted to live for herself, if only for a few years, a few months, even less than that.

Bai Fu was still bending her mother's ear. Lanlan did not even want to hear his voice. She knew what he was saying without listening. He'd either plead by looking pathetic or threaten to do something mean. That was all he could do. She knew every little thing that went on inside his head. He was too simple-minded to scheme. For Lanlan, it was better to put everything out in the open so he'd stop pestering her. She went into her parents' room and, with her eyes fixed on a large wardrobe, said to him:

"You know better than anyone what you've done. It'll be the next lifetime before I walk back into your house." That did not sound right. She wouldn't to go back there even then. "Not for eighteen lifetimes." She added. "I'd rather evaporate than spend another day in your house."

Bai Fu stopped his rambling and fixed a vicious glare at her, his default expression. Lanlan sneered, too used to his expression to be scared, "Whore." Bai Fu forced the word out through clenched teeth.

"You can eat whatever you want, but you can't say whatever comes to mind, Bai Fu, not in my house," her mother complained. "How is my daughter a whore? How can you say that?"

127

"I'll take from you double what you've taken from me," Bai Fu said to his wife, raising his voice to show his intention to fight to the very last. Lanlan smiled at her husband's shifting threat, from threatening her to scaring her parents. She was sure he was bluffing. Bai Fu did not have it in him to risk his life. She knew that was true, that he'd lost both his vitality and his spirit ever since taking their daughter out to freeze to death in the desert. He often screamed in his dream, haunted by the fear of a white fox coming to take his life, or racked by fear when he dreamed about police. Not Lanlan. Nothing scared her any longer. If death could not, why be afraid of living?

"All right," her mother said. "Your father and I are tired of living. If you'll do us the favor and deliver us from suffering, I'll kowtow to you. The earlier we die, the sooner we're out of this ordeal. You can stop trying to frighten us."

"Tell me, what do I have to live for?" He choked up. "I have nothing to look forward to, nothing." He sobbed.

Lanlan scrunched her nose in distaste; her heart had grown cold. Not anything, not even his death would sway her, let alone his tears. She surprised herself, a woman who had always been soft-hearted, a believer in the Buddhist principle of kindness to others. Some of the things that were ordinary to others would move her. And she saw the inherent good in most people. That did not include her husband. Love lingers forever between a couple who have been together for one night, as the saying goes. And the emotional attachment is deeper than the ocean for those who have been husband and wife for a hundred days. But not her. She found him repellent, and could not for a minute forget the beatings. For Bai Fu she felt only loathing. "Don't be so revolting, will you?"

Bai Fu stopped crying and sat, dispirited, a sorry sight. Looking at him now, she could not imagine how vicious, how violent he could be. The drastic change made him appear like two very different animals, a wild boar then and a sick deer now.

Her mother seemed to be relenting, glancing at Lanlan and then at Bai Fu. She wanted to say something, but changed her mind. Lanlan knew what her mother was thinking. If he hadn't been there, she'd have resorted to cliché and said, "A prodigal son who changes his ways is worth more than gold," and would have wanted her to reconsider. That was how her mother was, easily swayed by tears, with no sense of principle and fearful of confrontation. Lanlan, on the other hand, had hardened her heart, believing that was good for Bai Fu as well. He could start over and find a new wife to give him a son, since he was still young. If she dragged it out, she'd be holding him back, and who knew what amount of abuse she would have to suffer over that.

A dispirited Bai Fu got to his feet and sleepwalked his way into his sister's room. As Lanlan had expected, her mother whispered the moment he walked out, "You ought to think it over."

"Ma." Lanlan was unhappy. "Don't give him any false hope. He has to give up the idea altogether."

"I'm just afraid Ying'er will want to take the baby home with her. That's Hantou's heir, you know." Her mother sighed.

"It's her baby, you can't keep him here."

"Of course I can," her mother said stubbornly, "I won't let her take him. I'll take good care of her if she stays a widow in our house, but she has to leave her baby here if she wants to return to her parents' home." She softened her tone as her eyes turned watery. "How can this be happening? Our family is breaking up, one dead, the other gone away, and now we can't even keep the fatherless baby."

Lanlan knew that the tears would not stop once her mother mentioned Hantou, so she changed the subject, "Not so loud. Let's hear what they're saying."

Her mother stopped crying, cocked her ear, but could hear nothing. She went over to close the door before sprawling by the cat door to eavesdrop.

Lanlan was amused.

"Nothing important." Her mother got up after a while. "He didn't say anything, just bawled his eyes out. I have to say I feel sorry for him."

Lanlan was afraid she might be giving in, at least for her mother's sake. She'd been repelled by the way he'd cried in front of her, but was nearly swayed when hearing him sob in front of Ying'er. A man must be in terrible shape if he has to go crying to his own sister. Her flirtation with a change of heart ended when she was reminded of what she'd been through since the day they were married. Now he was weeping like a child in his own sister's room.

"Crocodile tears." She sneered.

"Don't say that." Her mother looked upset with her. "We're all humans and everyone has worries. We shouldn't gloat over others' troubles."

"I'm not gloating." For some reason, Lanlan's mood softened, though that did nothing to alter her decision. You muddle through life if necessary, she was thinking, but once you see the light, no one would want to continue living in ignorance.

Lanlan had been the victim of Bai Fu's spousal rape after they were married, which had gone on so long she'd lost all bodily desire. That was almost too sad to contemplate. As a mother, she'd suffered the pain of losing a daughter; as a wife, she'd been beaten into submission; as a woman, she'd deprived herself of a woman's heaven-ordained pleasure.

She was mostly upset with her father by how he'd worked so hard to convince her to stay with her husband, despite his brutality. Now that Hantou had died, she knew she must defy him. When she went back, she would file for divorce. This time no one or no one thing could convince her otherwise.

11

The merriment had taken everything out of them, and worries returned after the brief carefree indulgence. They wondered how far they would be able to travel, whether or not they'd ever reach the salt lakes. The more they reflected, the deeper the funk into which they sent themselves, so they put the questions out of their minds. As the sun's power lessened, they headed west. They would not allow themselves to be trapped and die in the ocean of sand. Getting on the road was the better option. Even a blind donkey runs into a haystack sometimes, so they might happen upon someone going to the salt lakes or a herder with his flock.

They passed a camel carcass at dusk; it was lying by a sand eddy. Lanlan was gladdened by the sight, for it signaled human traces in the area. Two black holes in the skull stared blankly, and likely had been doing so for a very long time. The bones were relatively intact, the teeth and ribs remained attached. Their camel shook its head, flicked its ears, and spit loudly. Laoshun would say it had seen a ghost. Could the soul of the dead camel be hanging around its carcass? They had heard of corpse-guarding ghosts that stayed by the bones until they were interred. Though frightened, Ying'er did not believe a camel ghost would be guarding its carcass in broad daylight.

"Look. It was carrying salt," Lanlan said, pointing to the bits of fabric by the carcass. "It may have died of exhaustion."

Ying'er saw no sign of salt transport, but was pleased nonetheless. It was good news to see something like that, for they had seen only sand, rocks, and a bit of desert vegetation, nothing with human connections for longer than they cared to recall. The carcass at least meant human traffic. That, however, did not tell them how far the animal had traveled before it died.

If it had died transporting salt, their objective could still be far off. Ying'er's despondency increased as she speculated the reason behind the camel's death. If nothing else, it meant there was neither a water source nor edible grass nearby. What other than thirst or illness could have killed the camel? Lying quietly in a sand trough, it had meekly met its fate. She sighed as she thought about what might await them in the days to come.

Lanlan had their camel kneel so they could climb on its back. It rocked and swayed before finally getting to its feet.

"So long," Ying'er turned to say to the carcass. "You had a tough life." The sad possibility occurred to her that she might meet the same fate before long.

No visible path appeared as they traveled on, but they encountered bones from time to time, either a whole carcass or leg bones sticking up out of the sand. Maybe, Ying'er said to herself, we're on a caravan route. Otherwise, where had all the bones come from? She felt better now.

Lanlan had hoped to shoot a rabbit, but oddly, the only live animal they'd seen in all the time they'd been in the desert, except for the sheep they'd encountered their first day out, and of course the jackals, had been the rabbit Ying'er had frightened off.

"Even a desert rat would be good," she said with a sigh.

Finally, they saw what appeared to be an actual camel route: a litter beside a carcass provided sufficient evidence. The wood had largely disintegrated in the wind, and beside it lay a pile of droppings that had been left who knows when. Lanlan felt her spirits rise, for no matter how they looked at it, they must finally be on the right track. Ying'er was happy too, if dubious, though her mood also brightened. Why were there so many camel carcasses along the way? Did this really lead to the salt lakes? If so, how far was it? And could their energy sustain them until they found water? All this was unknown. Lanlan must have been aware of the doubts, she just did not want to point them out.

What worried them most was their camel. The two of them could rely on the oil, but the camel's humps were sagging badly. How much longer would it last? It was carrying two adult humans much of the time, and when it tried to stand up with them on its back, it swayed and rocked before it made it. It wobbled when going uphill, as if it were about to fall. So, they climbed down whenever they were on an upslope and held the animal's tail to help them along.

After a break, they each took a sip of the oil and water before setting off for their nighttime journey. The camel carcasses infused the night with a sinister gloom; they were traveling along a path that was filled with signs of death.

"Moving slowly is better than standing still. Every step takes us closer, so long as we're heading the right direction," Lanlan said.

"Down, down." They called out for the camel to kneel.

It hesitated briefly before kneeling slowly.

"It's worn out," Lanlan said with a sigh.

After getting on the camel's back, Lanlan flicked the reins and shouted "Up, up." The animal swayed as it tried to stand, but managed only to raise its front legs once before settling back down again.

"You stay, I'll get down," Lanlan said as she got down off the camel. She called to it and pulled its tail, but it still could not stand.

Ying'er dismounted. The camel flared its nostrils, breathing slowly and laboriously. There were dry desert stalks on the

133

surrounding sand dunes, but it ignored them. Its throat was too parched to swallow stalks more arid than the sun.

Lanlan called out to the camel a few more times, but it just cried piteously, as if to say, You go on. I can't go any farther. Its humps were little more than leather pouches, and its ribs showed. Breathing hard, it kept sticking out its tongue, which had a thick, dark yellow coating. How Ying'er wished she could communicate with the camel or sense what it was feeling.

The many carcasses could have been signs to those coming after them that it was the newcomers' turn to die. A frightening warning. Ying'er recalled how, after falling ill, Hantou had held on to an illusion of getting better. At the time, the flame of his life had continued to burn, though feebly, always on the brink of going out. Apparently, camels are like that, she thought. They believe they will likely follow their comrades in death. Some might be strong enough to carry on, but the suggestion of death destroys what little hope remains.

How to save a camel that had lost the will or the stamina to go on? She had to think of something else. Ah, she thought, there's one thing they could do—give it some of their oil.

"But that's all we have left," Lanlan said with a frown when Ying'er broached the subject. "And we may have far yet to travel."

"We can't leave it behind. It came back after running off, that has to mean something. And we'll need it with us if we make it out of the desert."

"All right. Worst case, we die together," Lanlan said as she brought out the bottle and gave it a shake; the oil swirled, leaving streaky patterns on the sides. Ying'er's heart tightened at the sight of the shapeless liquid. There was enough for them to take a few sips each; it wasn't much but it was the only food they had left.

The camel gazed at the liquid with hungry eyes, which it had done each time they'd taken a sip. A desert stalk was repellent to a tongue that was as dry as the sole of a straw sandal, and a throat that was as parched as sandpaper. The liquid was different—smooth, it seemed, with a wonderful hint of coolness. It had only looked on greedily, watching the movements around the two women's throats as they swallowed. It could even hear gurgling sounds when the syrupy, shiny, sweet dew slid down their throats. Every cell in bodies that were as dry as smoke cried out joyfully. But the camel could only look.

The last thing it had expected was for the woman, whose lips were covered in dry, dark skin, to tip the bottle toward it, and it thought Lanlan was merely teasing. It had often been teased like that by villagers. The locals had a saying about hanging alfalfa on the skylight to make an old donkey yearn in vain. Village children would sometimes hold tender grass in front of a camel, and snatch it away when it opened its mouth, then laugh over their prank. In the past, it would shut its eyes with a haughty air when confronted with teasing, but at this moment, the appeal was overpowering.

To its astonishment, the bottle's opening was coming right up to its mouth. Sensing what the marvelous contents meant to the women, it gazed into their eyes and tried to apprehend the implication. It saw eyes brimming with concern.

When she tipped the bottle into its mouth, the smooth liquid coated its tongue as its taste buds cried out deliriously. It could hardly be called a taste, for it was more like a vortex of happiness, a tsunami of divine flavor. Its greedy taste buds opened feverishly to take in the smooth, viscous liquid that moistened its tongue. Now it could eat grass again. After that, it would be able to carry the two women once more.

When there was no more oil for either the women or the camel, Lanlan tossed the empty bottle into a sand trough. Ying'er picked it up, wiped its opening with her lapel, and put it into a sack hanging from the camel's litter.

Lanlan

Lanlan got another beating.

Bai Fu whipped her like flogging a donkey. Her body was crisscrossed with red and purple welts. The moment he left to go gambling, she struggled out and returned to her parents' house. When she walked in the gate, she was greeted by a yard littered with chicken droppings. So, she picked up a broom and started sweeping, making her arms and legs scream from the pain. She did not need to check to know how bad they looked. That's how it had been for some time. Ever since the death of her daughter, her mood had vacillated between brooding and angry outbursts, which naturally brought on more beatings. That was the only progress her plan for divorce had achieved.

Later that night, when the moon was up, she walked toward the Dasha River, where the squat houses, peeling walls, and dry dust on the ground were a blur, all fading into the moonlit night. In good times, the moon had brought her peace. Before her marriage, she had often gazed at it as she sat under the date tree by the gate. It had been brighter, fuller then, forever racing with the clouds in the boundless evening sky. The moon ran fast, hastily ducking into one puffy cloud and then another, as swift as the shuttle on a loom. When she grew up, she realized that the moon was also in bondage, tethered to an invisible rope, turning around and around like her mother at the stove or a donkey at the mill. And yet she envied it, until later, that is, once marriage and the distractions of daily life drove it from her mind.

Every time she looked at herself in the mirror, she was saddened by the sight: the rosy glow of youth was gone, replaced by a sallow hue. Crow's feet had crept into the corners of her eyes.

She would not accept the changes willingly. Her youth was gone before she'd made much of her life. And her husband turned out to be—to be—worthless. All this she would not surrender to its inevitability. She wanted something better.

She sighed at the thought of her marriage, which soured her mood. The Dasha River offered more soothing possibilities.

Back when water still ran in the river, there were water plants and clean rocks that could be fished out and dried in the sun to display their colorful patterns. She had collected many of the rocks and enjoyed looking at them during leisurely moments. Besides the rocks, the water was fine too, clear and cool, not a speck of impurities. She had been told it was snowmelt from the Qilian Mountains flowing through endless time and space to form a bend here, where it supported the livelihood of a whole village, before meandering on to who knows where. Waves of sand wriggled along the riverbanks and rose higher and higher to crest into an ocean of sand.

Then Lanlan changed, from a limpid young girl to a drab woman. Much like the Dasha River, whose water dried up, whose plants died, and whose trees thinned out. The stand of desert date trees was all that remained the same. Sturdy and hardy, unlike more delicate trees, they sank roots deep into the ground and, with tiny leaves and a modest need for water, they survived. When she was little, she had staved off hunger by gathering their dates. She and Huaqiu had come here often with other village children to cut green feed for pigs, knock down dates, and collect cow dung. Her mother had assigned the children each with a task, and those who failed to complete it would get a taste of her cloth shoe on their backsides. Sharp eyes and quick hands were essential in knocking down dates. One of the children would climb up a tree and swat them down with a switch, sending the others scrambling after them. Her mother did not care much about the dates, so it didn't matter how many she got. Cow dung was a different matter. It was their fuel, without which they could not boil water or cook a meal. The children often got into fights over it, until a rule was set that the person who spotted it got to keep it. Huaqiu, who had sharp eyes, often yelled, "The black yak-ox is raising its tail—I spotted that one for Lanlan." She'd run over, scoop it up, and toss it into her basket.

She clapped her hands, but there was no response. Huaqiu was late again. Leaning against a date tree, she looked into the sky, where an enormous moon hung amid sparse stars, the Milky Way barely visible.

She clapped again: *slap-slap—slap—slap-slap.*

A barking dog gave the only response. She was about to duck down when Huaqiu appeared from behind a tree. "Silly thing," she chided happily as she ran up and he took her into his arms. Lanlan liked the way he held and kissed her, passionate the way a man ought to be, but with his unique kind of abandonment. Her heart pounded like a startled fawn, a sensation that had all but disappeared since her wedding, for her senses had been dulled and her heart coated in a layer of dust

Dew settled in, its cool moisture seeping through their clothes. With their arms around each other, they were deep in the delirium typical of lovers. The village blurred in the distant night; everything faded around them. Their sorrows became a thread floating in the poetic night air, affording them a different kind of pleasure. Everything felt plaintive, the moon, the wind, the chill that the wind brought, as well as their racing hearts and sweaty palms.

"Time to head back." No sooner had the thought surfaced than it drove sharp pains into her heart. Happy, sweet moments like this never lasted long. How she wished they would last forever, but her parents were home, waiting for her. Their wrinkled faces, like the bark of trees, kept flashing before her eyes, each flicker cooling the blood in her veins.

"I have to go home," she said.

"Let's talk, spend the night, what do you say?" The temptation of his suggestion was nearly impossible to resist. All night—the whole night. Her heart pounded so hard she almost agreed to his request.

He put his arms around her, kissing her over and over, so eager and intense, nearly suffocating her. A violent, giant life force could breech any defense. She hated the thought of ending it now.

But she pushed away the hands groping her pants' cord and he let go of his hands. Sensing his disappointment, she said:

"Please don't be like that. It's not easy for us to see each other. Let's talk a while."

He did not reply, so she continued, "I used to dream about being with you, but after a while, I no longer even saw you in my dreams. I had so much to say to you, but I can't recall any of it now that we're face to face."

"What's there to talk about? I have to go home too. My woman didn't want me to come out, and I suspect she's looking all over for me."

Suddenly, she lost interest in talking to him, and began to regret agreeing to the meeting. Huaqiu had become a different man, she realized.

Men are all the same, she thought, as a sense of loss came over her.

Her mother was sitting up in bed, lost in thought, when Lanlan walked in. With a glance at her daughter, she sighed and said softly, "You should have worn a coat on such a cool night." Lanlan mumbled an acknowledgment. She spotted some sand on her lapels in the light of the lamp, a telltale sign of her whereabouts, so she flicked them off gently. She had an excuse ready in case her mother asked: she'd say she'd gone to see an old friend. But her mother did not ask; she sat deep in thought, after another sigh.

Everyone in the village had known about her and Huaqiu back then, but she had not talked about it openly with her parents, who in turn had never asked. Once she'd overhead them talking about them. Her father's attitude was clear; he did not want his daughter to choose her own mate. From minute details like a frown whenever Huaqiu's name was mentioned, Lanlan knew her father did not like him. On the other hand, he'd had plenty of good things to say about Bai Fu, who was as strong as an ox and a hard worker; he liked a good time, and often gambled, but that was not a problem in the villagers' eyes. Bai Fu did not steal, rob, or visit prostitutes. Playing a few hands of cards was nothing. To be sure, he'd taken these things too far, but everything would be fine once he turned over a new leaf. As for beating his wife, that needn't be a flaw at all. Every man in the village beat his wife, except for henpecked men who were ordered around by their wives until they had no standing among their peers. Laoshun himself had turned his wife's body into a bloody mat more than once. Which was why he tried to talk to his daughter about how men were ill-tempered during their youth, but would be better once they were older. But to Lanlan, it would be torture to spend a lifetime under Bai Fu's fist and whip, and she had no intention of turning into her mother. Maybe Mother would understand how she felt, Lanlan thought. She'd been young once, had suffered beatings, and had tried to get a divorce. Now she was old, in body and spirit. She sighed along with Lanlan or shed a few tears when she was feeling down.

She could not encourage her daughter to get a divorce, but could not sit by and watch her abused either. Caught in a bind, she could only say or intimate, "Don't worry about us and do what you want," or "You should know better, because we can't worry about you forever." The former encouraged her to go ahead with the divorce, while the later was intended to talk her out of it. Lanlan favored the former, naturally. It was true they could not be with her forever, and it was up to her to decide whether to listen to them or not. She had to make up her mind and walk her own path.

Before her wedding, Huaqiu had come to see her and, amid sobs, had told her all he needed was an answer. If she said yes, he would take her away, far away from the village, anywhere they wanted. But she could not cost her brother a wife, bring disgrace to her parents, and give neighbors fodder for gossip, all of which converged to become a barrier that kept her from eloping. Now she had awakened, and was no longer the same woman. Shedding her reserved nature, she did not shy away from a shouting match with her mother-in-law; forgoing her bashfulness, she went for Bai Fu's most vulnerable spot when he beat and kicked her; casting off subtlety, she became crude, and preferred blunt talk devoid of overtones, the same as other village women. Like a pair of scissors, life had shorn her of a young girl's nature, and only when it was quite late at night did she remember she'd once been young, with aspirations and romance. She would then be struck by a profound sense of loss. This was not a life she was prepared to accept.

She knew how hard it was to shake off her nightmarish fate, just as it had been for her mother and for all the women of Sha-wan. Yellow sand, local customs, violent husbands, and grueling labor were a corrosive fluid that ate away a woman's feminine self. Without knowing it, they had lost their best qualities and been turned into crones. Crones were not women, but machines to cook, to reproduce, and to toil. A woman lost something innate; her interest in life vanished and her share of joy was stifled. She was unfeeling, shrewd, slow-witted, quarrelsome, disheveled, hag-

141

gard, and gray, until she was finally reduced to a pile of bones. Such was the trajectory of life that women shared.

Most horrifying was the common belief that it was their fate. Fate was a turning millstone, while the women were ants on the stone, expected to accept their destiny. Whoever tried to break the set order would pay the ultimate price, dying a terrible death.

When she thought of divorce, the only one she could not bear to face was Ying'er, her sister-in-law. No matter how Lanlan felt about her own life and how much she wanted it to change, they had married each other's brother so the men could each have a wife. After Hantou died, Ying'er stayed in the home of her in-laws; despite her tears and sighs, she entertained no thoughts of remarriage, determined to remain a widow and raise her child. Lanlan would not want Ying'er to be a widow forever, and yet she was loath to let someone else take such a good woman as a daughter-in-law.

Bai Fu was, after all, Ying'er's older brother. Lanlan could not bring up such an awkward a topic. Nonetheless, she knew that Ying'er was the only one to whom she could open up, the one person who knew what went on in her heart, who understood the pain inside her, and who, more than anyone else, could grasp the traumatic blow to her spirit brought on by the death of her daughter. They were fellow sufferers, so naturally they found affinity in sentiments.

"You don't have to say a word," Ying'er once said. "I understand."

Lanlan knew exactly what she meant.

Ying'er was as quiet and serene as before; except for being somewhat gaunt, for the barely noticeable lines under her eyes, and for the occasional far-away look when no one was watching, she did not look like a woman who had experienced the tragedy of losing her husband. Lanlan naturally was happy to see her like that, but a shred of annoyance constantly cropped up: how could she recover so fast after Hantou's death? Maybe she'd never really cared for him.

During the infrequent times they were able to be together, they sang folk tunes. They shared a fondness for songs of separation and longing. Like a fine thread, the tunes tugged at their hearts and drew them out.

> A wolf bays three times in the ravine,
> A tiger runs out of the forest.
> I call your name three times,
> My heart nearly leaps from my chest.

> At Jiayu Pass, thunder claps.
> By the Yellow River, the rain falls.
> I cry so much my eyes are swollen
> When I see a stranger, I think it is you.

They wept when they sang tunes that echoed the sounds of nature; their emotions resonated with each other, though their minds were on different tracks. For Ying'er, sometimes she sang with such passion it was almost as if the words would never again be spoken.

Lanlan began to understand what went on in Ying'er's heart through these tunes. When she sang as she gazed tearfully, eyes half-shut, at the vast horizon or the surging ocean of sand, Lanlan sensed the agony deep inside her. It was, however, a forbidden place neither of them wanted to enter.

12

The women and their camel set off at dusk. The camel was able to walk, but was still too weak to carry them. Now they had to climb dunes that seemed to reach to the sky. Pain cut through Ying'er's calves again. Her feet sank with each step, and as the pain worsened, erupting from her soles, she began to limp.

Each step takes us closer to our destination, she comforted herself. But when she looked around, there was nothing but dark, soaring dunes. As usual, stars hung low, but they no longer interested her, lost along with the poetic sentiments she'd felt when they first entered the desert. Finally, she realized that such sentiments are a luxury, something you can enjoy only when you have enough to eat and drink and your survival is not in jeopardy. Poetic thoughts are an extravagance. They require suffering, but when that suffering presses down like a towering mountain, there is no room for them.

So, just keep walking.

Dragging her painful legs, she gazed at the blurry vista ahead under a dusty setting sun. She calcified her thoughts, froze poetic sentiments, stilled her heart, all to keep her hopes alive. Holding on to the camel's tail, she pulled hard only when going up a dune. On level ground, she strove to quicken her steps on leaden legs so as not to be a burden to the animal.

With the camel's halter in hand, Lanlan appeared to be leading the animal forward, but was actually helping herself along. Her father had made a point of putting on the halter before they left home. The woven leather strips put pressure on the head, but would not hurt the animal even if she pulled hard enough to propel herself forward.

Ying'er held onto the tail to keep moving, but the pain in her legs never let up, forcing her to shut her eyes every now and again. She was so exhausted she'd have fallen into a deep sleep if the sand had not tripped her up from time to time. At one point, believing she was sleeping on her bed at home, she let go of the tail and slumped to the ground. Fortunately, Lanlan had turned to check on her when they rounded a bend.

"You're lucky there was no wind. Otherwise, I wouldn't have been able to find you," she said. "It would have blown away all traces and howled strangely to carry off my voice if I called out to you. It could have made other noises to lead you astray. You'd have followed the sound until you'd gotten to a place where I could never find you. That's how many people stranded in the desert die."

To prevent Ying'er from falling behind again, Lanlan tied one end of a rope to Ying'er's waist and the other to the litter. The rope was long enough that it would be slack if Ying'er kept her hand on the camel's tail, but would tighten if she fell. If that happened, Lanlan, who was holding the rope, would stop and wake her up. To make it work, Lanlan had to keep the camel under control; otherwise, the animal would drag Ying'er along if startled. Despite her exhaustion, Ying'er had to admire Lanlan's ingenuity and marveled at the things her sister-in-law knew, not for the first time during the trip.

They stumbled along among hills of sand, half asleep. There'd been a bell on the camel when they set off, but it had gotten lost during their escape from the jackals. Now all they heard was the shushing of their feet on the sand, in addition to the occasional sneeze from the camel, which was loud enough to rouse a sleepy Ying'er.

Their flashlight batteries were running low. Lanlan turned the light on only to check the path ahead. Sometimes a carcass came into view under the column of light, a sight that would have sent them shrieking in the past, but was nothing unusual now. If they'd gone a long time without seeing one, Lanlan would grumble silently, afraid they'd taken a wrong turn again. They weren't all camel carcasses either. Some looked like dogs, but could have been foxes; they could not tell them apart. The flowing sand was supposed to bury the carcasses, but strangely it hadn't, probably because dunes to the north had blocked the gusting winds.

By midnight, they could not take another step, so they stopped to rest. Ying'er fell asleep the moment she sat down, while Lanlan remained standing to stay awake. She knew they'd be baked alive if they didn't cover more distance at night. But they were so thirsty, and the water in the jug was barely enough for a few more sips. Thirst, like a fire, scorched her throat, but she did not dare touch the water. We have so little left, she said to herself, we'll use it only to save a life. If one of us passes out from the heat, the other will revive her with the water. The few drops were not to be undervalued; sometimes a tiny amount can delay a looming death.

She was overcome by engulfing sleepiness, impossible to resist, like dark nights or death. So, she rested against the camel, thinking she'd wake up when it moved, either walking off or just lying down.

Then she shut her eyes and plunged into a colossal darkness.

Lanlan was still asleep when Ying'er woke up. The camel was on the ground, Lanlan resting against its side. The animal was sleeping in a cautious manner. It could have lain down and stretched out its limbs, the usual way a camel slept. Experienced camel transporters would never lie down next to a camel, for fear they would be crushed if the animal rolled over. But this was a smart camel that knelt to sleep clearly not wanting to crush Lanlan or startle her awake.

Dawn had arrived, bringing everything into view. Off to the side was a human skull with bared teeth, the two hollows of eye sockets staring at Ying'er. She ignored it. She wanted Lanlan to get more sleep, but knew it would be best to get on the road in the early morning cool. She had to nudge her awake. She was startled, her eyes snapped open, as if she could not believe it was daytime again.

"I slept like the dead," she said.

The fatigue had abated, but thirst returned. Hunger receded to the background when thirst raged. Lanlan had wanted to keep the water to save one of them later, but the thirst was too powerful to ignore, so she changed her mind. Pouring some water into the cap of the jug, she handed it to Ying'er, after which she drank a capful herself. They tried to moisten their lips with their tongues, but that was futile, for their lips were too dry to be rehydrated.

After getting the camel up, they were on their way again. The body must not be pampered. If you keep moving, even if there are aches and pains, your body will get used to them. But take a break, and the fatigue and pain will be aroused, which was how Ying'er felt at the moment. The soreness felt worse than it had at night. Now that she was sore all over, thirst and aches enveloped her like two whirlwinds, but she was able to walk in relative wakefulness. She had no time to worry about the path they were taking; just resisting the thirst and bearing the aches and pains used up all her mental energy.

The dune was less steep as they walked on, and had little vegetation, mainly desert stalks, which even the camel ignored. They started seeing camel droppings. Lanlan crushed a few of them, and they all looked ancient. Clumps of a thorny plant on which camel hair had snagged appeared near a sand eddy. The plants were long dead, meaning there was not enough underground water to sustain their growth.

Ying'er focused on other things to divert her attention from the maddening thirst and aches. The first was Lingguan, who had left her and the village, and not been heard from since. His face now appeared before her, sweating, his lips as swollen as Lanlan's. The image had been transplanted in part from Lanlan, who so closely resembled her brother.

Her thoughts abruptly turned to the salt lakes. To be sure, she could conjure up no image of the place, but for that very reason, it carried a mystique. It had become a kind of totem, after so much suffering, hardship, and searching. She hoped the trip would change her destiny, at least change her present life. When the family was hard up, her father-in-law would take a camel to the salt lakes and bring back hope each time. But what did it look like? The more they traveled, the more concerned she grew. She'd had many things to look forward to in her life, a different one for each phase. In the end, all had turned to soap bubbles, bright and colorful when they floated, but leaving unbearable disappointment and emptiness when they burst. She hoped it would be different this time with the salt lakes. Her weary heart could not take another blow.

They stopped to take a break and swallow the last sips of water. It had been two days since they'd last relieved themselves, meaning the little water they took in remained in their bodies. Neither said a word as they drank, for they knew what it meant.

"Let's get going," Lanlan said.

They walked with the camel until noon. Ying'er wished they could resume traveling at night, but the flashlight batteries had died, and they could not afford to make a wrong turn. Besides, their bodies would continue to use up energy even if they lay in a deep pit when they ran out of everything.

"Maybe we're close," Lanlan said. She was always saying maybe: maybe we'll run into someone, maybe we'll find water, maybe we'll get some food. They were hopes, these maybes, and all they needed was for one of them to deliver them from privation.

But noontime closed in on them before they met one of the maybes.

The sun would not stop spewing its flames just because they lacked water, and their bodies would not retain moisture simply because of all the maybes. Dehydration showed its first sign in their heads; they started to doze off and began seeing things. Hallucinations were not a problem, unlike dozing off, which was a maw ready to swallow them up. Lanlan kept telling Ying'er not to fall asleep. Stay awake. Ying'er knew she would never wake up once she succumbed to sleep. So, they reminded each other, though the raging thirst was gluing their eyelids shut.

The camel was the first casualty. With its eyes half open, it flared its nostrils, breathing heavily, as if a bellows were moving slowly inside. It had done well, Ying'er thought. The energy from the little bit of oil had sustained it enough to help them over several dunes. She hoped it did not fall, because they were helpless to save it. The salt lakes weren't far, she thought—of course they weren't, at least in her mind, so the camel mustn't die. Lanlan stared at it and let out a long sigh.

The camel shuddered and slowly lay down. It stretched out its neck and limbs, its breath drawn out. They would have to pay the owner if it died, but money was the least of their concerns. Ying'er worried about the camel's survival in the same way she'd watched over her husband during his last moments. But her mind wasn't clear enough for her to feel sad, even though she knew the camel was dying and that the two of them would be next.

She sat down. She didn't want to, but her legs made her do it. It was hopeless. If the camel had remained standing, she'd have been reassured. Now that it had fallen, she could not climb over the next dune by herself; besides, what good would that do? There would be one more right after it. She could not be bothered with thoughts of death or survival; all she wanted was to close her eyes and have a good sleep. It's what her brain wanted, and there was nothing she could do about that.

Gritting her teeth, Lanlan glanced at the camel and then at Ying'er. Lanlan's gaunt, shriveled face was sweat-stained, and black dust and dirt lined the sides of her nose. Ying'er knew she too was in a sorry state, but it no longer bothered her.

"Hang in there," Lanlan said. "I'll go look for water."

"Where are you going to find water?" Ying'er wanted to say, but looking for it was better than doing nothing. Lanlan might not find any, but not trying meant accepting death.

Without waiting for a response, Lanlan took the bottle and dragged her feet over to a sand trough in the north. Her progress was painfully slow, her joints creaking noisily, looking like a moving skeleton to a dazed Ying'er. She won't make it back, Ying'er said to herself.

Lanlan trudged around a sandy hill and vanished from sight, leaving Ying'er with the impression of a drop of water soaked up by the sand.

Don't leave me out here alone, Lanlan. A mild sense of sadness stole up on Ying'er and she felt like saying to the departing Lanlan that if this is how it would end, we should die together.

With its eyes nearly closed, the camel breathed heavily, the hollow of its belly rising and falling erratically.

All was quiet. She recalled how the sun seemed to shriek at noon, like chirping cicadas. But now it was silent. Not a sound in the sand trough; even the camel's puffs were fading. Its belly continued to rise and fall, but was making no noise. Ying'er felt that she was being dissolved in an enormous quietude. Wondering if she was still alive, she looked up at a sky so blue it took on the quality of satin, against which shreds of silky clouds were either racing each other or vying to look foolish. As always, they withheld the water they contained. She decided not to worry about it.

Lanlan must not have been truthful. She wasn't off looking for water; she'd discarded her body and gone to another world.

150

That was a bad thing for her to have done, as they should have left together. Ying'er was too drained to be resentful, for lethargy had woven a large net and cast it into the air, ready to drop down on her. It had done that many times already; once it was like a spider's web, at another time a fishing net, increasingly dense and tight. She knew that this time it would capture her soul. It would not be a bad thing if the net of drowsiness took hold of her.

A crow landed on a nearby sand hill and cawed. Ying'er knew she was dying. She had heard that crows loved the flesh of dead humans and, with a superb sense of smell, could detect the scent of death on a living person, like a vulture. That was why people considered it to augur bad luck. According to Lingguan, however, crows were supernatural birds, underlings working for Mahakala, the protector of the Buddha dharma. I'll feed myself to the bird, then, if you say it's supernatural.

She'd heard that a crow will go first for a person's eyeballs, a disturbing thought. Before she breathed her last, she told herself, she would crouch down and bury her face in the sand. She could not bear the thought of a black bird's beak reaching for her beautiful eyes. But then she wanted to laugh at her own foolish thoughts.

More crows landed, all cawing and fixing their gaze on her. The camel opened its eyes when it heard the birds, the implication not lost on the animal. It looked at Ying'er, who looked back, tacitly sharing a sense of helplessness. Her eyes felt drier than ever, and a rumbling noise echoed in her head.

The birds must have pecked clean those human bones she'd seen along the way. They could have found nothing more delectable in the desert than human flesh. They surely hoped this human would die of thirst in their midst. Let me fulfill your wish, then, she said to the crows. But, could they have already gotten to Lanlan's eyeballs before coming for mine? She could almost see Lanlan, keeled over in the desert, her face a bloody mess. That was how her brain worked now—it would not show a picture she wanted to see, instead giving her bloody, abhorrent scenes.

She shook her head with difficulty.

In her haze, she watched a few of the crows circle above her. They were in such a hurry. Did they think she was already dead? She waved the flashlight, but it was a poor weapon, so she reached over and snapped the whip off the camel's halter, a spare whip for lashing the camel's nose if it refused to obey an order. Neither of them had had any use for the whip, for they'd had two docile camels. A black shadow swooped down on her just as she held the whip in her hand. Quietly she mustered enough strength to swing it upward. Obviously, the crow thought she was dead, and had not expected an object to strike out. It also did not know it was flying so fast it would be stunned when it smashed into a waiting whip. Imagine the force as it sped toward it.

With a muffled thud, the crow fell and rolled into a trough.

The other crows cawed and flew back to a nearby hill.

The fallen one twitched a few times and went still.

It felt unreal. The odds of actually hitting something were like noodles falling into a starving blind man's mouth. What a surprise she'd hit her target.

She crawled over to the dead bird and saw it was much smaller than a grown chicken. With its wings spread, it had looked like a real bird, but on the ground, it was a scrawny little thing. There were a few drops of its blood on the sand. Maybe it's what could keep her going a while longer. A timid person by nature, she was emboldened by her dazed, sleepy state, and grabbed the bird. Rationally, she wanted to twist its head off and suck out its blood. But she couldn't break it off, no matter how hard she tried. She began to retch when she imagined her mouth smeared in its blood. Nothing came but dry heaves, but her stomach and esophagus went into a frenzy of action and drove away her sleepiness. I'd die before I ate this, she told herself as she flung the bird away; it made a dark but short arc in the air before falling into a sand trough.

As she recovered her breath, she squinted at the crows in the distance, which were staring back at her. A mutual fear had developed between them. While the human and the crows faced off, the camel seemed above it all. It had seen her feat, but showed no surprise. After all it had been through on this trip, nothing would surprise it.

Ying'er was dead to herself. She would soon be crow's food. She had been terrified days before that she would become jackal food, but now it was all the same, no matter which one got to her first, so long as they didn't start before she died. She sensed her soul drifting away, as drowsiness overwhelmed her wakefulness.

The crows cawed loudly, too eager to wait, though none was bold enough to challenge the whip. The camel continued to pant like a bellows. When it opened its mouth, Ying'er could see its tongue, dark as a strip of tanned leather. It was nearing death too, she knew. That would be all right; they would keep each other company, and she would not be a lonely ghost. Don't leave me too soon, camel, she wanted to say.

But no sound came. She was cocooned in a dense net of drowsiness. The crows had stopped cawing. She felt that the large birds were swooping down and that the wind beaten up by their flapping wings had formed another net descending on her.

Lingguan

The house looked empty with Hantou gone; everything was replaced by a dull sadness. His mother continued to sob and Ying'er kept drying her tears, both trying to hold back and not cry out loud.

Lingguan still could not believe his brother was gone. When he was inside, he kept expecting Hantou to walk through the door and when he was outside, he thought Hantou would soon be on his way out. When a bird called, he wondered if it was a messenger from Heavens to tell him that Hantou was still alive and that he'd crawled out of his grave. As he squatted on the southern loess hill, he had the illusion that his mother would come with a smile to tell him, "Your brother has come back alive."

But it was just that, of course, a cruel illusion.

He dreamed about his brother often.

In the dream, Lingguan was surprised to find him alive. Surprised and delighted, he would run up to his brother, but Hantou would avoid him with a grim look on a dark face, unsmiling and quiet. Lingguan was heartbroken. But at least, Hantou was alive in his dream. Lingguan was glad of that, and wouldn't mind if Hantou ignored him, just so long as he wasn't dead.

Waking from a dream like that was the absolute worst. Everything around him rankled, for it would remind him of a reality he could not accept.

He had been avoiding that reality for days and did his best to ignore it. It was a thorn, and even accidental contact caused heartache. He was staggered by the recollection of how Hantou had worked as a common laborer to provide for his brother's education, of his guileless smile when he came into the city with food for him, and many other long-forgotten, painful scenes. He tore at his hair, cursing himself with clenched teeth.

An older brother is like a father, he knew, and what Hantou had done for him knew no bounds. It was a debt he could never repay.

His dreams nearly drove him out of his mind. His throat was dry, his ears rang. Spasms went through his heart when he thought about how grim-faced Hantou had avoided him, and he could hardly breathe.

No wonder he avoided me. No wonder he wore a grim look. And no wonder he refused to say a word before he died. He must have known, he must have. It's so obvious. She—she's pregnant. No wonder. You're a bastard, Lingguan.

He was so ashamed of himself when he recalled what he'd done with Ying'er in the sand hollow when Hantou was in the hospital. He'd smiled and fallen in love as he listened to her sing. What kind of animal are you? How can you go on living? Why— why don't you put an end to your useless life?

What he found most difficult to think about was Ying'er.

Every "romantic" recollection gnawed at him, evidence of his sin. He couldn't bring himself to look at her, so he did his best to avoid her.

Obviously, she had been avoiding him too.

She spent her days in the room she'd shared with Hantou, sobbing until she was hoarse and could barely catch her breath. Maybe she was feeling the torment of her soul too. His partner in sin.

Lingguan could almost see her face, which was now impossibly sallow. It was a scab on his heart, a trigger for self-reproach, and a dark cloud over his mental sky.

Worse yet, her pregnancy was approaching full term.

A new life would soon be born, his child.

For Lingguan, it was a punishing reality, an unavoidable cruelty, an eternal nightmare, an unforgiveable sin.

He wondered if ghosts really did exist. He sincerely hoped so, for then he would be able to see his poor brother and ask for his forgiveness.

He wished he could disappear, leaving not a figment of his repugnance behind.

But nothing could be done now.

His existence became a burden.

Lingguan began to ponder how he would live out the rest of his life.

The villagers concluded that Lingguan was crushed by Hantou's death. He was often seen lost in thought on the loess hill, his eyes glazed over and fixed on something in the middle distance. He moved like a sleepwalker.

One crimson evening, a whirlwind blew under a blood-red sun in a sky with leaden clouds that seemed about to drop to the ground. Grayish shadows were cast on a lonely sand dune, where a solitary figure stumbled along. The dust kicked up by his feet was like a fog that turned him into an indistinct, spectral shadow. That was Lingguan.

The evening sun perched gingerly on the tip of distant mountains, providing a bleeding backdrop. His shadow grew longer on the sand as the sun continued to descend, and merged with the shadows in the horizon to spread out like water. Little by little, an evening mist fell with the dust and covered him in the hazy black desert.

Shawan villagers thought they heard shrill calls from a wild animal or a large bird in the east that night; they went on for a long time. The next day, Lingguan was gone.

No one was sure what happened to him. Someone said he went to Shenzhen to see a school friend about finding work, but failed in his quest and was reduced to begging on the street. Another said he went south and worked in a feed lot. Yet another said he performed odd jobs at a museum while studying languages. But, according to a profiteer who often traveled into the desert, he'd heard that someone from Liangzhou had died at Pig's Belly Well in the heart of the desert. The body was tossed into a sand hollow and gnawed out of shape by foxes, eventually reduced to a pile of bones. Could that have been Lingguan?

Laoshun was too busy to listen to the gossip. White Dew, which marked the fifteenth solar period, would arrive soon, and the rabbit hawks would be coming down again. His time was taken up by weaving nets to trap them. Besides, Ying'er had just given birth to a baby boy, who now filled the large void from Hantou's death and brought his grandparents enough daily matters to keep them busy. More importantly, he and his wife had faith in their son; they believed he had left for the wider world, but knew he'd be back one day; Lingguan would come home no matter how far he'd traveled.

He'd left because he wanted to return.

Ying'er was their only cause for concern. Day and night, she sat blankly, humming a tune known to every villager in Shawan—

> *The log-carrying pole is broken,*
> *Drops of clear water fall to the ground.*
> *Soiling my body and turning it black,*
> *You left, walking down a broad, open road.*

13

A faint sound came from far away, it sounded like her grand-mother calling back her soul when Ying'er was little. Back then, if something was not right, her Grandma would say her soul had strayed. She'd call it back as Ying'er looked on.

Grandma's voice came from a great distance,

"Ying'er—ai—your soul was frightened away, but come back now—"
"Come back now—" there would be an echo.
"Ying'er—ai—your soul was frightened high up, but come down now—"
"Come down now—"
"Ying'er—ai—your soul was frightened in the heat, but come back cool—"
"Come back cool—"
"Ying'er—ai—your soul was frightened when hungry,
but come back full—"
"Come back full—"
"Ying'er—ai—the three souls and seven mortal forms return now—"
"Return now—"

Grandma could come up with many more such incantations. Starting from a relatively distant place, she called all the way back to their kitchen, where she put flour in a porcelain bowl and wrapped it in a piece of red cloth to press against her chest, back, and shoulders. A dent would appear in the bowl after a while, and

158

Grandma would say:

"See how much is gone?" She would add more flour and repeat the incantation, pressing until the flour was even in the bowl to conclude the soul-recalling rite.

Her mother, usually the one who echoed Grandma, would not let Bai Fu repeat what the older woman said. Her brother, a prankster, would invalidate the effort by saying the opposite of "come back," and they would have to find another auspicious date to start over.

Grandma's drawn-out voice was as sweet as mung bean soup and went straight to Ying'er's heart. Later, when Grandma died, there was no one to perform the rite for her.

But the voice appeared again. It brought a warm, cozy feeling to her hazy state of mind; she thought she was dead, because people said you can only meet dead relatives when you are in the underworld. How wonderful! I'm going to see Grandma again. Grandma had doted on her. When she was little, Grandma had held her in her arms, calling her "My sweet little girl" and giving her loud kisses. Magical as an old witch, Grandma always had something rare on her, like sesame candy or peanuts. She had endless ghost stories to tell, usually at night after turning out the light, scaring Ying'er so much she hid in Grandma's arms.

To her, the drawn-out voice sounded like silken threads wrapping around and tugging at her. The wind of life was taking her forcefully to an abyss, while the voice, an audio string, tied her down. She was drawn closer and closer toward the person calling out to her, when she sensed a change in the voice; it sounded more like Lanlan.

She struggled to open her eyes; it was like turning a rusty door latch. A blinding light splashed into her eyes when she forced them open, too bright to see what was before her.

"Hurry, take this." Lanlan sounded urgent and happy.

Finally, Ying'er could see Lanlan, who was holding a black stick. Ying'er did not move, so Lanlan scraped the stick with the whip handle to rub off the black surface and reveal a watery whiteness underneath. Ying'er had seen those before. In the winters, after slaughtering a goat, the villagers would slow-cook them with mutton. What were they called? Oh, yes, they were suoyang.

Lanlan broke off a small piece and put it in Ying'er mouth. When she bit down gently, Ying'er felt sweet juice spread. Lanlan gave her the whole piece she'd scraped clean, telling her to eat it all, while taking out another piece from the carrying bag she'd made from her head scarf. Ying'er could not believe how much Lanlan had gathered.

Lanlan broke off a piece and put it up to the camel's mouth. Still breathing fitfully, the animal stuck out its dark tongue and labored to move the juicy pulp into its mouth.

To Ying'er, these roots, like the reed roots before them, were among the best things she'd ever tasted. A gentle bite sent juice oozing between her teeth to be lapped up by greedy taste buds. They were ecstatic, like hatchlings seeing their mother return with a worm, mouths opened wide as they chirped loudly. The sweet, aromatic juice summoned back her stomach's lost memory and sent it into a frenzy of movement.

Able to eat the black sticks on its own, the camel crunched loudly, white juice flowing down the corners of its mouth, making Ying'er lament the waste.

"Finish yours now," Lanlan said spiritedly. "We'll go dig more after we rest. There are loads of them in a sand trough just over there."

Lanlan stopped her from having another one after she'd finished the first. She tried to pull up the camel; it struggled to its feet on shaky legs, after eating the piece Lanlan had given it. Suoyang roots were the best remedy they could imagine for thirst and hunger, and a great tonic. After eating them, the camel's lifeline began to return slowly. Ying'er still had a headache, but was no longer feeling drowsy.

"That's enough," Lanlan said. "Let's not eat too much. We'll have more later."

They took the camel to the sand trough, which was just around a bend in the sand, not far, as it turned out. There was soil mixed in with the sand, a perfect home for the plant. Lanlan located a crease in the ground and stomped on it, making a hollow sound.

"The ground is full of them," Lanlan said. "I dug those we just ate from one spot."

Ying'er saw creases all around her, similar to the ground surface broken by potatoes. Some of the roots had poked through the sandy soil.

"Heaven never seals off all the exits," she said emotionally.

"It's the Vajravārāhī who saved us. Believe it or not. After I walked past the bend, I knelt down in the sand trough and prayed. I said, Vajravarahī, please help me leave the desert alive. If you do, I'll renovate your temple and gild your statue. I prayed for a while and then I saw a red figure nearby. I thought it was a herder, and I chased after him all the way here, where I discovered suoyang instead. When I go back, I'll collect donations to repair her temple."

Lanlan was earnest and sincere. Ying'er suspected, however, that she had simply been seeing things, though she chided herself for blasphemy. If the Vajravārāhī had in fact shown Lanlan the way here, the deity would be hurt by her doubts. "Then, we should both thank the Vajravārāhī," she replied.

Lanlan dug into a crack to reveal the stems inside. Suoyang is a parasitic plant that can grow to a foot in length. A deep red, it thrives in sandy soil and usually grows in clusters, the larger of which can be quite dense and heavy. They did not have to work hard; digging and pushing away the sandy dirt revealed clusters underneath. Lanlan scraped off the dirt with her whip handle before tossing a piece over to the camel. It cried out, seemingly in great excitement, no longer looking tired and miserable.

They unloaded the litter and dug a pit on the shady side of the sand hill. After eating some more of the plant, they tethered the camel, climbed into the pit, taking care to make sure it was safe, and slept. When they woke up, they had some more suoyang and went back to sleep, and then did the same when they woke up the second time. With enough sleep, and aided by plenty of nutritious suoyang, they soon regained their vitality.

The following morning Ying'er saw seashells on gobi rocks. Obviously, there had been water at some time in the distant past. Maybe the desert had once been an ocean, she said to herself as she dug up more of the fleshy stems. They would have the camel carry as many as possible, even if they had to walk. Once done, they would keep traveling in the direction they'd chosen.

Ying'er

A restless mood settled over her parents' house when Ying'er returned. Bai Fu spent his days with his unsavory friends; Father had his eyes on antiques, as usual, running off to see tomb raiders all the time; and Mother was forever whispering with Pockmark Xu, the village matchmaker. She was hoping her daughter would marry Zhao Three, the Butcher, thus bringing in enough money to get her brother a second wife.

Xu had once brought Zhao to the house. A fat, greasy man with a head like a pig's, his bulbous nose turned bright red when he had a bit to drink. The very sight of him set her teeth on edge. She knew it was his affluence that had earned him her mother's exorbitant praise. After being a butcher for more than a decade, he'd slaughtered enough pigs and cows to wear his four-inch knife down to a willow leaf, so, naturally, he had acquired considerable wealth. Now he'd opened a gold panning site at White Tiger Pass, and people said it would bring him a fortune. He'd let it be known that he would spend lavishly to make Ying'er his wife, and would double his offer if she brought her baby along. Gaining a son and growing a beard are hard for any man. His first wife had run off after he beat her for not giving him a child. Lacking an heir, he was unsettled, unsure if he might ever have a son. This was likely his last best chance, for which he would spare no expense.

Ying'er's mother knew she was justified in bringing her daughter back for a visit. The baby was a different matter; he was Hantou's son, and they would never give him up, even at the cost of their lives. She'd been unnerved by the fearless way Ying'er's mother-in-law had snatched up the baby, and she was not hard-hearted enough to send her son over to seize the infant for Zhao's money.

"Everyone knows the baby is your daughter's," Xu argued. "Go ask a judge who should have him, now that his father's dead, his grandparents or his mother? It's clear, it's the law. It's your right."

"Really?" Ying'er's mother was dubious. She could not believe that the law would sanction snatching other people's family line.

"If I lied to you, my ancestors are donkeys," Xu swore.

She wanted to believe him, but wasn't sure if she should pry that baby out of the woman's arms.

"The witch would fight to the death," she said. "The baby means more to her than her own life. She wouldn't let my daughter bring him home. So, let's forget that. Zhao can think until his head hurts, but he will never have that boy. The baby's worth more than gold; we want him, but they want him more. Besides, they've lost their eldest son. How would it look if I snatched their grandson from them?"

"But he's your daughter's child. That wouldn't be snatching." Zhao had promised Xu two thousand yuan if he could manage to bring the baby along. That was many times more than the fee of a regular matchmaking deal, so, naturally, he had to do his best to make it happen. "It's only fair that the baby goes with the mother. It's immoral to pull a baby off his mother's breast."

Ying'er's mother felt her resistance softening. Ying'er had wept for days now. Her mother had steeled her resolve and kept her at home, but she felt sorry for her daughter, especially when she saw how her face had turned sallow and had begun to shrivel, despite her youth. She also felt bad as she recalled how Hantou's mother had cried her heart out over his death; yet her heart turned to stone when she reminded herself of the shrew's red, angry face when they argued. And so it went: her heart softened one moment and turned stone cold the next.

Ying'er thought she was losing her mind. She could hear her

baby crying and calling out to her.

At the sight of Pockmark Xu, she walked out the gate and down a small village path, ignoring the dirt, not caring if it got on her shoes, her socks, her pants' legs, her whole body. She couldn't think straight, her mind a confused blur, as if she were living in a different realm. Her aspirations as a girl had been nothing but a fantasy, as were the burden of being a young wife and the sorrows of being a widow. And then there was the blissful happiness, those few moments of overpowering joy; but they too were mere fantasy.

The trees along the path had gone bald, all the leaves blown off, their branches pointing into the sky to present a disorienting sight. After the wheat harvest, the field lay in disarray, a mirror image of her feelings. People in the distance were blurry, yet so were those nearby. She could only mumble a response when someone greeted her. She was no longer the Ying'er of the past.

It had been a long time since she'd last been on this path.

She'd often walked down it as a student memorizing her texts and dreaming of a future, a now bygone future filled with potential. Sometimes she would lead the sheep over and lean against a tree to read books that made her young heart quicken. The future was beautiful; she'd longed for it, called out to it.

She could not have anticipated that in that future she would be married as an exchange, to be Hantou's wife, and later a widow, as a mother without her child, to be bartered off like a farm animal and bereft of hope. From this moment of her life she could see all the way to the other end. Her mother's present was her future, but she would suffer more than her mother, because she'd been to school and had sketched out a future for herself.

After sobbing against a tree trunk, she squinted into the overcast sky. The great desert was not far off; it spread ripples of sand, higher and higher until they turned into a mountain. The adorable Yindi had perished in a chilly corner of the desert. Ying'er still grieved over the thought of her little niece. Lingguan once said that Yindi had been born with a trying fate. Women in a similar situation, he had added, managed to survive, but not Yindi, who had been deprived of that right. That is pure nonsense, my love, Ying'er chided silently. No matter what a woman does, she can never overcome her fate, so it is best to be released from suffering at the earliest possible moment. What is so good about growing up, or getting married? What is there to enjoy in life? Sometimes she thought it would have been better if she hadn't been born, but that had not been up to her. By the time she understood that, she was all grown, accompanied by endless worries.

When she walked in the door her mother told her what Pockmark Xu had said. "I'll leave if you're thinking I'm eating too much of your food, Ma." She continued unhappily, "I don't believe I can't feed myself out in the wide world."

"How can you say that?" her mother replied. "You're flesh and blood. Who else would worry about you if I didn't?"

"Why don't you save yourself the trouble this time? I'm old enough to know what to do. Can't you let me take care of my own business just this once?"

"What do you know about taking care of your business? It's clear what the Chen family has in mind. They want to sell their daughter again, but they want my girl for free. They're not going to have it their way. I tell you."

"Would you stop that, Ma?" Ying'er frowned. "All I hear when I walk in is you complaining about this or cursing that."

Her mother's lips moved as if to get more air, while tears welled up in her eyes. "You too? The old man says it, the young one does too, and now even you join in to tear me apart. Every day I get up before dawn and work till midnight. Who do I do it for? For you two, of course. Now you won't even let me say what's on my mind."

Tears sluiced down Ying'er's face, but she had no response, so she ran into her room and cried until she could hardly breathe.

"Don't worry, I'm not long for this world." Her mother's voice came from outside. "The lump in my belly is still growing, probably the same problem as the one that got your dead husband."

"Enough, already." Ying'er's father bellowed. "Would you shut up? Look at the state she's in. How can you prattle on like that?"

"Since you want to be the good one, you can deliver the girl to the Chen's door, but you'll have to find your son another wife."

"Sure. When the antique—"

"Ptui!" She spat before he finished. "A disgrace to your ancestors is more like it. You've been going on about big business deals all these years, and I think you've got a screw loose. I haven't seen a single coin from you, while you've squandered everything I ever got from raising pigs along with my soy bean and vegetable seed money. Where do you get the nerve to bring up that antique nonsense of yours? All day long, antique this and antique that, you're pathetic."

The old man's face reddened, his mouth hung slack. He pointed a finger at her, but was completely deflated.

"You're a witch. You've mocked me all my life. Stop pushing me around. You can know what's gold and what's silver, but you can't know what's in a person's heart. When I make it big, I'll—"

"You'll swallow me whole and shit me out, is that right?" She spat again. "I can see through you. You're a master of big talk and empty words, but you're not worth a single toe on my foot when it comes to doing anything serious."

"Well—well—" He shrank back and scowled, like a man who refused to fight with a petty woman.

Ying'er listened with a blank look, disgusted by what she heard. It occurred to her that her mother had said so many different things she'd lost focus; now it seemed the only remaining issue was the baby. It took Ying'er some effort to extract herself from the scenario her mother had created. Why had she been thinking about leaving the baby? Why can't a woman remain a widow if she wants? She was a married daughter, the so-called spilled water, and to the villagers remaining a widow was right and proper. But unless Lanlan came back to Bai Fu, her mother would not let her go. But Lanlan was Lanlan and she, Ying'er, was Ying'er, and that was that. Worst case, she went back to her in laws and set up her own household. She would work herself to death, sell herself, if necessary, to make enough money to find Bai Fu another wife and buy her own freedom. But what a childish idea. A family working the field for a year can barely make enough to get by. It made her dizzy just thinking about the amount needed for a man to have a wife.

The wind began to howl in the afternoon, sending clusters of sand flying.

Was her mother really that bad? Her ideas and her actions were all meant to benefit her son. To be fair to her mother, Ying'er knew it had been hard for a woman who had to marry off her daughter to save her son from a life of bachelorhood. They were just too poor. The little they got from the land was barely enough to fill their bellies. Her mother was simply trying to survive. She knew that if her parents had a better solution, they would not be so hard on her. As a little girl, she had been her mother's favorite, her father's too, and they'd always made sure she was well treated.

Matchmaker Xu came by again that night. An incurable sot, Xu would trade his life for something to drink. And so they drank.

When the noise rose to an unbearable level, Ying'er got down off her bed and went into Lanlan's former room. Her legs felt rubbery, her steps unsteady. Exhausted from mental torment, she lay down with difficulty; she had trouble catching her breath as she dragged the blanket over. She stared into a dark night ripped apart by lightning, followed by heart-stopping thunderclaps and splashing water. The sloshing seemed to fill up the void in the world,

She heard her mother's crisp laughter, loud enough to drown

out the wind and rain. Ying'er frowned; she choked up when she thought of Father's face, leathery as the bark on a desert date tree. What has he worked for all his life? He's been cheated so many times, and yet he never seems to regret it. Maybe that's the right attitude, that it's better to at least have a dream, unlike Mother, who is always complaining and blaming others for everything bad that happens. She is forever in a bad mood; if she had any dreams, they were long forgotten. Without dreams, life is unbearable, no matter how modest they are. Ying'er was more like her father, willing to be swindled, even with full knowledge that what she hoped for was only a sham. Far better to have a dream than to have none. But now even reality was trifling with her pathetic dream, making it impossible for her to go on. Night closed in on her and the black rain came down in full force. Lightning strikes lost their intensity, but the wind continued to howl. The night felt strangely heavy, overwhelming the gaiety in the outer room, and pressing down on her eyelids.

She fell into the deep, heavy darkness.

Suddenly, the darkness felt heavier, twisting and tearing at her. She awoke to a groping hand; the smell of liquor assailed her nose. Pockmark Xu.

"Ma—" she cried out.

"Shh—be quiet." he whispered. "They're asleep. Here, take this and buy yourself something nice."

Ying'er felt paper thrust into her hand. It disgusted her. She flung it to the floor.

"Get out!" she yelled.

She wanted to sit up and slap him, but the man's audacity so outraged her she went limp, powerless despite her wish.

"Get out, you bastard!" She'd never in her life cursed anyone like that.

"Be quiet. Don't fight. Just a little while, it only takes a little while." Xu was breathing hard as he threw himself on her and

169

tried to tear off her clothes.

"Pa—" She shrieked her plea, choking up. She heard voices through the door, a man's and then a woman's, but soon they went quiet.

"Elder Brother—" She screamed, her voice rising over the sound of the storm outside, but failing to penetrate the silence out there.

"They, um, know. Don't be afraid. You're no virgin. I'll buy you a new pair of pants tomorrow, all right? Something made of fine material. I'm a man of my word." He pinned her hands under her while unbuttoning her blouse.

She spat and cried. One of his hands was on her breast. She was powerless to fight him off as his other hand went for the pants cord.

She wailed, sounding barely human, surprising even the hands into a momentary pause. She sent all her strength to her vocal cords, the only way she could fight back.

"Be a good girl, don't cry." Unnerved, Xu covered her mouth, giving her a chance to free one of her hands to scratch his face. It obviously hurt, but he pinned the hand back. The stink of alcohol pressed closer as something scratchy brushed against her face, followed by a powerful stench.

"Ma—" She cried out again, a voice that rent the night, but still failed to rouse her mother. Why? she wondered. Have they told him it was all right to do what he was doing? Are they really so afraid of upsetting Pockmark Xu, afraid of ruining the family's great prospects? She despaired, her will to fight fading. I'll just die. It's better to die. She sobbed helplessly.

The stench followed her sob and found her; it was revolting beyond words. Suddenly a light went on in her head and she took a big bite.

An animal-like howl erupted.

She was calm now. After all her pleas for help had failed, she actually regained her composure. "Get out!" She hissed through her teeth.

The man muffled a reply.

She let go of her teeth. A lightning strike gave her enough light to see a twisted face, accompanied by moans and heavy breathing.

"Get out!" She screamed.

The muffled moan began to recede.

Ying'er felt like throwing up, but nothing came, only tears. She wept as she put on her shoes and walked into the yard, where she keened in the pouring rain.

Every pore of her body was nauseous. Rain came down, like someone splashing water on her. She was quickly soaked, her clothes stuck to her. How she wished she could strip naked for the rain to wash her clean, inside and out.

After a brief and bitter exchange with her parents, Ying'er walked through the gate into pitch darkness all around. The rain had let up, but the wind was chilly and harsh, seemingly blowing right through her. She shivered, and an itchy nose told her a cold might be coming. That was nothing, now that she'd shed a heavy load inside. She never expected she could leave her parents' house so easily, and had thought that only the threat of death would release her. Xu's rape attempt provided her with all the reason she needed, her family's complicity gave her the justification she desired. The nausea, on the other hand, seemed to have taken root deep inside her soul, and she felt like retching when she thought about what had just happened.

The narrow path, vaguely visible in the rain, was muddy and slushy, but did not deter her; she didn't mind tripping and falling now and then. One was meant to stumble through life. What worried her was not falling down, but the possibility that the disgust would never leave her. It was so repellent, and it wasn't going away, even after she'd washed her mouth countless times.

The muddy surface improved once she turned onto the main road. Sandy soil had its advantage, for, after being drenched by rain, it wasn't slushy. A desert date tree on the roadside was inky black, like a phantom. This spot was rife with ghost stories. She wasn't afraid. You're just a ghost, nothing more, she said silently to the imagined specter, nothing to be feared. She walked on, following the road.

The rain began to let up, from a storm to a downpour, then to a shower. Morning light in the East grew brighter, like a drop of ink spreading on rice paper, small at first then larger, its hue turning brighter, as it licked at the curtain of darkness. Shades of the night dissolved slowly.

Ying'er dried her tears, ruing the thoughtless things she'd said to her mother before walking out. It's hard enough on Ma already, she thought, and she had no choice but to go along with the disgusting Pockmark—and yet Ying'er had said so many spiteful things to her. She bit down hard on her lip. She knew she ought to turn back and kneel before her mother until she forgave her. She almost turned around, but then forced herself to stay the course. Leaving this time might bring a change to her life; if she stayed, she'd never be free.

She stumbled along. The path had turned uneven, now that she was near her in-laws' village, filled with potholes, and she might trip and fall if she walked too fast. It didn't matter. She would get up if she fell, the bruise would disappear and a wound would heal if she hurt herself. But the pain she was feeling hung on. She had been blinded by outrage against her parents, but now her mind had cleared, and she had to be more forgiving, after all the hardships they had endured. If given a second chance in life, she would dedicate herself to finding ways to make them smile and enjoy life. But it was too late for that. All she could do now was watch helplessly as her father and mother snapped at each other, like two spiders in a jar, tormenting one another as mortal enemies.

And it was all caused by poverty.

Finally, she understood why Lingguan had left. He'd done what she wished she could do.

Lanlan

The time had come for Lanlan to do what she wanted to do.

Divorce. Even saying the word had a stunning impact on her. In the village, divorce was more mortifying than walking naked on the street. As the saying went, a true steed accepts but one saddle and a virtuous woman stays with one husband. As far as she knew, a woman got divorced usually because she had made unforgiveable mistakes or had irreparable defects, such as adultery or childlessness. She drove the notion away every time it popped up, but it came back with a greater force, like pushing a ball deep into water. But then she began to take the idea seriously.

With a different perspective, she fantasized about life after a divorce. A crack opened up in the oppressive sky over her head, to let in refreshing air and bright light. Divorce still sounded scary, especially when she thought about village gossip. She could even see with her mind's eyes the odd looks they'd give her. But it was seductive compared to the passage of life that led straight to a pile of bones. Especially for Lanlan, who had never wanted a boring, monotonous life.

Life loses its pleasure when you follow a preset course and pace. The field, the yard, the kitchen stove, and the toilet were transformed into a gigantic rut in the mill for Lanlan, while she became the mule that turned the stone round and round. She seemed to have traveled far, but she opened her eyes to see herself walking in a circle on a preset track. The only change was the fading of the rosy glow on her face. She refused to head to life's end life like that.

But she was reluctant to bring up the subject, since her marriage had been the result of an exchange. She knew that the moment she asked for a divorce, her mother-in-law would force Ying'er to remarry. For the sake of the young widow and her family's reputation, Lanlan had to put up with things as long as she could.

She was disappointed in her parents, but knew that her father was simply old-fashioned, stuck with a mind that had always resisted new ideas, and became more hostile to them as he grew older, however protective of her he had always been. Her mother's ambivalence did not make her decision easy, but neither did it present an emotional obstacle.

Her mind was made up. She would never again share a bed with the man who, she believed, had "murdered" her daughter.

Lanlan went back to her in laws' hoping it would be the last time. The sight of their gate provoked an intense loathing in her; everything seemed oppressive and depressing. The house looked irretrievably ugly to her every time she walked in, with its peeling walls, a back fence darkened by smoke from heating fires under the kang, and the long-handled wooden hoe she'd been made to use in the field year in and year out. Her mother-in-law was sweeping the yard. Lanlan walked by, feeling the older woman's beady eyes following her.

Despite Bai Fu's beatings, Lanlan feared her mother-in-law the most, the type of woman who was generally called a Dragon Lady in popular fiction. From between her thin lips could emerge expressions that would make a person blush, but she knew how to deal with people, plying them with perfunctory chitchats. With a honey jar for a mouth and a pincushion for her head, she would gossip with anyone about anyone. Soon after Lanlan married into the family, everyone in the village knew what she was "really" like. Many of the older women were quite surprised. "Oh, she looks so sweet. I can't imagine she's actually like that."

Now fortified with resolve, Lanlan walked straight into their room. She was greeted by the stench of Bai Fu's feet. He was still asleep; he could sleep until noon when he didn't have to work in the field. Snores escaped from his open mouth. Thanks to an excess of fluids in his throat, nauseating sounds erupted as air passed through. She could not believe that this was her husband. Her mood lightened at the thought that the marriage would soon be ended. But her heart sank when she was reminded of all the unpleasantness that would follow the inevitable showdown. The last thing she wanted was for her mother-in-law to punish Lanlan's family by forcing Ying'er to remarry and take the baby away from them. The fleeting good feelings vanished.

Lanlan picked up a rag to wipe the unsightly dust off the large armoire. It was part of her dowry, the sole object in the house she cherished, the only thing that truly belonged to her. But she knew she would have to leave it behind. Her parents had spent more than they could afford to have it made, and she would hate for the Bai family to keep something so precious. But giving it up might be easier. Besides, how would it look if she were to have it trucked back to her parents' house? Imagine all the villagers coming out of their houses to watch, the reverse of a bridal procession. She looked at herself in the mirror and saw dark circles under her eyes; sadness overwhelmed her when she noted how haggard she'd gotten. The best years of her life were over, and she had trouble believing, let alone accepting that.

No argument followed Lanlan's announced plan to seek a divorce. The room was eerily quiet, as if they had been waiting for her to bring up the subject. The silence dragged. With his beard quivering, her father-in-law brought out his tobacco pouch with a trembling hand. His hand shook shamefully as he pinched and twisted the tobacco, but missed the bowl again and again. Bai Fu stared at her coldly, his face muscles twitching scarily.

"I've been prepared to die for a while now. My life for yours."

"What's the big deal, son? Go ahead, get a divorce. There are plenty of girls in the world for you to choose from." Her mother-in-law sounded tough, but her eyes betrayed a hint of uncertainty.

Usually, the woman was like a fully inflated ball, bouncing right back when you pushed her down. But on this day, the ball was punctured by Lanlan's demand.

Naturally, Lanlan knew what her decision meant to the family; she felt a measure of satisfaction when she intuitively grasped the truth behind her mother-in-law's forced nonchalance. Normally, as truculent as a wolf or a tiger, Lanlan noticed, this time she gave her husband a look, obviously unhappy with his performance.

"Sure," she said with a strained laugh. "Go ahead. But don't think you can get off easily. We'll drag it out until the donkey dies and the saddle rots."

"You can drag it out all you want, and the outcome will be the same," Lanlan said with a smirk. "The Bai family does not rule the world. There's always the district court if it doesn't work out at the county office, and if that doesn't work, there are courts above it. I don't believe I'll be denied a place to make my case."

"You damned well think you've got a case, don't you?" Bai Fu kicked a white rooster that was pecking by his feet out into the yard, where loud cackles erupted.

Sensibly, she held her tongue, for she knew what would happen next. Bai Fu fixed his furious eyes on her, a clear sign that his anger was building, and that all he needed was an excuse to use his fists on her. She wanted very much to explain her reasons, but in this family, reason always lost out to clenched fists. They could not rise above their propensity for violence.

"What do you think you're doing?" Bai Fu's mother shot him a look. "Vent your anger where it belongs. That rooster didn't do anything."

Sensing the woman's intention to incite her son, Lanlan wished she could talk back, but anything she said now would be the spark that set off the explosion. The frightened rooster was still crowing in the yard; a dog was barking. A tractor rumbled by, shaking up everything. All the noise crammed into Lanlan's head nearly suffocated her.

Her father-in-law jammed his fingers through his dirty, straw-like hair, and broke down; he began by sobbing, but soon he was howling like a cow. Lanlan was unnerved. She had anticipated the likely outcome of her demand—a beating from Bai Fu—but had never expected the old man to cry. In her eyes, he was the only decent member of the family, besides Ying'er, so perhaps it was no surprise that he would lose control. He was wailing without tears, yet to her it sounded as if he were mumbling curses at Heaven, at earth, at everything.

"Life stinks." It was the only phrase she heard clearly.

Her mother-in-law did not know what to do about her husband's loss of self-control, except to glare at him, vainly wishing he could act like a real man. In her view, they had lost a great deal of face when Lanlan made her demand, and the most powerful counterattack was indifference. She would have liked to kick Lanlan out like throwing away a worn shoe, so everyone would know she'd been cast out of their house. Then, she wished, she would buy her son an even prettier wife. Unhappily, she could sell everything they had, and still not have enough to pay the exorbitant cost of another wife. Her head hurt just thinking about it. Besides, her son had never lived up to her expectations. If you raise a pig, you know its nature; she knew very well what people thought of Bai Fu. All these depressing thoughts made it impossible for her to do what she really wanted. She was resentful, and would not allow the slut to have her way. A woman who had wanted to outdo everyone all her life, she simply could not bring herself to admit defeat to a younger woman. Her husband's sobs fueled her anger. Worthless man. Losing face was worse than anything.

She knew he was crying not only over Lanlan's demand. Things had not gone well for them in recent years. Their disappointing son was addicted to gambling, and had such terrible luck that their doorsill was nearly worn down by creditors. Then there was the death of her granddaughter Yindi—all this was enough to make her lose heart. Her husband was always saying that life stinks, owing to all his frustrations, and he needed an outlet. The problem was his timing; he should not have cried before that slut, and definitely not right after she demanded a divorce. Finally, she could hold back no longer. "That's enough," she screamed at her husband. "What are you crying for?"

He stopped, but seemed glued to the spot, staring blankly and shedding silent tears. Bai Fu gritted his teeth and balled his fists, prepared to release his anger. Lanlan felt strangely calm. She too knew that her father-in-law cried not simply because he did not want the divorce to go through. So much had happened in the family in recent years that her demand was the last straw. She felt her heart soften, not forgetting that she had not given her in-laws a grandson. Never someone to flinch under a verbal or physical assault, she lost her resolve when treated with a smiling face and kind words, let alone tears. She was about to give in.

Bai Fu chose that moment to jump to his feet. Lanlan did not have time to react before she felt her face burn with a numbness, followed by excruciating pain on her scalp that soon spread to the rest of her body, legs, eventually all over.

He began his usual exercise.

Normally his mother stepped in when he beat Lanlan, but not this time. She might not have wanted to ruin a piece of "property" in the past, since it would cost them money to repair the damage. Now that their daughter-in-law wanted to leave, she deserved to be beaten more than anything else.

Bai Fu was doing his best; sending Lanlan back down each time she got up. He could keep it up without breaking a sweat, as she knew only too well. Her ears rang, her nose was bleeding, and pain shot throughout her body. It felt as if a large platter had settled over her head, heavy and stifling, making her dizzy.

Neighbors ran over and formed a wall around them.

In the past, Lanlan would rather be beaten to death than run away, for she had not wanted to be a laughingstock among village women. It was different today, now that she had made up her mind. Face no longer meant anything to her; instead, she wanted as many people as possible to know what Bai Fu was like. In addition to having enough witnesses at court, she also wanted them to see for themselves that she had asked for a divorce in order to survive.

14

Finally, a dazzling whiteness appeared before Ying'er and Lanlan.

It was harsh on the eyes after days in the yellow sand. As they got closer, they realized it was alkali soil, where nothing grew. The alkali had heated the ground and made it spongy; even the air gave off a salty ocean smell.

"We're almost there," Lanlan said happily.

Ying'er's mood should have been buoyed as well, but she felt a strange calmness and foreboding instead. She was afraid of another disappointment after all their searching.

As they walked on they saw towering hills of salt crust. Lanlan said it was dredged from the lake. The sun shining down on them sent off prisms of reflected rays. Everywhere they looked was a brilliant white, like a crystal palace. Their camel cried out spiritedly.

There were people walking to and from the mounds, but from a distance they looked like ants. Ying'er spotted the salt lakes when they drew closer. Bodies of dark green water, dozens of feet wide and hundreds of feet in length, out of which workers scooped salt with slotted ladles that allowed water to drip through when they were lifted out. Long stretches of dry land separated the lake, where salt crystals were arranged in rows of pyramids.

The men, dark-skinned and wearing only shorts and sandals, turned to look at the new arrivals, bedraggled, obviously weary, leading a gaunt camel. They looked hungry, thirsty, and in desperate need of rest. When one of the men walked up to them, Lanlan asked for water. He went back to where he had been working, picked up a metal bucket and said,

"There's plenty here. You and your camel can have it all."

Having gone so long without water, they nearly wept out of gratitude. The camel let out a long cry when it smelled the water. Lanlan dunked their bottle into the bucket. Air bubbles rose noisily, as it took a long time to fill. She handed it to Ying'er, who drank despite knowing it had once been in the camel's mouth. The water was tepid, but it was real water, much more satisfying than the juice of suoyang. After finishing, she handed the bottle to Lanlan, who did the same. She was about to refill the bottle for the camel, but the worker moved the bucket over so the camel could bury its mouth in the water.

Lanlan felt bad about using up so much water, but the man said:

"Don't worry. We've got plenty. Are you here to buy salt or did you come to work? You definitely aren't just passing through, not at a place like this."

That gave Lanlan the germ of an idea. "You're right, we came for the salt, but we can work too, though we're not strong enough for what you're doing."

"There are plenty of things you can do," the man said. "The women here sew hemp sacks, pick impurities out of the salt crystals, things like that. We can always use the help."

Lanlan whispered to Ying'er,

"It would be great if we could make some money while we're here and still take salt back when we return. How does that sound?"

Ying'er nodded, not quite sure how they'd manage, but she trusted Lanlan and was in no hurry to load up and go back out in the desert. A change of scenery and activity didn't sound bad at all.

"All right," Lanlan said to the man. "We can try it out for a couple of days. We'll stay if we can manage the work."

"Then let's go see the boss."

When the first man explained to the boss what they'd talked about, he said, "Sure, you can spend a few days here and give it a try."

Ying'er noticed with surprise a number of women, all with sunburned faces, clustered around a nearby rammed earth building.

"You can bunk with them," the boss said. Ying'er wondered if, like her, Lanlan also felt relieved that the shepherds' caution about the kind of men they might run into never became a problem. She felt safe here.

They led their camel over to the building and unloaded the litter. Its back was festering again and giving off a terrible stench. Lanlan scooped up some salt water to wash the wound.

It was a medium-sized building without regular beds, just a row of good-sized rooms with doors in which railroad were ties laid side by side. Lanlan and Ying'er had set off with two mattress pads, but one had been torn to pieces, the other doused in kerosene to use as grenades. Their bedding had been on the camel killed by the jackals, leaving them with only a single pad to use as a mattress. The railroad ties were knotty and rough, and their padding was thin, which they knew would make sleeping uncomfortable. But being away from home meant they couldn't be choosy. To earn enough for a dignified return, they'd have to put up with an even more austere existence than they were used to.

They were to be put up in one of the rooms with a woman who welcomed them with a friendly greeting. Sansan was a big woman who looked like a worker herself. Few women were willing to come all the way out here to work, so those who did show up were treated like visiting kin. Sansan led them out of the room, where she dumped some noodles into boiling water and added salt to make a meal for the newcomers. Vegetables were a rarity in the area, they were told, trucked over to the management station some several li away, producing long lines for workers eager for a more balanced diet. The two travelers' stomachs, shriveled by thirst, had been awakened by the suoyang plants, so now they were ready to eat some real food, which they did until sweat dappled their foreheads. It had been a long time coming, and they rejoiced in the simple fare.

After they ate, Sansan sought out some hay for the camel, which she tethered to the door.

"Get some rest. Your camel's safe. No one comes here but people in the market for pure salt."

Ying'er and Lanlan went inside and lay down for a nap and enjoyed a deep sleep, their first in days. When they woke up, they were surprised to see a couple of men standing nearby. Sansan noted the looks of alarm on their faces, and rushed to put them at ease.

"These are some of our hardest workers. They're here for me to stitch up the wounds on their legs. You don't have to look."

Lanlan and Ying'er were shocked to see peeling skin on legs as hard as armor, like the calluses on an old cow's neck. The skin was thick, grayish white, and covered with bloody cracks; some of the wounds were deep, scary red, open sores the size of a child's mouth. Though they weren't bleeding at the moment, they were still an alarming sight, and obviously painful.

Sansan told them that a full load of wet salt crystals was too heavy to simply pull out of the water with the ladles, even with both hands. So they rested the handles on their thighs to use as a lever, raising it to let the water pour through the slots. Over time, a layer of calluses formed on their skin. And as they worked, the hard surface cracked and bled, bigger and bigger, until they needed to be sewed up. Since the wounds were bathed in salt water, they were painful, but there was no fear of infection.

Sansan worked expertly with needle and thread, and there was little if any blood. For some of the men, the procedure would have to be repeated within days.

Ying'er gasped and looked away, as she recalled how, when they were making their way across the desert, the salt lakes had always seemed almost idyllic, just waiting for them. How disappointing to be greeted on their arrival by such a repellent sight.

Seeing a look of curiosity, not disgust, on Lanlan's face, Sansan asked if she wanted to help. Even though she enjoyed considerable praise for her needlework, applying it not to fabric but to bloody wounds, she passed for the time being. One of the workers chuckled as he took a threaded needle and put on a show of poking it through the thick skin to pull the gaping wound high up on his thigh together. He was being playful, but the beads of sweat rolling down his forehead betrayed the discomfort, if not pain. Ying'er and Lanlan could not believe what they were seeing, but they'd get used to that and worse over the days to come.

The men walked off cheerfully after the suturing. Sansan lit a kerosene lamp. "There's no electricity in any of the buildings," she told them, "except for the management station, where the lights are turned off at ten at night. The generator you're hearing in the background is reserved for the hoist. It's dark in here much of the time, no matter how brilliantly the sun shines outside.

"The man who gave you and your camel water earlier is Daniu. He's the lead worker. He's the best, he can scoop up ten tons of salt a day. Fulltime workers like him are allotted the most food, of course, since they need plenty for the hard work they do."

For Ying'er and Lanlan, fresh from village life, this was going to be a new and, they hoped, profitable adventure.

While they were talking, Daniu came in to say that the boss

offered to put them to work as soon as they were ready. The salt crust—the hard ground surface—had to be removed before aged salt could be harvested from the alkaline water. Grains of salt and sand fused to form crystals called salt roots during the process, and Ying'er and Lanlan would join several of the women in picking them out of the salt crystals. They would be used as filler for the potholes in the roadway. They'd earn one yuan a bucketful and be paid at the end of the month. He also gave them canvas uniforms and dark glasses.

"It's the easiest work around here," Sansan said encouragingly. "You're lucky a couple of women just quit and left. Otherwise you'd have to fight for the job."

Before they turned in, Lanlan gathered wheat stalks for the camel. The needle grass on nearby sand dunes had been planted to shore up the sand, and was not for camel consumption. With plenty of water, the camel didn't mind the dry stalks and chewed away happily.

"The salt lakes were a dowry from a Mongolian lord to one of his daughters a hundred years ago," Sansan said as they got ready for bed. "It was the best dowry any girl could hope for, like a treasure chest. The salt continues to grow no matter how much you scoop out. It really is an endless supply."

After a simple breakfast the next morning, they went up to the salt mounds. Mostly aged salt, the crystals were large, mined from recently dug pools, where they had steeped for years. After the aged salt was scooped out, new salt would grow in the alkaline water in a few years, but the crystals would be smaller. Aged salt tasted better and fetched a higher price.

Picking out the salt roots was a job for women, some of whom were out there already, wearing the same canvas work clothes Daniu had given Ying'er and Lanlan. He handed them buckets and said all they had to do was copy the others.

185

They watched as a hoist transported a pile of salt mixed with salt roots onto the mound. The crystals were white but dirty, the roots much darker. Ying'er spotted a dark shape in the salt, picked it up, and tossed it into her bucket. Her routine was underway. As she worked, the hoist made a loud noise that seemed to drill its way into her head; loud noise had always bothered her. After a. while, her ears were buzzing and she felt somewhat disoriented. Yet she had to ignore the din, as the salt kept pouring down, cascading like water. Since salt roots rolled down the side of the mound among the crystals, she was forced to work nonstop. Inundated by the racket, she wondered how anyone could count this as an easy job.

"Hey there! Are you blind?" Someone yelled as she lost herself in the work.

Ying'er turned and saw a menacing face staring at her. The man pointed to several salt roots still on the mound. Not used to wearing dark glasses, she had trouble telling them apart from salt crystals. She took off her glasses and gave the man an apologetic smile before climbing up to remove what she had missed and add them to a still modestly filled bucket. She straightened up and was knocked to the ground by a great force, while needles shot into her eyes. She covered her eyes with her hands and rolled off the mound.

"Why did you take off your glasses?" The man chided her. "They give you those to protect against salt spray. But that's all right, don't worry. The salt water stings, but it won't do any serious damage." He called over a worker to take her place and told her to rinse her eyes with fresh water from the bucket.

She did what he said, and the pain subsided after a while. Wiping her face with a towel, she thanked him and walked off, but he stopped her and asked where she was from. She answered, reluctantly, wondering if that was the rule around there. She couldn't be sure if his question was well- or ill-intentioned.

Most of the men kept darting glances at the two new arrivals, who appeared to be ill-equipped to do much of a job, especially the prettier one, Ying'er. For some, it was simple curiosity. Since they were all from somewhere else, they wondered where Lanlan and Ying'er were from and what they were doing here. Others may well have harbored less innocent thoughts.

It did not take long for Ying'er to realize that picking salt roots was hard, relentless work, especially with the sun beating down mercilessly. One reason was stress: as the salt flowed down, she had to stay focused and act quickly or the roots would be buried in the salt. Another reason was a sore back from bending over. The long ride on their camel had already caused discomfort in her back, and now the pain was intensified. And then, even with the protective glasses, salt water kept stinging her eyes, producing a constant flow of tears. When she was bent over picking up salt roots, water would ride along the crystals and splash in her face. By blinking quickly, she managed to avoid much of the direct contact with her eyes. Yet, the all-invasive water always found a way to steal in and make them burn. Thanks to the outfit she'd been given, she was relatively dry underneath, though the heavy material was drenched, and she was sweating head to toe. She stole a glance at Lanlan and found her forever resilient sister-in-law hard at work, seemingly unaffected by anything. Lanlan is a survivor. The thought flashed past her mind. What about me? Ying'er asked herself silently.

She was getting dizzy. And this was considered the easy work, she reflected. She had to agree, of course, that there were harder jobs, as she recalled the sinister gaping wounds on the workers' legs. That helped make the work seem less taxing, and she knew that if she wanted to earn enough money to pay for the lost camel and to finance her brother's remarriage, she'd have to put up with the hardship, and for quite a while.

As the sun rose higher, the mound of new salt turned into a steamer. The smell of alkali grew stronger and spread around them, a pungent, acrid odor reminiscent of the ocean. The salt lakes must be a dead ocean, Ying'er thought. She recalled the seashells they'd found when digging for suoyang. That triggered a recollection that, like a warm current of water, rippled through her. Lingguan had once promised to take her to see the ocean, which she'd only seen on TV, a never realized trip to an azure blue that stretched across the horizon. The ocean in her imagination was cool, with breezes brushing her face, pleasantly ticklish, unlike the sweltering, stifling hot salt lakes. The work was tough, but she'd pretend it was the ocean he'd promised to show her. That would help, she hoped.

"Hey! Don't fall asleep on the job!" The man screamed at her again.

Ying'er snapped out of her reverie to see all the salt roots brought over by the hoist, sprinkled on salt. She quickly picked them out, until she felt like she'd never be able to stand up straight again.

15

Before long, they felt they might as well be wearing a suit of armor, for the heavy clothes they'd been given had stiffened when the sun licked off the water splashed on them. A layer of white salt obscured their clothes' original color and began to restrict their movements. Unavoidably, water had seeped in under the outer garments and, though generally salt-free, had wetted the clothes underneath.

Finally, noon came. The women went into a changing room made of grass mats hung on four sides. Ying'er and Lanlan took off their work clothes and found that both the top and bottom could stand on their own. After changing, the other women took off their work clothes and rinsed them in buckets of fresh water, where the salt dissolved without any scrubbing. They spread the uniforms out to dry and changed into the clothes they wore away from work, before starting on lunch.

Ying'er and Lanlan had flung their changes of clothes at the jackals, so they had nothing but the set they were wearing and the one blue blouse Ying'er had held back. New to the work, they hadn't known to take off their own clothes before putting on the uniform, so everything they were wearing had turned stiff. They had no choice but to rinse their uniform and keep their clothes on, which rustled as they moved.

"Did Dirty Old Man say anything to you?" Sansan whispered to Ying'er.

"Who?"

"The boss. The one you talked to when you arrived."

"Why do you call him that?"

"For good reason, but only in private." Sansan giggled.

Sansan went on to tell her that the boss seemed redundant, but enjoyed a great deal of power, though he answered to an even more powerful boss who was in charge of all aspects of the salt reclamation project.

"We call him Dirty Old Man because he likes a bit of you know what."

"No, what?"

"Well . . ." Sansan covered her mouth and giggled again. "What else could it be? He's always summoning female workers to his shack. He can do that out in the open, since his wife died. You know what men like most, don't you? A promotion, getting rich, and a dead wife. Dirty Old Man has all three. Naturally, he's quite eligible, and, naturally, he's on the lookout for another wife."

The man they were talking about approached in the middle of their conversation and walked in to drop off two sets of gently used clothes for Ying'er and Lanlan. How did he know we have no change of clothes? Ying'er wondered silently to herself.

He looked at Sansan, who said nothing until he left. Then she whispered to them,

"Do you think he heard what I was saying?"

"Let's hope not." Ying'er tried to reassure her. "He was outside, after all."

"So what if he heard?" Lanlan said. "If he's unhappy and doesn't want us here, we could find jobs like this anywhere."

"Why *did* you come here?" Sansan asked Lanlan, who gave the same answer she'd given Daniu and the boss when they arrived.

"It's actually easy for a woman to make money just about everywhere, if you don't mind what you do." Sansan continued. "But if you want to keep your reputation, then you have to work like a donkey. Here, at least, you get to see your hard-earned money every month, without fail. At some places, you work for nothing, because a

190

dishonest boss will find a way to take it from you."

Ying'er wondered if the boss had given them his dead wife's clothes, which made her uneasy. Lanlan had already changed into one of the sets. Seeing Ying'er hesitate, she said:

"Go in and change. You gather firewood on the mountain you're standing on. Give me what you're wearing and I'll wash everything."

Ying'er changed out of her wet clothes, and washed them in a bucket alongside Lanlan. After they laid them out to dry, Sansan checked around before she whispered:

"Don't underestimate Dirty Old Man. He's got plenty of money, and has lots of ways to get more. He's running a scheme with one of the truck drivers. For every four-ton load of salt, they chalk it up to six and split the money."

"How do you know?" Ying'er asked.

"You can't wrap a fire in paper." Sansan sneered. "It's an open secret. We don't own the salt lakes, so no one really cares that much. These days, anyone who's got the ability can get what he wants."

Lunch was ready, and they were about to eat when the boss showed up again. With a glance at Ying'er, he dropped off bags of pickled mustard greens before walking out wordlessly. Looking at Ying'er, Sansan was about to say something, but decided against it.

It was still boiled noodles, but delicious; they were famished, and the addition of the pickled vegetables made for a real lunch. It had been quite a while since Ying'er and Lanlan had enjoyed several hot meals in a row.

In the afternoon, when they knocked off for the day, someone came to weigh the salt roots the women had collected. With only twelve buckets, Ying'er fared badly. Lanlan had fifteen, while some of the others had more than twenty. If the hoist dumped about the same amount of salt roots into each woman's area, Ying'er reasoned silently, then she'd come up terribly short, not a very good start.

To add to her overall discomfort, she suffered leg cramps that night as she lay on her lightly padded railroad tie bed, her muscles twitching and jumping to keep her awake. Beyond the physical effect, to the villagers, muscle twitches usually signaled something unexpected or unpleasant.

What could it be this time? Her baby? Was something wrong? She tried to shake off her concerns and told herself that her in-laws would never allow anything to happen to the little boy.

After working for several days, they'd each made a hundred yuan or so, but would have to wait till the end of the month to get their money. Sansan told them that not many temporary workers stayed for long. "Not even a wolf would choose a place like this to shit," she said. "They come out here, work for a month or two, and leave right after they get paid."

Permanent workers who scooped salt, on the other hand, were very well treated. In addition to their wages, they were allotted a monthly ration of three hundred pounds of coarse grain, until the boss told the grain station to supply them with only finer grains, wheat and rice instead of millet and sorghum. They were also given a steady supply of meat at no cost. Everyone else had to pay for their food.

Daniu came to their room each night, either to chat or for Sansan to sew up the cracked wounds on his leg. He kept stealing glances at Ying'er, telling her she was as pretty as a painting. There were other women at the salt lakes, to be sure, but the elements had turned their faces dark and rough. The men had gone a long time without seeing a good-looking woman. Even someone with Lanlan's more careworn looks was rare. She too could be considered a pretty woman out here. Appearance meant less to her than it did to Ying'er, and she was not bothered by the loss of beauty. Events in the desert had convinced her to return to the Vajravārāhī Cave when she was back home. She'd begun chanting sutras again, her heart filled with gratitude over the gift of suoyang when they had resigned themselves to death in the desert. The Vajravārāhī gave me back my life, she said to herself, and I'd be unworthy of her if I didn't keep up with the practice.

Besides her religious practice, Lanlan constantly fretted over her parents back home. To ease her mind, she asked the boss to place a call to the small shop in her village for them to tell her parents that she and Ying'er were doing fine, working at the salt lakes, so they shouldn't worry. In Lanlan's eyes, her parents were a contradiction; they seemed to always do or say something stupid when she was around, but once she was away, she had only positive thoughts about them. Parents were like your hometown; you only felt its warmth when you were away from it. Ying'er had no such feelings about her home, save some sympathy for her father.

Daniu was a model worker. He had a thin face, but had mostly ropy muscles, which rippled when he worked. The only physical flaw were his sunburned skin and legs covered in callouses and gaping wounds. He had been at the salt lakes long enough to tell stories, mostly about the other workers. He also talked about the boss, who had promoted him to be a sort of deputy. It wasn't much of a promotion, but Daniu was in close proximity to power, and his status among the workers was elevated. Whenever one of them had a problem, they came to Daniu, who talked to the boss to resolve whatever it was.

After becoming a model worker who scooped ten tons of salt a day, Daniu got special treatment from the man who measured salt production. When the workers brought up the salt, it was stacked by the water. When he was too lazy to do it himself, he had Daniu do it for him and double checked his figures from time to time. So Daniu was vested with considerable authority, and whomever he favored would benefit. Naturally, he was mightily pleased with himself.

"Come see me if you ever need anything," he said to Ying'er and Lanlan, thumping his chest for emphasis. He acted like he could swallow the sky and spit out the earth.

Ying'er did not grasp the import of that comment at the time, thinking it was no more than a simple boast.

16

There was to be a movie showing at the management station one night soon after they arrived. After gobbling down their dinner, the women dressed up and got ready for some entertainment. Ying'er hadn't wanted to go.

"We're going," Lanlan insisted. "I don't care what they're showing, it's something to break up the monotony."

So, they fed and watered the camel and then followed the crowd to the station.

The road was flanked by bunch grass and other desert vegetation, its potholes filled with the salt roots they and the other women worked so hard to gather during the day. Daniu was particularly attentive to Ying'er as they walked, constantly checking on her, though she ignored him as best she could. The temporary workers whispered back and forth, frequently roaring in feral laughter. Assuming she was the source of that laughter, Ying'er frowned and tugged on Lanlan to put more distance between them and the disgusting men. Daniu cursed the workers, who merely laughed and walked off.

"Don't mind them," he said. "That's just how they are. If they don't see a woman for three days, they think every sow is a rare beauty."

"What's that? Are you saying we're a couple of sows?" Lanlan asked.

"No, no. What I meant was, there aren't many women around here, and pretty women like you two are a rarity, so of course they're acting like hungry wolves," Daniu explained anxiously.

"Then, do they plan to eat us?" Lanlan laughed.

"Don't worry. With me around, they wouldn't dare."

Lanlan pinched Ying'er and smiled with a hand over her mouth, "Listen to him. He wants to be our protector."

The management station was not large, just a row of single-story buildings, including a commissary kitchen and a sundry shop that sold a few food items, tobacco, and other necessities. There were no chairs in the large room they called a movie theater, so the workers brought their own stools. Temporary workers were reduced to standing to the side, where they crowded into the women, with feigned innocent looks.

Dirty Old Man was there too. He handed two stools to Lanlan. Ying'er saw how a hostile look replaced Daniu's fawning smile when the other man turned his back. After the boss walked off, Daniu murmured:

"You'd better watch out, he's got his eye on you. He's a terrible womanizer, always using the excuse of finding a wife in order to sleep with one woman after another. When he's finished, he tosses them aside."

His warning, however self-serving, was not lost on either woman, Lanlan in particular. Her disheartening experiences with Bai Fu and Huaqiu had soured her on men in general. Two sisters-in-law, one who had attracted the attention of more than one man in their still unfamiliar surroundings, the other on alert to protect her from unwanted advances.

Once everyone was settled, the movie started, a story about a group of prisoners. Ying'er was sickened by some of the ribald activity behind them, with coarse workers getting frisky with women who either cursed them or giggled. She was grateful to the boss for having brought them stools, allowing them to stay clear of the groping.

As the first reel was being changed, Daniu elbowed his way up through the crowd carrying a tree stump as a makeshift stool. When some people complained, he apologized as he pushed through.

The movie started again, but Daniu's head now blotted out part of the screen, which incurred more complaints, so he crouched down. Ying'er was not pleased that he'd decided to sit by them. It was not uncommon for women to appreciate male attention, she knew, but that was never welcome with someone not to their liking.

Lanlan made room for Daniu, who sighed happily as he sat down. That made Ying'er wince, as she sensed people behind pointing at her. People see what they want to see, she knew, and explaining away her innocence in what they were thinking would be hard if not impossible, thanks to Daniu's conspicuous attention. Inevitably, romances or casual physical involvements occurred among the workers, but she wanted to avoid even the hint of those sorts of entanglements. Her reading of popular novels as a girl had inculcated her with a strong belief that casual intermingling belonged to the animal kingdom, not human.

Daniu was breathing loudly, irritatingly, sending breath from his nose directly toward her. How repulsive. She couldn't help it, she'd been like that all her life. Even as a little girl, she'd refused to drink from a glass someone else had used without first washing it, even if it meant going thirsty. The same attitude held with bedding and clothes. Granted, there was an exception; she never minded anything Lingguan had used. Then again, reality had forced her to make adjustments. She'd put on someone else's clothes the boss had given her, had drunk from the same bottle used by the camel, and had eaten from a bowl that others had used.

She felt a scratch on the back of her hand. Thinking it was accidental, she ignored it. But the scratching got more insistent, and her face burned when she realized what was happening. She scooted over to avoid the fingers, but her reaction only encouraged them to grasp her hand. The grip tightened when she tried to free it. Outraged, she gave Daniu an angry glare and saw a lewd look on his face. If she hadn't worried about embarrassing him, she'd have screamed. Now that she couldn't free her hand or curse, Daniu got bolder; he stuck a finger into her palm, which he then balled with another hand. The finger thrust back and forth, a gesture with meaning clear enough to humiliate her. Infuriated, she tried to pull her hand back, but no matter how hard she tried, she couldn't get loose. Helpless tears welled up in her eyes.

The hand on hers was damp with sweat. She tried again, but still failed to fling his away, so she jumped to her feet, blotting out the screen, and immediately drew curses that felt like slaps in the face.

"I'll be right back," she said. Both hands were exposed as she got up, and finally she was free.

She walked away from Daniu at a crouch. People were staring at her, so she pretended she was going to relieve herself. She hadn't had the urge, but once outside she actually did have to go. Looking around, she found a secluded spot, but before she reached it, two powerful hands clamped down on her. She heard Daniu's heavy breathing.

"Let me go," she snapped at him.

"I want you so much I could die." He was panting. "Take pity on me."

She struggled, but could not get away. Those hands, which were used to working with a metal scoop, could easily take her by force, so she changed her tone.

"Let me go and we can talk."

He did as she asked, but still tried to put his arm around her.

"Be a gentleman," she said as she dodged away.

"I'll be good to you. You can believe me. I mean it. If I'm lying, my ancestors are donkeys. You believe me, don't you?"

"Something like this can't be forced. I have someone back home."

"If it can't be open, we can do it on the sly."

"How can you say something like that?" she was incredulous.

He responded by picking her up and walking into the dark. She struggled, but could not fight him off. She screamed, but got no response from anyone. His heavy breathing overwhelmed her senses. As she continued to struggle, she threatened,

"I'll kill myself if you don't stop."

"You women are all alike," he panted and said. "You fight at first, but soon you won't want to let me go."

She tried to bite his arm, but he blocked her each time. She started to cry.

"Daniu! Hey, Daniu!" A shadow came out of the theater.

Daniu let go of her and vanished into the night.

Ying'er could tell it was the boss. Drying her tears, she walked out of the dark, not courageous enough to relieve herself.

"Is that you, Daniu?"

Ying'er said nothing.

Clearly, the boss had his eye on her too.

Daniu stayed away over the next few days, bold enough only to gaze at her from a distance. At night, Ying'er made sure the door was securely latched. Lanlan had misread the whole thing. Something had indeed happened, just not what Lanlan thought. Ying'er had not wanted to bring it up, but to clear herself with Lanlan, she had to tell her sister-in-law everything. Lanlan gnashed her teeth.

"I'll handle him if he comes again."

Sansan was treating her differently. Before Ying'er's arrival, she and Daniu had had a history of sorts, enough to cause gossip. Daniu had wanted to keep it a secret, but Sansan told others he'd tried to seduce her and that she'd turned him down. That was a loss of face for Daniu, who was so outraged he revealed their sexual relationship. But now he had his eye on Ying'er, so Sansan turned cold toward her. She did not force them to set up their own kitchen, since they'd lost their cookware in the desert, but she no longer treated them as friends.

Lanlan talked it over with Ying'er and decided it was time to become more independent in their communal setup. After she asked around about buying cookware at the shop, the boss showed up with a few items, saying it had been left behind by some temporary workers. Sensing there might be friction, he asked if they wanted to move out. To Lanlan, it was better to have someone around, so she told him they'd stay with Sansan.

After several days at the salt lakes, some of the inconveniences became more urgently apparent to Ying'er: they did not have their own changes of clothes, no feminine products, and so on. Worst was the loss of the blanket that had been on the dead camel. The desert baked in the day and froze at night. When the sun set, a desert wind began to howl, and their building felt like an ice cellar in the early morning. Sansan had shared her wool blanket with them when they first arrived. Since the night of the movie, Sansan had unobtrusively drawn the blanket to her side, and Ying'er knew that the other woman thought she had stolen her lover.

And then there was their camel. It had been a handy boat in the desert, but turned into a burden at the lake, for they had to keep searching for grass. To help them out, the boss asked a Mongolian herder to graze the camel for the time being. They knew the farmer they'd borrowed it from would want it returned soon for spring planting. Lanlan was thinking that if someone from Liangzhou came to buy salt, she could ask them to take the camel back for them, while they would stay to work. She had done her math: they could earn something carrying salt back, but not as much as working at the lake for a few months. Besides, they were paid in cash here, while salt must first be traded for grain that would then have to be sold for cash. Too much trouble.

Lanlan asked the temporary workers to keep an eye out and let her know if someone from Liangzhou showed up. But she soon discovered that her knowledge of the salt lakes was dated by ten years. There hadn't been a highway back when people from her village had come for the salt. Now there was. Trucks could carry several tons, while a camel managed only a fraction of that. She felt like a fly in a bottle; the outside world had changed, but her understanding of it was stuck in what she remembered.

Now she thought she understood why there were so many jackals in the desert. In the past, salt carriers would travel with rifles and pick off the animals, preventing them from forming packs. Now with trucks rumbling down the highway, there were fewer camel caravans to shoot them. She also understood why the camel carcasses along the way had all been bleached and why there hadn't seemed to be any new ones. Camels had stopped coming here to transport salt long before they began their harrowing trip.

She'd already been through so much—marriage, beatings by her husband, the death of her little girl, asking for a divorce, not to mention all the miseries on the trip across the desert. Now she was faced with a dramatically new world. If she hadn't made this trip, she'd have believed the world was the same now as it had been since before her wedding.

Changes had come to the salt lakes as well. Manual excavation was slowly being replaced by machines. A rabbit had been enough to exchange for a load of salt, now it had to be paid for with cash. Other changes weren't so striking, except for the trucks that made the lumbering camels look pathetic. She finally understood why transporting salt on a camel's back had become a rare trade. To think that she had been so proud of her idea before they left!

She would work for a while, she figured. If they liked it here and someone could return the camel for them, they'd stay longer, at least until they'd made enough to return with a bit of dignity. But would she be exchanging one set of troubles for yet another? And what about Ying'er?

The next day, a worker came over with two woolen blankets. The boss had heard they'd arrived with no bedding and only a single change of clothes. To Ying'er and Lanlan, it felt like receiving coal on a snowy day. Yet, they were unnerved by the boss's awareness of everything happening around them. What didn't he know?

Before long, Ying'er sensed that some of the workers were whispering behind her back. She was getting the hang of the work and was picking up more buckets of salt roots. She actually gleaned more than the others once in a while, drawing odd looks from the women. Something was wrong, as she discovered that her piles grew visibly larger every day after the lunch break.

One day, instead of napping after lunch, she cracked the door open to keep an eye on the spot where her salt roots were stacked. Half an hour later, Daniu showed up. He approached stealthily, with a sack over his shoulder, and, after checking around to make sure no one was watching, dumped a load of salt roots onto her pile. What an eye-opener! He must have picked them up along the road to the management station and carried them over as a gift.

Her face flushed with embarrassment. How would she face people if they found out?

She asked Lanlan to tell Daniu to stop. Lanlan was worried,

knowing that Daniu was more than casually interested in Ying'er. They were still outsiders here, unfamiliar with interpersonal dynamics. Beyond that, they had planned to stay only as long as it took to earn enough money, and this had every sign of making that difficult. She told Ying'er she'd talk to him as soon as she got him alone.

"He said you needn't worry," Lanlan returned to tell Ying'er the next day. "He said you'll get a couple of hundred more each month this way." Making light of the situation did not sit well with Ying'er.

"What does he take me for?" she said unhappily. "I don't want that kind of dirty money."

When Daniu came for a repeat performance the next day, she was ready. She went up to him and, with a stern look, told him to stop what he was doing. No matter what he thought, his favoritism was making her look bad in the eyes of others, especially the women engaged in the same job as she.

"Sure, all right," he replied, surprised by her displeasure. "I just wanted you to know how I feel. I really do like you a lot and I'll do anything for you. Everyone knows how wonderful it is to nap after lunch. I don't mind going out there for you, as long as you can make a bit of extra money."

"I'll report you to the boss if you do that again," Ying'er threatened, afraid he wouldn't stop.

"All right. I said I'll stop." Finally, she'd put some fear into him and he slinked off.

She was drenched in a cold sweat when she went back inside; people would think she'd willingly get something going with him. Why else would he miss his mid-day naps?

Sure enough, she overheard one of the workers say to another,

"See that pretty woman, the one who arrived recently? She's

Daniu's new love interest."

The comment angered and humiliated her. There could only be two sources of the rumor, one of whom would be Daniu himself. She heard that the temporary workers were all like that; the scarcity of woman had enriched them with fertile imaginations, and they enjoyed making up salacious stories. The other likely source would be Sansan, who acted as if Ying'er were a true rival.

Sansan rarely looked Ying'er in the eye now, nor did she talk to her, though they still shared a space. Ying'er and Lanlan could not keep using her stove any longer, so Lanlan found some bricks to make a small stove by the door. The plants around the lake were reserved to shore up the sand and hence were off limits. For fuel, they had to scrounge camel droppings after work. It was wonderful fuel, since it burned slowly, and only a few pieces lasted a long while. But the temporary workers had to cook their own meals too, so they also gathered camel droppings, as did the permanent workers' children. With so many people out gathering, the droppings were scarce. Sometimes it took an hour to find enough to cook a meal.

One day they decided to take their search for fuel farther than usual over their lunch break. They borrowed a hand cart and set out for the herders' area. To their disappointment, there wasn't much left there either. Obviously, they weren't the first with that idea.

"If we'd known camel droppings were so precious, we could have saved those from our own camels on the way," Lanlan said, half seriously.

"Back then we had no control over our own lives. We couldn't have been thinking that far ahead," Ying'er replied, though she too felt bad about leaving the droppings on the way. Human hearts are remarkable, she thought. Sometimes the desire is as great as a bottomless pit, but at other times it is too easily satisfied. Now the sight of camel droppings would send them running ecstatically.

As they walked along, pushing the cart, its wheels kept sinking into the sand, and soon they were sweating. At work, bending over constantly had led to sore backs. Now, during their midday break, they would have loved to lie down to rest, but there were things they must do, even if they didn't feel like it. Eyes wide open, they searched for anything that could be used as fuel.

After a frustrating hour, Lanlan was ready to give up. "Let's go back, so we won't miss work."

"We're already way out here, so let's keep looking. Just a little longer," Ying'er replied. "I don't believe the herders have plugged their animals' rear ends." Lanlan looked at her wide-eyed, surprised by Ying'er's coarse expression.

They both smiled broadly when they spotted a pile of camel droppings in a nearby sand trough. Overjoyed, they ran forward with the cart. Part of the droppings were dry, other parts were still wet, but that did not bother them. They scooped it all up, wet and dry, and tossed into the cart.

"What a strange camel. Why did it keep shitting at the same spot?" Lanlan wondered aloud. Ying'er was wondering the same thing.

"We all have our habits," she said, "so maybe this camel is the same. It has a favorite spot to use as a toilet." Buoyed by the find, Ying'er wasn't at all embarrassed by how foolish that sounded.

As they were leaving, they heard a cough; they jumped in surprise. An old man was rounding a corner of a sand eddy where, Ying'er realized, a small house stood. It was a tiny structure with walls made of salt slabs, blending into the background and nearly hidden from sight. They'd both missed it.

"Hey, you thieves, stop right there. That's my fuel," he demanded.

Ah, this was no toilet, it was a fuel repository. They were mortified by their mistake. When he came closer, Lanlan explained that they'd recently arrived at the salt lakes, planning to take salt back to their village in Liangzhou, but had stuck around to work for a while. They'd had trouble finding fuel close to home, and had stumbled onto his pile. They wouldn't have dared take it for their own if they'd known it belonged to someone else.

"Ah, Liangzhou, you say. I had a job there once, a good job, and a good life too. It's a great place to live."

"What brought you way out here?" Ying'er asked him.

"Well, my wife died, and I sort of fell apart. I lost my job, and roamed around for a few years, getting by the best I could. Eventually, I wound up here, close to the salt project, but living on my own. My son stayed in the city, and he makes sure I've got enough to get by. I have two camels, and that's where they do their business or where I take them if they're out grazing. There's more of their droppings than I can use, so take what you need. Consider it a gift."

"We can't do that. You have to cook too," Ying'er protested.

"Of course, you can." The man smiled and continued, "My camels will give me more. It's not like their rear ends are sewn up."

They looked at each other, smiling over his use of Ying'er's expression. They thanked him for his generosity when he gave them two sacks to fill with the dry droppings and repeated their thanks as they toss the sacks onto the cart.

After walking awhile, they realized they'd neglected to ask the man what it was about Liangzhou that prompted his kindness. Suddenly, they noticed that the topography had changed. They'd taken a wrong turn somewhere, and panicked because they had to be back at work soon. Ying'er said, "Let's just retrace our steps and follow the ruts we made on our way over." That is what they did. The detour caused them to be an hour late for work.

The boss told them he was about to send some temporary workers into the desert to look for them, when they finally showed up. Everyone was relieved to see them back safe. Being lost out there can be serious, he said to them. Lanlan had expected to be reproached, or worse, by the boss. To her surprise, he only cautioned them not to stray too far into the desert in the future. He did not need to say more, not after what they'd been through.

They placed the sacks with the dry camel droppings under the raised railroad ties on which they slept so the temporary workers wouldn't come in and steal them. There was enough for a good many days, maybe even weeks. Sansan was constantly short of fuel, so Ying'er gave her some whenever she needed it, and that softened the woman's attitude toward them, at least a little. When her family came to see her, she even shared some of the desert rice they'd brought.

The droppings from the old man's camels weren't worth much, but his charitable act warmed their hearts every time they talked about it. There are still more good people than bad in the world, Ying'er comforted herself. Over the coming weeks she wouldn't be so sure of that.

In the meantime, when word got out, the anecdote of two women picking up the old man's fuel became a joke among the workers, who laughed every time someone mentioned it. Oddly, being the butts of jokes made Lanlan and Ying'er feel they finally belonged, that they'd been accepted as regular workers.

17

It was raining, so the women who gleaned salt roots got the day off. Ying'er asked Lanlan if she wanted to take a walk. The rain was refreshing, a pleasant respite from interminable steamy days. Before they set out, a couple of workers arrived for Sansan and Lanlan to sew up their wounds. Lanlan had seen enough that she could do the job now, and didn't mind it at all. Ying'er, on the other hand, could not imagine threading through someone's skin with a needle. With the new arrivals, the room got noisy and boisterous, so she walked out.

In the several weeks they'd spent at the lakes, their work had kept them tied to their quarters and the pyramids of salt, except for their midday escapade in search of fuel. Finally, a change in the weather gave Ying'er a chance to be out and about.

Not everyone viewed the change in the weather as a simultaneous break in the routine. The temporary workers were paid by the amount of salt they scooped, the more they produced, the more they earned, so most continued to work in the rain. A few were hard at work removing crusts that had formed over the salt lakes, a sort of tough shell. Explosives had to be used to blow away the hardest layer, and then drills were brought out to remove the softer ones before the sheet of sand and salt could be taken away to get at the aged salt steeped in alkali water.

"Hey—Here's a crystal for you," a man shouted from a distance.

Ying'er thought he was calling out to someone else until he repeated himself to assure her he was talking to her. I've got all the sand roots I need or want, she said to herself. But when the man got closer, she saw he was holding a brilliant object about the size of a sand root, but with light reflected off of what looked like facets, nothing like the dull, ugly things she gathered. She walked over. The worker, a young man with fair skin and pleasant features, handed her the crystal. It had a glittery translucence, as if carved from ice. She thanked him, earning a bright smile from him.

"No need to thank me. You can thank the salt lakes," he said. "They created it. These are fairly rare, and still, most of the workers just toss them onto the pile. We're too busy trying to make a living to care about objects of beauty." He had a shy, almost apologetic look.

Ying'er saw something in his eyes that reminded her of Lingguan. It was the look of an educated man.

"You seem different from the other men. You look like a city boy who's had some schooling."

"Baozi was a talented student," commented another worker who had walked up while they were talking. He answered her before the young man could open his mouth. "He passed the college entrance exam, but it cost more than his family could afford."

Baozi's face darkened. Not wanting to add to his unhappiness, Ying'er looked away.

The long strips of water reminded her of the wheat fields back in her village. In the rain, the emerald green water that had once stung her eyes was especially picturesque.

Baozi went back to work. Intrigued, she watched him lower a board into the lake to clear the salt from the sand, which was washed away. Then he began harvesting salt with his metal scoop. When it was full, he anchored the handle on his thigh to pry it out, the way she'd seen other men do it, but he barely managed to break the surface. So, he poured out some of the salt. Even half a scoop proved to be much for him, and soon he was panting from the exertion. He won't earn much that way, Ying'er said to herself. But maybe in a few years he'll be working like Daniu. If so, would he retain the present look? Or will he be as coarse as Daniu?

Daniu must have been watching her. For not long after she'd arrived on the scene, he came up to her. Seeing her eyes on Baozi, he gave the young man a sullen look.

"Can you believe the way this kid works?" Daniu said. "Like a scrawny dog trying to piss. Here, let me show you." He snatched the scoop from Baozi and in no time had extracted a dozen full scoops of salt. Despite her antipathy toward a man who had tried to violate her, Ying'er had to admire his strength.

He gazed at Baozi with a condescending, superior air.

"Give me a year," the younger man said, "and I could be just like you."

"Like me?" Daniu guffawed. "In your next life, maybe. I was born with supernatural strength." He pulled Baozi over, lifted him up, and flung him into the water. "Shut your eyes," Daniu shouted.

"Why on earth did you do that?" Ying'er demanded. The words were barely out of her mouth when Baozi floated to the surface, which made the other workers laugh.

He spat as he climbed ashore.

Ying'er was happy to see him unharmed, but livid over what Daniu had done. Knowing that he was capable of doing something even more outrageous if she stayed, she walked off and found a spot to sit and admire the crystal she'd been given. Soon her heart seemed infused with its luminous sparkles.

A fine rain, little more than a drizzle, fell on the lake, making a shushing sound. She was slowly taken in by the tranquil beauty. For too long she'd been restless and hurried. Toiling away and rushing about all the time, she rarely had a moment of quiet to herself. It was wonderful here, taking in the deep green water, a cooling rain, sand rippling imperceptibly in the mist, and a world blurred by the drizzle.

Everything sounded different in the rain, like ice melting in the spring. The sound grew louder as she listened carefully. She imagined a scene of ice cracking and wondered if the salt crystalized into mirrors before breaking into shiny shards. She was mesmerized by the scene, the world around her glistening in the rain.

Fortunately, Daniu did not follow her. She sat in the fine rain, caught up in the transformative visions created by prisms of wet salt crystals, dreamingly sitting outside of time, until she heard Lanlan call her in to dinner.

Even after finishing the simple meal, Ying'er could not let go of the tranquility by the lakes, so she invited Lanlan to return to the site with her and share the beauty of the water, the salt, and the gentle rain. But before they could leave, Sansan showed up with the woman known as Wu Jie—Big Sister Wu—who weighed their buckets every day. She had always been friendly to Ying'er in particular, sometimes jotting down an extra bucket or two than Ying'er had actually gathered. Ying'er was grateful. It meant only a few extra yuan at most, and though the act was borderline dishonest, Ying'er was grateful.

Wu told Sansan and Lanlan she wanted to have a private chat with Ying'er. After the two women left, Wu surveyed the room and said,

"I had no idea how hard you have it here. That's my fault. Just let me know if you need anything, and I'll do my best."

Ying'er knew the woman wanted something from her, or she wouldn't have braved the rain. But she had to wait for her to bring it up.

After some inconsequential chit-chat, Wu finally revealed what she'd come for.

"What do you think of our boss?" She asked Ying'er.

"Which one?"

"The one they call Dirty Old Man." Wu laughed.

Ying'er had not called him that, and felt sheepish about hearing it from others. "He's fine. See this blanket? He lent it to us."

"He's really a very nice man, you know," Wu said emotionally. "Every worker has benefited from his kindness. They call him 'Timely Rain.'"

Ying'er had never heard the nickname, but she said nothing.

"You probably didn't know that his wife died."

Now Ying'er got a sense of what the woman was about to say, and her heart raced. Sure enough, Wu came out with it.

"He has his eye on you. He's been watching you for days. He thinks you're a fine woman.

"He's met many women, and he likes you more than all the others.

"If you say yes, you'll eat and drink only the best. No more hard work for you.

"There's a cart-load of women who would like to fill the empty spot. If you're willing, he'll marry you right away."

On and on she went.

Ying'er was quiet the whole time, trying to think of an acceptable excuse to turn him down without hurting his feelings. But she came up with nothing. I'll tell the truth, she thought.

"It sounds wonderful, but I'm afraid I'm not lucky enough to be that woman. I have someone already."

"Oh, where is he?"

"Working in the provincial city."

Ying'er did not know where Lingguan was, but she had to say something. She simply said he was "working," which was open to interpretation. Being the provincial governor was working, so was washing dishes. Wu would have to guess what work Lingguan was involved in.

Wu could not press the issue for now, so after more chit-chat she told Ying'er to give the matter some more thought before taking her leave.

Sansan walked in, looking like a new person, her cold demeanor gone already. She had been eavesdropping.

"Why didn't you say yes? He's like a gold nugget. Do you know how many women can only dream about being the one he chooses? Didn't you hear her say he would like to marry you right away? How could you turn down something so good?" Sansan wasn't done yet. "You think he's too old. Is that it? Actually, he's not that old. It's just the wind and sand here, which has turned his skin dark and coarse. We women can't be picky about such things. We take the good with the bad. With his protection, you'd never have to worry about any of the workers getting ideas, including the temporary ones. I could tell you stories about women who came here before you and left in disgrace or simply disappeared. Just look around. You're young, you're pretty, and, as far as everyone is concerned, you're available. You're not too young to know what that means. Not only that, a man in his position can be the best thing to happen to you or the worst. I know I wouldn't want to make an enemy out of Dirty Old Man. If you marry him, you're not the only one who will enjoy a better life out here. Everyone knows that Lanlan is your sister-in-law. He would make sure she's well taken care of too."

Lanlan listened without saying a word.

When Sansan left, after urging Ying'er to think it over, Ying'er asked her sister-in-law out for a walk. Under an umbrella they'd borrowed from Sansan, they went to the spot where Ying'er had sat earlier in the morning. Rain continued to fall, heavy enough to wet their clothes, yet which gave the world around them a charming beauty. They sat down, but for Ying'er, everything looked different now. It was quiet. Her mind, however, was

212

anything but at peace.

"That's a pretty good deal," Lanlan said to break the silence. "Don't be thinking too far into the future. I know you're still thinking about Lingguan, but you have no idea where he is or what he's doing. You don't even know if he will or even can return to the village. Most men who leave don't. I probably shouldn't be saying this, but have you thought about how so many things are beyond your control?"

Ying'er's heart sank when she realized what Lanlan was getting at. She squinted into the distance. With the workers gone, the area around the lake was quiet, except for the sound of raindrops falling on their umbrella, and the occasional noise of salt cracking and breaking off.

"I want to tell you something," Ying'er said. "When I was little, my pa bought me a jade pendant. I loved it. One day my brother spat on it to spite me, because he knew I couldn't stand anything filthy. It was soiled, so I smashed it. Do you see what I'm saying? I know that living requires compromises. You have to go along with people and muddle through. But I can't do this. We're on earth for only a few decades, why can't we lead a clean life? Something dirty can never be cleaned. Don't you think?"

Lanlan heaved a sigh.

"You must have something in your heart that can't be soiled, don't you?" Ying'er asked. "Well, even if you don't, I do, and if it's gone, life won't be worth living any longer.

"I don't want to give up my reasons to live for some good food and drink, or for some clothes, or for a life of ease.

"I'm willing to die for what I live for."

"Listen to you. What are you talking about? This isn't about dying. Don't think like that." Lanlan knew no one could change Ying'er's mind, not if it meant giving up thoughts of Lingguan and an idealized future.

213

Sansan spread the word, and now everyone at the lakes knew what the boss had in mind, and also knew that Ying'er had not accepted the proposal Wu had offered her for him. It was a great loss of face. Men are like that; face matters more than anything. A stream of people, some well-intentioned, some not, came to see Ying'er, repeating what Wu had said to her, with even more reasons for her to accept. Whatever they offered turned to dust when it encountered Ying'er's notion to die for what she lived for. But she never let on; she treated them all with silence, which, strangely, made her seem even more attractive to the boss. Some spread word that he would consider his life lived in vain if he could not make her his woman.

Now that everything was out in the open, the boss stepped up his pursuit, first by sending Wu over with greens, the most coveted commodity at the lake. Only once a week were vegetables trucked over from the city. To get them for their meals, family members of permanent workers were turned into full-time shoppers who lined up early on the days the truck came. The temporary workers sent people over to buy the cheaper greens, though they were still many times costlier than elsewhere. Ying'er naturally longed to add greens to her diet, for the skin on her palms kept peeling, which, according to some, was caused by a lack of vitamins and minerals in vegetables.

The boss had many trucker friends, who brought sacks of produce each time they came. He told Wu to take some to Ying'er, who rejected them, leaving them on the floor. She would not even allow Lanlan to touch greens that started out crispy and fresh, but yellowed and wilted within a day. Sansan chastised her for wasting food; she washed the withered vegetables, cooked, and ate them herself. Ying'er let her be.

Wu kept bringing more, and Ying'er kept saying no. Everything Wu brought was fresh. Once she left, Sansan went ahead and washed them before they rotted. Ying'er doesn't want them, she'd say, so someone has to eat them and not let them go to waste. Gradually the temporary workers heard and swarmed over to divide up that day's take once Wu left after her delivery.

Soon everyone at the lake knew that Ying'er turned down things the boss sent to her. An admirable woman, they said. But those were fresh, crisp, lush greens. If she could turn down the boss's offer, then Daniu stood no chance with her. They began to doubt rumors of her fondness for him, rumors he himself originated. As they talked about Ying'er, she slowly became a sort of mythical figure.

Daniu mistakenly assumed she'd turned the boss down because she had fallen for him. The imagined scenario moved him so much he nearly wept each time he thought about it. Whenever he saw she was alone, he found an opportunity to walk up to her.

"I'll treat you as well as you treat me," he said, adding, "Just wait. I'll show you what I'm made of."

Ying'er was confused, with no idea what he meant by the way she treated him.

He was convinced that she admired his strength. He could not forget the look she gave him when he scooped up huge quantities of salt the day he flung Baozi into the lake. It was a look of astonishment, which he mistook as fondness. Day and night, he thought of that look, which, in his mind, evolved into even more of the same. Immersed in those imagined facial expressions, he indulged himself by working even harder.

Anyone who yields to a world he has created in his head can concoct many reasons why someone should be in love with him. She has no reason not to love me, he told himself. He was powerfully built, muscular, and energetic, and he made plenty of money, second only to the boss, though to him, the boss's money was dirty, from an illegal source. Who knew when the proverbial snow would melt to expose the bodies, and the government would confiscate the boss's money? His money, on the other hand, was hard earned, with his blood and sweat; he was the rightful owner of whatever he had. Besides, he'd heard that women liked strong men. The boss had passed his prime, and wasn't "strong," like him.

There was an autoharp in one of the workers' rooms, along with a tattered book of songs. One day a very bored Baozi awakened the instrument. At first it creaked and groaned, but it came alive in a few days, the notes from the old instrument swirling in the air everywhere. Daniu listened along and learned to hum tunes, which he did when he was out walking, even when he was working.

Everyone who saw him said, Daniu is lovesick.

Wu came again, but not to bring vegetables this time. She told them the first two women had returned to pick salt roots, so Ying'er and Lanlan would have a new job.

"All right. We can do anything. If there's no work, we'll just go home." Ying'er replied with a smile.

"What are you saying?" Wu laughed too. "The new job isn't as dirty as picking salt roots. It's still hard work, but no salt water in your eyes or hot, sweaty uniforms."

Lanlan said they'd do it.

Their new job was to hold down blowing sand that would kill the salt lakes if it settled in large quantities.

There were two ways to go about creating a barrier: one, they could haul dirt up to a dune to form dirt ridges, or two, they could press wheat stalks into the sand like netting. Wheat stalks were scarce, so dirt was the common material. The management station had set the width and length for the ridge and paid by the meter. No matter which method they used, it was only temporary. As soon as flowing sand buried the man-made barrier, the dune came alive again, so holding back the sand was an unending task.

Once they got there, Ying'er saw that this was a much harder

216

job than picking salt roots. There was no shelter to block the sun's harsh, relentless rays, but that was not the most difficult part. That was the job of transporting the dirt up the slope of the dune in a canvas stretcher. They filled it with dirt before swaying their way up. After each step forward in the sand, they sank back half a step.

Every time they moved a load up the dune, the carrying poles bit into their hands, pressing deep, seemed to crush their bones. The weight of the dirt dragged them down the dune. As their feet sank into the sand, it seeped into their shoes and cozied up to their feet. They were an unsightly pair after only a few steps. Gritting her teeth and holding her breath, Ying'er managed to carry a load up the dune with Lanlan. She slumped to the ground when she got to the top. When she noticed other women looking at her, she ignored them and their mocking stares, as she tried to catch her breath.

"Let's try it for a day," Lanlan said as she mopped her sweaty forehead. "If it's too hard for us, we'll settle up and go home."

"What can we do back home?" Ying'er said. "Look at those other women. They can do it, why can't we?"

They clenched their teeth and picked up the stretcher. Ying'er felt that her legs no longer belonged to her. Sweat gushed from her pores and her eye sockets. The worst sensation came from pain in her calves with each step.

By noon they'd sweated enough, but the ridge hadn't seemed to grow. After a rough calculation, Ying'er knew they wouldn't earn much, if anything, the way their work had gone so far. That, they both realized, was how the boss retaliated against Ying'er's rejection.

Told that the spot was far from camp, they had decided to bring water and food for lunch. They'd thought they could work over the lunch break, but neither could manage to stand after a brief rest. When they checked to see how others were doing, they were chagrined over their own lack of progress.

They smiled bitterly at each other when Daniu came with Baozi to see them. Daniu hailed them when he ran up the dune. Lanlan gave him a friendly greeting, while Ying'er smiled, making him feel welcome—sort of. He and Baozi picked up the stretcher and started carrying loads of dirt up the dune. Soon the ridge was much longer than before, after the women had worked all morning.

"You're doing this all wrong," Daniu said. "Want to see how the others managed? I'll show you." He went over to dig up the ridge someone else had built, and Ying'er saw the trick. Their neighbors had pushed sand together to form a ridge, then covered it with dirt, which allowed them to build a long section with only one load.

"But the work is wasted when the wind blows the dirt away," Lanlan said.

"Do you think they care how long the work lasts?" Daniu continued. "How much do you think you'll earn your way?"

"But won't the management station find out?" Lanlan asked.

"Depends on how you go about it. Give the inspector a carton of cigarettes and he'll turn a blind eye. That should take care of it."

"That's cheating," Ying'er said. "We can't do that. We didn't come all the way out to the desert to earn that kind of ill-gotten money."

Daniu and Baozi continued to help the women until they were bathed in sweat. Before they left, Daniu said to Ying'er,

"I'll go talk to the boss and ask him to give you lighter work. A job like this could kill a donkey."

The women got back to work after the break. Ying'er was at a point where her body would no longer do her bidding, and she crumpled to the ground halfway up several times. The dirt was gone, of course. Lanlan was also panting from the tiring trek. Soon they were exhausted, not an ounce of energy left, but neither would consider cheating.

"There was once a religious man who offered incense to the Buddha with profound sincerity it seemed," Lanlan said, "so the Buddha came to test him in the disguise of a salt-peddler. The man used a rigged steelyard to get an additional few ounces of salt. The Buddha smiled and said, three years of incense burning cannot compete with half a *jin* of salt." She continued, "The man's three years of good karma were wiped out by that little amount of salt. Honesty is the key to religious practice."

"I don't care about good karma," Ying'er said to her more religious sister-in-law. "I simply can't bring myself to do something like that. Being poor is nothing; we're worth more than that little bit of money."

They kept building the ridge with real dirt, but had little to show for a day's work. They did not have to calculate to know that, if not for the dirt Daniu and Baozi had carried for them, they would have made less pressing the sand all day than picking salt roots for one morning.

18

There was news about Daniu, bad news.

When they returned to their room at dusk, Sansan told them he'd slugged the boss. The reason was simple. Believing he had a close personal relationship with the boss, Daniu had gone to speak on the women's behalf so they could continue collecting salt roots. He forgot that he was still a worker, no matter how strong, and that friendship could only apply to people with equal status. So, the boss just glowered at him.

"Dirty Old Man has been unhappy with Daniu for some time," Sansan said. "How could an ordinary worker dare fight him over a woman? The boss was looking for an excuse to get rid of him, and Daniu made it easy. He stared daggers at Daniu, word has it, and said, 'Whose pants' crotch has rotted away to let you out? Just who do you think you are?' That really pissed Daniu off."

They'd heard from Baozi that Daniu had been unhappy with the boss for quite a while also. Ying'er recalled what Daniu had said, "You wait. I'll show you what I'm made of." Baozi had told them that Daniu had long wanted to have it out with the boss, and when the boss made it known he wanted to marry Ying'er, Daniu had gnashed his teeth and said that the boss should take a piss to look at himself in it, that he was an old donkey salivating over tender alfalfa. That and more was reported to the boss by a worker who wanted to get on his good side. The boss called Daniu a useless dick.

Daniu was incensed over this, but nothing bad would have

happened if he'd just slunk out of the boss's office. The boss was always cursing someone, so being called a useless dick was no big deal, and Daniu should have let it go. But he'd promised Ying'er that he'd get her lighter work. He was a man of his word, and could not break his promise, certainly not to a woman. So, this time he decided to let loose with everything that was on his mind. In the past, when the boss got drunk, it was always Daniu who carried him back to his room. The boss called him Brother and even got him involved in deals he couldn't ask anyone else to do—there were people watching him, their eyes firmly on his position. As a result, Daniu was privy to some of the boss's secrets. A man of personal loyalty, he never talked about them to anyone, except to Sansan, to whom he'd complained bitterly one day when he'd had too much to drink. Daniu had wailed, "This fucking world is so unfair. A few tricks and he rakes in so much money, like sweeping up leaves, while I work myself to death but barely manage to get by."

But this time the boss scowled when he mentioned Ying'er and told Daniu to get out. He'd have left if the boss had stopped there. But no, he shoved him and more than once, and Daniu shoved back.

"You know how strong Daniu is," Sansan said. "The boss banged up against his desk and nearly knocked it over."

"Even that would have been okay if it was just the desk flipped. But the boss picked up his chair and threatened him with it, and with that, he was no longer the boss. He was just someone who'd picked a fight with Daniu, who didn't want to fight, but whose hands could not stop. He swung and the chair was in pieces. Then his fists went for the boss and knocked out his front teeth.

"Daniu broke the law," Sansan said. "Knocking out someone's teeth isn't a serious offense, but it's still personal injury. Serious or not, he hurt the boss. When the police came to arrest him, he fled into the desert.

"Daniu's done for," she continued. "That one punch changed his fate. The management station docked his pay for the boss's medical expenses, so they said. The money was nothing. But then they fired him. He'll go to jail if he's caught, and running away makes his situation worse. He'd probably rot in jail."

Ying'er felt terrible. Daniu was in trouble because of her and Lanlan, no matter how she looked at it. If he hadn't tried to intercede for them, he'd still be the model worker, still have his job, and not be guilty of a criminal offense, even though they hadn't asked him to do anything for them. She heard he'd put the salt lakes in such a good light that when provincial officials came to visit, they all wanted to watch him work. He was a great asset to the place and the boss would surely have agreed to his request if it had been anyone but Ying'er. But two male lions will fight to the death over a female, and so, it seemed, would two grown men. Ying'er was indignant over all the unwanted attention, whose consequences an attractive woman like her often had to suffer through no fault of her own.

Late at night the three women were still awake, each with her own worries. Outside, a wind howled. There were few trees to stand its way, and the wind charged at the walls around them, bringing with it frightening sounds. "Daniu was doing so well, why did he have to get into trouble?" Sansan sighed. "His sister is still in college and depends on him for support. Now with this, her education is over."

Lanlan and Ying'er wondered if Sansan was blaming them.

There was a knock at the door, a cautious one that was barely audible in the gusty wind. They exchanged a look.

"Who is it?" Sansan asked.

Silence, except for another knock.

"Go away," Sansan demanded. "I'll scream if you don't stop knocking."

"Sansan." A familiar voice.

Sansan cried out and jumped to her feet. The latch was off as soon as she reached the door.

Daniu slipped in.

Ying'er couldn't believe her eyes. The police were looking for him, and yet here he was.

He was covered in dust. He found a bowl, filled it with water, and gulped it down.

"I can't stay here," he said to Ying'er. "Come to Xinjiang with me."

Ying'er did not know what to say.

"Xinjiang is huge. I didn't kill anyone, so they'll give up chasing me. I can't stay here. You know Dirty Old Man bears grudges. Even if the police stopped looking for me, he'll do something, so come with me. I'll be good to you for the rest of your life. I mean it."

Sansan looked at Ying'er with envy and indignation over her failure to appreciate Daniu.

Ying'er smiled unhappily and glanced at Lanlan, who knew what her sister-in-law was thinking. She turned to Daniu.

"She has someone already, didn't you know that? Her heart belongs to him."

Daniu's face fell. "How come you've been so nice to me if you have someone else?"

Ying'er shook her head. She felt like saying, What did I do? What did I say? I never promised you anything. How was I "nice" to you? But she knew it would be a great loss of face for him if she said that.

"What has she done?" Lanlan spoke up for her. "That's how she treats people, it's why everybody likes her. You let your imagination run wild, that's all."

He sat woodenly for a moment.

"I don't care who you like. I like you, and I'll make you mine even if it means my life."

Hearing him say "make you mine" visibly upset Ying'er. What do you take me for? she felt like saying.

"Like they say about relationships, a melon picked before it's ready isn't sweet," Lanlan said to him. "Look. Sansan has been so nice to you."

Sansan's face brightened as she gazed at him.

He frowned. "Let me think." After a moment, he said, "I'll be back if I can't figure things out."

He was quiet, but then started weeping. He reached up and his hand came away wet with tears. How could he weep like a little girl? Obviously, this was so hard to take he uncharacteristically lost control in front of the women. After wiping off more tears, he said with a grimace, "I'm done for. They'll beat me to death if they catch me. Those animals torture their prisoners. You know the boss's son is a policeman. Besides, I'd be killed by other prisoners even if the police spared me. Prisoners are worse than the police. They have so many ways to make you suffer." He sucked in air through his teeth and fell silent.

"Even if I make it out, no one will want to hire me. How will I face my parents? They treat me like a money tree, and my sister relies on me. I can't think any more, I'll die if I do."

"A grown man shouldn't talk like that," Lanlan chided. "It's not going to cost you your life. It hasn't worked out here, but this isn't the only place where you can find work."

"That's easy for you say. In this day and age . . . I know it's my fate. A fortuneteller told me I'd face a steel threshold, this year. I tried my best, but failed to avoid it. I'm not afraid of a beating. I just don't want to lose face. You may not know it, but anyone who's been in police custody is tainted in my village. No matter how hard you try, you can never wash off the stain."

"Then go apologize to the boss," Ying'er finally said. "Maybe he'll forgive you."

"No, he won't. I know what he's like. When everything's going good between us, he's great to be with. But if something goes against his wishes, he'll bear a grudge for the rest of his or your life. He's lost a lot of face this time, so how would he let me off? Besides, I know too many of his secrets, and he's wanted to get rid of me for a long time."

Then he turned to Sansan with a glum look. "Don't reveal any of those things I told you to anyone. You'll lose your head if they know." He finished with a long sigh.

"Make everything public," she said. "You'll be safer that way."

"It involves too many people. I don't know what to do." He turned to Ying'er, "Give it some thought, won't you? Xinjiang is really a great place."

Ying'er knew she had to stop him from having more fanciful thoughts, so she said, "I'd rather die than go with you. I've made up my mind, so leave me alone."

"I envy those bandits everyone talks about. I'd be one of them if I could. I'd kidnap you to be my wife." He sighed and took down a leather flask from the wall—Lanlan had filled it with water—before grabbing some steamed buns. He gave Ying'er a long, hard look and walked out with a sad smile.

The three women stood there silently. The impact of Daniu's departure affected each of them differently. Sansan was already in tears, tears more for herself than for him. She detected a sense of finality, the end of a nascent hope that she might somehow win his heart, however fanciful the thought might be. She had admired him for so long, she sometimes felt that their union was inevitable. Now he had walked out, taking with him not only that hope, but all her feelings of envy or animosity toward Ying'er, whose fragile emotions threatened to overwhelm her. Self-reproach over the cruelty of her rejection of Daniu's offer weighed heavily on her, but she could not accept a man out of pity. Her marriage to Hantou had taught her that. Lanlan, battered, embittered, pious Lanlan experienced a sense of foreboding. This will not end well, she was thinking. Any thoughts of staying to earn the money that would ensure her independence evaporated with Daniu's departure.

Believing that only she could put things to right, since Daniu's reckless act had stemmed from his feeling for her, Ying'er went to see the boss the next morning to plead Daniu's case. Human hearts are made of flesh, she thought. Some good words should warm his. She'd say as much as she needed to help Daniu.

Without his front teeth, the boss looked older. She knew the teeth meant nothing, for they would likely be replaced with gold ones soon, and that would make him look even more imposing. What mattered to the boss most was the loss of face over being beaten up by an ordinary worker, for his underlings and his rivals would take advantage of that. He did not occupy an especially high-ranking position, but it was one with great monetary potential.

Ying'er took a good look at the boss, a first for her. He had an unusual face, of a kind she found least appealing,

"I've come to plead Daniu's case," she said as she lowered her eyes.

"Fine," he replied unhesitatingly.

She looked at him with surprise, for she'd expected him to turn her down flat.

"Fine." His eyes glowed brightly as he stared at her. "The one who tied the bell has to untie it. He came to plead your case, and now you're pleading his. One favor for another."

"Thank you," Ying'er said.

"But it all depends on you, on your agreement to a condition."

"What's that?"

"What do you think?" He continued, his bright eyes still on

226

her, "Maybe I'm too impatient. How's this? We won't get married yet, because you need to get to know me. We'll try it out for a while. If it works, we'll go ahead; if not, we won't."

The mention of "try it out" made her sick to her stomach. She understood exactly what it entailed. She felt a hand clasping her throat, and she had to fight for air. "No, I can't do that," she strained to say.

He walked out from behind his desk and came toward her. She backed to the door, afraid he might try brute force. With one foot in the room and one foot out, she planned to hold on to the door jamb and scream if he dared force himself upon her.

He knew what she was thinking and smiled. "Then I'll have to let the law take care of things. Just think how many people work here. If everyone wanted to slug me, would I have any teeth left?"

Ying'er felt a pounding in her head as she struggled to continue, "I'm just here to do what I can. Please don't be too harsh on him. Give him a way out and be lenient."

The boss chortled. Ying'er felt a powerful wave of fright and disgust sweep through her head, so powerful she thought she might pass out. She backed out the door, only to see some workers watching her. They knew why she was there, for sure, and she felt she'd let them down. "I'm worthless," she thought.

She headed back to her room. It was only a short distance, but it felt interminable. The pounding in her head continued. I did the best I could, she said to herself.

Men disgusted her. Why do they all have to be like that?

"Hurry, everybody. It's Daniu, he's dead!" The shouts shattered the early-morning calm.

Ying'er went out the door with Lanlan to see a large crowd clamoring around one of the lakes. Sansan ran up and let out a frightening howl. Baozi was already there, sobbing.

Daniu's body was floating in the water. It was hard to see if he was injured. The dark green water presented only a silhouette. The workers all stared blankly. Some sighed now and then, drawn-out but hollow.

Ying'er noticed signs of a disturbance on the ground in front of the lake, in which Daniu's body moved in a gentle arc. Had there been a struggle? A fight? Did he fall in accidentally? No, he wouldn't have drowned if he had, but would have floated safely on the salt-saturated water, just as Baozi had when Daniu had flung him into the water to impress her.

The police arrived from town, bringing along a medical officer. The workers parted for them impassively, but then were told to fish Daniu out. They did, and laid him out on the ground, face-up, his sightless eyes staring into the bright sunlight. There were no marks on his face, which was already slightly bloated.

After telling the workers to remove Daniu's clothes, the medical officer asked the women to leave the scene. Then he set about examining the body.

Sansan had stopped crying, as Lanlan, her face ashen, laid her hand on her arm. Ying'er was choking up. She could not understand how Daniu could be dead. He'd been making plans to run off to Xinjiang, with or without her. Clearly, he'd died under suspicious circumstances, she thought, but no one was saying anything. Such a simple, straightforward man, could he have lost his life over a couple of teeth?

Sansan shuddered. Ying'er could tell how deeply she'd cared for him. Not a particularly good-looking woman, she brimmed with vitality and would have been a good match. Daniu, Fate did not treat you well, Ying'er said silently. She recalled how he'd felt about her, had been annoyed by how he'd attached himself to her, and at times almost felt defiled by his attention. But as she

228

thought back now, she was touched by his sincerity and devotion. The pain turned into something warm, which in turn led to tears.

Ying'er put her arm around Sansan, who was staring blankly, her eyes sunken and dry. The desert wind and sun had sucked the moisture out of her skin and sprinkled her face with sunspots. She would never have fair skin so long as she worked under the blistering sun

In the distance, the medical representative was still examining Daniu's body, with curious workers looking on. Ying'er could not bring herself to look, and was reminded of the callouses and gaping leg wounds Sansan had so carefully stitched for him.

Baozi came over to squat by Sansan.

"He has no visible wounds, only a few bruises here and there, but his shirt was in tatters, torn to pieces, actually. It looked like a monster had reached out from the water to drag him in." Baozi dried his tears and continued, "The doctor said he could tell that his lungs were filled with water, so he'd drowned. But you have to agree, that's odd, because it's damned hard to kill yourself in that water. Daniu must have been forced under after he fell in. That has to be it.

"Even the boss can only shake his head. He said he'd asked the police to stop their investigation, it was only a couple of teeth . . . who could imagine Daniu would die like that?

"Maybe he really wanted to kill himself. He could have wrapped his arms around a chunk of the salt crust before jumping in to keep himself under. When he died and let go of the crust, the water pushed him to the surface."

The question people would be asking themselves and others for days was: Why?

Daniu was to be cremated.

All the workers went to see him off. His parents came, and wailed like cows. Two shriveled people, like dehydrated eggplants.

It was hard to imagine how they could have produced a son like Daniu. The old man howled, as tears dripped from his stubble, while his wife beat her chest. When sent for by the management station, they had only been told that Daniu had had an accident, and were stunned to see that their son had already turned into a corpse covered by a red flannel sheet. To avoid saddening them more, the workers tried to keep them away from the body. He had drowned, that was certain. Following the lead of the boss, the medical examiner declared that it was a suicide; the police held a different opinion, but nothing more was done.

There were various views of why he would take his own life. Maybe he hadn't wanted to be caught and tortured by the police. Or maybe he despaired over the loss of his job at the salt lakes. Hopelessness was thought by some who subscribed to the suicide theory that he felt he had nothing to live for after Ying'er's rejection. That last view got the police interested in talking to Ying'er, who told them what Daniu had said the last night she saw him.

Those words would stay with her for a long time.

19

Lanlan and Ying'er felt as if they were falling apart physically, after several days of working on the sand ridge, and in spirit after seeing how little their hard work had accomplished. They did not want to cut corners, so their ridge was much shorter after three days than the ones others had managed in one.

"The way we're going, we won't make any money after paying for our meals. This doesn't look like somewhere we can stay for long," said Lanlan. "What do you say we settle up and go home?"

Ying'er felt terrible about what had happened to Daniu. People were pointing, she discovered, and the pressure was becoming unbearable. The work was hard, and, for the first time, she did not feel like staying. They decided to hold out till the end of month, and leave for home after receiving their pay.

They prepared for their departure by turning their remaining flour into steamed buns, and broke them into walnut-sized pieces, which they fried into crispy bread. They also pickled some scallions that were old but still edible.

Lanlan asked Wu to return the wool blankets and cookware to the boss for them. Feeling bad about how things had turned out, Wu gave them three sacks of salt. According to convention, Mongolian herders got free salt for themselves and for their camels, so Lanlan accepted the gifts. They went looking for the herder, paid him for his effort, and got their camel back. Its hump had grown back after weeks of rest and grazing. But it didn't look the same to Ying'er, though she couldn't say why. It was just a feeling.

Daniu had taken their leather flask with him the day he'd walked out, so Lanlan had to buy a plastic jug for water at the management station shop. The camel would carry the sacks of salt, so they would not be able to ride.

"We can walk," Ying'er said. "That's what legs are for."

Lanlan assured her that so long as they were not bothered by jackals or other wild animals, they would travel in a straight line and not get lost again.

Ying'er legs went soft at the mention of jackals. But she managed to hide her fear from Lanlan, for she knew that the terrifying ordeal that had cost them a camel and nearly their lives was always on her sister-in-law's mind too. For now, they had to keep up their morale and avoid anything self-defeating. If either of them openly admitted their fears, fright that had yet to become real would be enough to terrorize them, even keep them from venturing out into the desert again to return home.

Lanlan checked their weapon supplies: they had half of a sack of gunpowder and some buckshot. She was afraid of predators, but there was nothing she could do about that; they had to either traverse the desert or take a long detour. Traveling in a straight line meant they'd reach home in less than a week, if they didn't get lost. Taking a detour was harder to predict, but would require at least three weeks.

"Let's follow the short route taken by the ancestors," Lanlan said.

Ying'er agreed.

To fill out what they'd need, they bought kerosene, batteries, and other supplies. The kerosene was for the lantern, whose shade had been smashed during their encounter with the jackals. Luckily, the shop also carried glass shades. They bought bicycle ball bearings to use as ammunition on wild animals, as well as firecrackers that would be more effective than her musket in scaring them off.

"Anything else will merely cost money and add to the camel's load," Lanlan said. Ying'er agreed with everything Lanlan said, since her sister-in-law was a more experienced desert traveler, despite their shared experience a mere few months before. They'd make do with the buns and water for the few days it would take to get home.

After returning the borrowed cookware, they said goodbye to Sansan, who still had not gotten over the death of Daniu, and was sorry to lose the companionship. Baozi had given up the life at the salt lakes shortly after Daniu's cremation and returned home. He did not even have the heart to say good-bye. The boss, whose role in Daniu's death was heatedly talked about by the workers, was seldom seen outside the management station after the rushed cremation, making it unnecessary for Ying'er to avoid him. She could not forget how he'd looked at her when she'd gone to plead Daniu's case. Had her rejection of a mean-spirited suitor led to the death of a decent one? She desperately hoped not.

After drawing the pay for their last month, they set out early one morning before the sun began sending down its relentless heat. Ying'er felt a sense of emptiness as she considered what the few sacks of salt and the little bit of money they were returning with had cost them, physically, mentally, and emotionally. She recalled the high hopes and sense of adventure they'd started with. So much had happened since then that their departure could be considered a sort of retreat. But they had survived encounters with wild animals, burying sand, the loss of half their transport, and prolonged hunger and thirst in the desert. Unlike the vast majority of women in their village and beyond, they had worked at jobs they never could have imagined back home, and had been paid for their effort. They were tougher than they'd been when they set out.

Now they were back in the desert. Their hard work had infused them with stronger legs, and they walked with light, springy steps the first couple of days. The camel, however, looked to be straining, even before they'd traveled far. The load would surely be too heavy if they had a long way to go, but they figured it ought to be able to carry a couple of hundred kilos for this short trip without trouble. To conserve their animal companion's strength, Lanlan chose gentle slopes, and yet the camel still panted hard and salivated visibly.

Dark, late autumn clouds blocked out the sun to keep the heat down. The sky had not been so overcast when they left the salt lakes region, only some puffy gray clouds. They would have waited before taking off if had there been dark clouds like these, for large drops of rain could be hiding in them, given the mercurial change of weather in the desert. They hoped the clouds would be blown across the hills by the desert wind. Neither of them worried much about it.

Their steps were light, but not their hearts. The shiny broad road in their dream had darkened. What would they do when they got home? Lanlan said she'd come back to the salt lakes if life got too hard back home.

"What would you do there? You'd be like the temporary workers, exhausting yourself day in and day out to earn enough to survive, trading your youth for a life that would gradually be whittled away. Is that really what you want?" Ying'er said.

"When you look at it that way, religious practice is still the best option," Lanlan said. "I'll return to the Vajravārāhī Cave and gain some peace of mind at least."

Before they left the village, there had been two places with frequent crowds and a bit of excitement: the first was the Vajravārāhī Cave, the second was White Tiger Pass. The former, a grotto containing a trove of documents and cultural relics, had been discovered by villagers digging in the mountain. After they reinforced the cave, an official from the Department of Religion declared it to be a site in which to perform Buddhist rites. Later on, the wealthy entrepreneur Shuangfu put up the money for power lines and moved a dozen old houses from Liangzhou to the grounds outside the cave to attract villagers, who loved novelty. For Lanlan, the Cave was a refuge, a place where she could gain serenity.

"What's the point of religious practice if it's only the 'best option'?" Ying'er asked pointedly.

"I still think I'll go back to it when we return. It's something I know."

Compared with a host of other things in life, Ying'er discovered, what Lanlan wanted was still more meaningful than what she could think of for herself. No matter what, the accumulation of good karma would not vanish just because the body was gone. Could it be that the earliest practitioners had come up with the idea of looking for meaning in a largely meaningless world after experiencing a sense of helplessness? Like us? Religion, for Lanlan, provided an answer. For Ying'er, answers were more elusive.

"I guess we have to travel down some paths in life whether they're meaningful or not," she said and decided to put off talking about their predicaments. She knew she hadn't earned enough to get her brother another wife. The salt wasn't likely to make up the difference either. Then there was the lost camel. Lanlan, on her part, knew they would be back where they'd started and felt terrible about what would happen to Ying'er once they returned. She realized that she was fortunate; her parents would take her in and let her stay for as long as she wanted. Her father hadn't been supportive of her Buddhist practice, but she didn't think he'd object if she worked on their meager plot and took over the household chores. For Ying'er, whose son was in the care of Lanlan's mother, who would not give him up no matter what Ying'er decided to do with her life, the options were far more limited.

In the end, the rain came.

It started with muffled rumbles from the dark clouds, but those few thunderclaps bought down a surprising cataract of water. Not a single drop had fallen from the sky to soothe their parched lips on their way over, and now, with enough food and water to keep them safe and alive, eager to go home, there was a cloudburst. The rain bucketed down with full force; with no warning, a curtain of geysers was pulled straight down on them, and they were drenched before they could react.

Being the careful sort, Ying'er had put together enough provisions, including water, steamed buns and other staples, for ten days of travel. She had forgotten about rainwear. They had not expected to run into any rain, let alone a deluge. It felt as if the gods were picking a fight with them or pulling a prank when they least expected it. Yet another setback, a supernatural one on their journey. Ying'er's mother would say that with fortune as an adversary, nothing they did would ever work out. Fortune, she'd say, does not smile on the needy or the deserving.

"Is this what fate has had in store for us all along?" Lanlan wondered aloud.

The rain seeped into the sand. Their path wasn't muddy, but the wet sand stuck to their shoes and made progress harder than usual. It was tough going, but tolerable. The worst came from rain that seemed to assault them from all directions, with water flowing down their hair and into their eyes. It was white as far as the eye could see, while the sounds of pelting rain filled their ears.

The raindrops were big and powerful, almost like whips. At first, their skin felt the pounding of each drop, but soon they were numbed by rain so cold their teeth clattered. It was, after all, late autumn. When the sun showed its face, the chill moved away, but then the clouds took over. Their faces were pale, their lips purple, and goosebumps covered their exposed arms. It was terrible.

Lanlan looked tiny as she walked along holding the camel's

reins. Her clothes were plastered against her body. Gritting teeth tautened her cheeks, an uncanny copy of her mother. Ying'er was fond of her sister-in-law and fearful of her mother-in-law, who was cunning and headstrong. Would Lanlan become just like her mother? Ying'er wondered. Hard to say. She had found that so many pleasant girls unknowingly turned into severe mothers-in-law; they lost their femininity and gained the shrewish qualities of a crone.

Please don't turn into your mother, Lanlan. Ying'er said silently. On second thought, she wondered if she herself would become her mother. She'd heard from villagers that her mother had been a beauty known far and wide. Yet life had turned her into a notorious harridan, though Ying'er knew she'd been forced to change. So Lanlan's mother could have been like Lanlan now, and life had made her into a mother-in-law who made Ying'er's knees buckle at the mere thought.

She felt something warm in her eyes. Please don't ever become your mother, Lanlan, she repeated silently. Then she realized that Lanlan would not want to change, but your clothes are tainted yellow when you walk through a rapeseed field. Change or not, oftentimes isn't up to the individual. Then how about Lingguan? Would he become another Laoshun? Again, hard to say. Even if he were to return so they could actually spend the rest of their lives together, who could guarantee that they wouldn't become his parents, sniping at each other like fighting scorpions? There must have been a great force in life to change his parents into people they hadn't wanted to be. She despaired at the realization.

Her thoughts made the rain more bearable. The rainstorm would stop at some point, while the "change" she refused to accept might be something beyond human control. How awful. She took a closer look at Lanlan, who, she discovered, did resemble her mother, but had something that was absent on her mother's face. Maybe it had to do with the Vajravārāhī. She'd heard that you can hardly change your fate unless you have a spiritual belief, something that has the power to alter your destiny.

The going was getting tougher. Their shoes were weighted down by the wet sand, compounded by the fact that they were walking up a dune. They would have taken a break earlier and waited for the rain to pass if they'd known it was coming. But it had started before they'd reached the halfway point of the dune, when the slope was gentle and the climb was easier. Now as the slope grew steeper, they were having a great deal more trouble. Ying'er wanted to find a spot to rest, but knew the rain wasn't going to stop any time soon. They'd have to wait until they reached the downslope to rest.

She held on to the litter to help her move forward. The camel was soaking wet. It had molted during the summer heat. When they first came into the desert, the camel had been molting, but not noticeably, and now it had shed all its hair, looking like a plucked chicken. It then dawned on her that the herder must have sheared off the camel's hair, which was quite valuable. He had gotten more than his fair share out of the arrangement. She recalled how, when they first got the animal back, it had looked strange to her, but she hadn't let that concern her, and it was too late now.

Lanlan stopped when they reached a swirl in a flat area.

"Let's take a break to eat something," Lanlan said, as she opened the sack, only to see that the buns had turned mushy.

"I don't mind. Mushy's better than nothing." Ying'er said encouragingly.

The buns were sticky and not very tasty, but they ate as much as they could, with the help of the pickled scallions.

The camel was huffing, stopping to lick the rain dripping down its shoulder.

"The salt is melting," Lanlan said indifferently.

Sure enough, the salt sacks were not as full as when they'd

started out. What a shame, Ying'er thought, but she said, "Let it melt. If that's what Heaven wants, there's nothing we can do. At least the camel's happy," she commented wryly. The salt was nothing compared to camel hair that that could have fetched several hundred yuan, she felt like saying, but didn't. She didn't want Lanlan to feel bad, but to her surprise, Lanlan brought it up herself.

"Did you just realize that?" Ying'er asked.

"I noticed back at the lake, but what could we do, two women from out of town? Besides, we'd turned our camel over for him to graze without getting anything in writing. If we upset him, he could refuse to give it back to us, and we couldn't do a thing about it." Lanlan sighed. "Worse case, we pay for the camel hair with the money we earned."

After making the camel lie down, Lanlan opened a sack, scooped out some salt and put it in a plastic bowl for the camel. It stretched out its lips and with a slurp, began to chew noisily and happily.

The women, however, looked wretched, their wet clothes felt clammy. Rain flowed down from hair plastered to their faces to wash their blue lips. The salt bowl was quickly filling up with rain, but the camel screwed up its lips and slurped up the wet salt, looking cheerful and unhurried. Ying'er felt a calmness when she looked at it. Camels are such good-natured animals, she said to herself. Come rain or wind, they always look unhurried; they must know that anxiety is useless when dealing with a world beyond their control.

After slurping up the salt crystals, the camel kept drinking the increasingly tasteless salted water. Hoping for more, it gazed at Lanlan, who said it was enough for now and got up to tie the sack. The salt continued to melt, but she was in no mood to do anything about it. What they wanted most at that moment was not money or love, but a warm bed, for which they would have to wait. Humans can be quite frail. When Lanlan was well fed and warmly clad, what she treasured most was the Vajravārāhī. But at this moment, even her favorite deity was less attractive than a warm bed. The animal side of human nature demands creature comforts.

Ying'er discovered that their feet were being buried in a sand flow.

Shifting sand was coming their way.

They did not know that's what it was at first, for they'd only heard about shifting sand in stories. They had no idea how sand shifted. When a gusty wind blew, they saw sand travel up the edge of a shady trough over to a sunny one, which was how a dune moved. The sand could bury houses and crops, but the villagers never called it shifting sand, for a dune moved at a glacial pace, a process mostly gone unnoticed by people. This was a carpet of sand that shifted before their eyes. Likely the surface of the dune was too saturated to take in all the falling rain, so the water flowed down the slope, taking enormous amounts of sand with it.

The watery mix rose above their feet before they noticed it. Ying'er froze in terror; she'd never seen anything like it. Death had not frightened her up till now, but she was terrified at the thought of being buried alive in wet sand.

Lanlan was less flustered, as she quickly freed her feet. The sand felt solid, unlike gooey mud. It had such a powerful pull it took great effort to get her feet out, so she told Ying'er to move hers. By straining hard, Ying'er managed to get one foot out, and Lanlan helped her with the other. "We'll be buried alive if we stay here," Lanlan said. She got the camel up and they trudged up the steep dune, despite the rain.

Shifting sand does not occur everywhere. Since it follows the flow of water, it builds up in hollows. Lanlan avoided depressions, choosing to travel on prominent rises. They managed to skirt a few treacherous spots, but that made Ying'er dizzy. The sand

240

seemed to encircle her and the sky was spinning. She thought she might pass out.

When she looked up, she could not see the top of the dune. The rain had blurred everything, spreading a gray pall over the horizon and the entire landscape. She had no idea what time it was, just that it must be afternoon. Without the rain, they'd have been able to guess the hour, but rain had slowed time down. Had a few minutes passed, or a few hours? All they knew was they must crest the dune if they did not want to be buried by the shifting sand.

Lanlan kept to flatter areas and shaded troughs, following a zig-zag route to make the trek easier, but still sometimes they had to walk through sand in motion. Gradually, Ying'er realized that it wasn't as scary as she'd thought, that she'd be safe if she moved her feet fast enough. The camel, on the other hand, was heavy, and its feet kept sinking into the sand, with a dull, unpleasant sucking sound as it lumbered along behind them. Its sides rose and fell as it breathed noisily.

The sky had darkened, either because of the clouds or because dusk was descending. Jagged edges of lightning stung their eyes, and the rumble of thunder kept drawing closer. Sometimes an explosive thunderclap frightened the camel into tossing its head. Its feet were making sucking sounds, and the shifting sand appeared to be building. Ying'er's legs were sore; she was dead tired, but she did not dare slow down. Lanlan reminded her to take smaller steps to increase the pace of movement. The rain did not appear to be stopping anytime soon and, worse yet, they still could not see the top of the dune. Drained of energy, Ying'er gasped for air, swallowing rain water, and yet thirst dogged her. At least she didn't feel cold anymore, and she may have been sweating. Lanlan was swaying and stumbling on shaky feet, dragging the camel along with her movement. Things did not look good,

241

Ying'er knew.

Suddenly, she saw Lanlan throw down the reins and sit down on the sand, looking about to act up, or "play a dead dog," in the local term, a common ruse among Liangzhou women. Liangzhou had many well-known cases of miscarried justice; some had been rectified, thanks to a woman's "playing a dead dog." When all appeals had gone unheard, the women would sit down, wrap their arms around the municipal party secretary's legs and not let go until the grievance was redressed. Was Lanlan using the tactic on the gods? Ying'er wondered, when Lanlan called out to her, "Hurry, lie down." Ying'er hesitated as she saw sand rising to her ankles. "Lie down," Lanlan shouted again. Now Ying'er understood. She lay down and would have laughed at her silly thought about Lanlan "playing a dead dog,' if the situation weren't so perilous. The sand surged under her, so with a twist of her body she began to float atop it.

Their camel stood dumbly. Lanlan called to it, but it seemed not to have heard or understand the command. The sand quickly submerged its feet, then rose nearly up to its knees. "Kneel, kneel," she shouted. The animal was too frightened to move, however, and the sand quickly rose up to its belly.

Though the rain continued to fall, the western sky had brightened. Sheeting rain looked more like columns of misty smoke rising from the desert into the sky. Elsewhere everything was hazy, as if the rain had turned to steam. Ying'er felt better. It was a wonderful sensation to be carried along by the sand, almost swimming on a dune, like the time they'd "flown down" on their way to the salt lakes, nearly tearing the seats of their pants, a rare lighthearted moment.

They stopped at a relatively level spot. Ying'er sat up gingerly and found she wasn't sinking, so she stayed put. Her teeth clattered and her exposed arms were covered in goosebumps, with a greenish tint, like Lanlan's face. They could freeze if the rain continued through the night. They had a cigarette lighter to start a fire, but where would they find anything to burn?

The red hue had disappeared from the sky, and the rain had died down a bit, while the sand had stopped moving. Seeing Lanlan asleep in a heap, Ying'er woke her up so she wouldn't catch cold. They sat blankly, wordlessly, before crawling over to the camel. Its legs were almost completely buried. When Lanlan tugged at the reins, it tried to get up but could not move.

They shouted commands; it stretched out its neck, but its legs remained stuck. It had taken nearly all their energy to fend off the chill, and they were too exhausted to do more.

"Forget it for now. We'll spend the night here and dig its legs out tomorrow," Lanlan said.

It was a relatively safe place to rest, so after eating some water-soaked buns and feeding the camel more salt, they leaned against their immobilized companion and fell asleep as it crunched away.

20

The chill woke Ying'er up. Wind coming off the dune cut like ice water; the rain had not stopped, though it had lessened. Wet clothes against their skin was nearly unbearable; the parts of her body resting against the camel were warm, but the rest of her was chilled to the bone. Her throat hurt and she was racked by shivers. This was a terrible time to catch cold, she thought, as she rubbed the pressure points on her hand between the thumb and the index finger, then her temples, and finally her knuckles. I can't get sick, I'd be a burden to Lanlan. Please don't let anything happen to me now, she prayed to Lanlan's Vajravārāhī, despite her lack of faith in the deity.

Lanlan sneezed and woke up. She groped her way over to hold Ying'er tightly. "Someone has to take the headwind, so it might as well be me."

"We'll take turns," Ying'er replied, feeling warmer now, with Lanlan in front and the camel in back. She tightened her arms around Lanlan, to bring some warmth to Lanlan's back.

It was too dark to see stars. The raindrops were smaller, but denser, giving their faces no chance to dry. Ying'er was grateful for the warmth from the camel. After a while, she made Lanlan turn to lean against the camel and put her arms around her. Lanlan said no, but Ying'er insisted.

Lightning continued to crackle in the distance, accompanied by the dull sound of thunder. The camel was snorting comfortably, but sounded like a dying old man. They managed to keep their fronts and backs warm by switching around, but they were sitting on what felt like ice. "I wouldn't be greedy and ask for a warm bed now. A bale of wheat stalks would be enough," Lanlan said. Ying'er merely smiled.

"I feel closer to you than to anyone else in my life," Lanlan said emotionally. "There are my parents, of course, but we're so different they can never understand me. You and I have looked death in the eye together. You can't go on without me, and I can't live without you. We're inseparable."

"I feel the same. You have to agree that the gods were kind to give us each a companion we can rely on."

They changed positions again, and Ying'er felt herself plunged into an ice cellar. The wind blew against her chest, with nothing to block its path. She shivered, wondering when dawn would arrive. "Why don't you take my place?" Lanlan said. "I'm used to staying on the outside."

Ying'er would not have it. "You're flesh and blood, like me."

Lanlan tightened her arms around her and said, "Let's keep talking. At a time like this, if we can't stay awake, we could die in our sleep."

That sounded like a good idea to Ying'er, but neither of them could find anything to say. The few things they forced themselves to talk about quickly bored them.

"Let's light the lantern," Lanlan suggested. She took off her vest and told Ying'er to use it to block the rain, concerned that the heated shade might explode if it came in contact with the rain. She groped around the load on the camel to find the lantern and then the lighter. It lit with a single flick to light up the darkness. But lighting the lantern was harder, since the flame could not reach the wick. Ying'er rolled up some camel hair they'd saved and dipped it into the kerosene; finally, the lantern was lit.

The light that split open the surrounding darkness somehow warmed Ying'er. She put the vest away and leaned forward to shelter the lantern from the rain with her body. The pungent odor of the kerosene did not dampen her spirits. Besides bringing light, a lantern was a good heating device. When she put her hands close to the glass shade, a warm current wormed its way into her palms, and from there to her heart through her arms. "Lanlan, warm yourself with this," she called out.

The heat from the lantern was limited, but a hedge against the cold. They realized that their hands were warm, but by leaning forward they left the warmth of the camel and began to shiver. Ying'er felt raindrops on her hand and saw them splatter against the lantern shade with a sizzle. She cast a worried look at Lanlan. Lanlan adjusted the flame to make sure they did not burn their hands; when the shade lost heat, she turned up the flame, and when it was too hot, she turned it down.

It was getting light out. They ate more mushy buns with scallions and then tried to dislodge the camel. The wet sand still had too great a pull for it to free its legs on its own. "It'll die if we can't free it," Lanlan said. "The sun's blistering heat will kill it before the day's out if it doesn't move."

They started digging, scooping out wet sand that held the camel motionless. Possibly sensing they were helping, it neither struggled nor complained. Together they freed one leg at a time, until, with a shout of relief they helped their companion escape the trap that had held it overnight. It cried out happily the moment it was free. Ying'er saw that the salt on its back had melted in the rain and that the sacks were completely flat. That did not concern her. So many things mattered so little to her now that she had flirted with death, the wind and the rain. She could not tell if the feeling came from her weary heart or if it was part of the aging process. But it made no difference. It was the same for Lanlan. Meditation in the Vajravārāhī Cave had taught her how to avoid the trials of daily living, and in their moments of crisis, had brought her a sense of calmness.

Afterward, Lanlan said that as far as she was concerned, the lantern had saved them from dying in their sleep on that cold, wet night. Another perilous incident survived.

They resumed their homeward trek the next day, the last day and night they would spend in the desert. On the following morning, after another breakfast of sodden buns and water, for them and their treasured camel, the sight of a bit of foliage—Artemisia and desert rice—cheered them and infused their legs with strength they did not know they had. Their camel, too, no longer burdened with heavy bags of salt, seemed to glide over the sand. Despite the scorching heat, with the sun directly overhead, they saw signs of life in outlying fields. They were greeted by village dogs. Their return had not been anticipated, and would not attract much attention. The villagers' minds were preoccupied with gold that had recently been discovered nearby at White Tiger Pass.

A month before they'd set out, Shuangfu, the village's preeminent entrepreneur, had brought dozens of young men to White Tiger Pass to dig pits and build wooden enclosures, telling people they were panning for gold. He had been ridiculed by everyone, including Laoshun, Lanlan's father, who had said, "There's no gold in this corner of the desert, a place where even wolves won't shit." His fellow villagers agreed, mocking Shuangfu, who met with resistance when he tried to hire village boys.

Everyone waited to see Shuangfu make a fool of himself. To their amazement, a month later, he actually produced some gold.

Water zigzagged its way from the village reservoir like a silver snake to the panning trough, where loose sand was washed away, leaving behind a thin layer of bright yellow flecks. So this is gold, they commented when Shuangfu displayed his newly unearthed riches.

With that craze occupying the villagers, young and old alike, the return of the two weary women went unnoticed. Seeing a single bedraggled camel with soggy, empty sacks across its back, Laoshun demanded to know what had happened to his camel. When he was told it had ended up in the bellies of jackals, he nearly exploded with rage, but had to remind himself that Lanlan and Ying'er's safe return was worth more than a camel. Their appearance made it abundantly clear that they had been punished by the desert and all that had befallen them over the months they had been gone. Listening to Ying'er recount their experience fighting the jackals, he smiled, unable to suppress his pride over Lanlan's bravery, while his wife sighed and cried out in fear over the most frightening parts. Lanlan sat silently, keenly aware that she had returned in disgrace, with nothing to show for her plans, no salt, a dead camel, and so little money for their work at the salt lakes as to be meaningless. It had been easy to brush off familial pressure and declare her plan of working the family plot and meditating, but now back at home she was immediately besieged by demands from within and without. Dealing with the intended divorce, once again forced to live in the same village as Huaqiu and his suicidal wife, and facing an uncertain reception by family and her fellow meditators would be trying. She knew it would be even worse for Ying'er.

Laoshun rued the loss of his camel for days. What a shame that such a fine camel, good enough to be a stud, had ended up killed and eaten by jackals. He choked up every time he thought about it. But not openly. He kept it to himself, telling the two women to pay for the camel hair and not mentioning his camel again. In his eyes, it was another disaster the heavens cast his way, and he'd just have to take it. He could not bring himself to fault two frail women who had actually escaped from a pack of hungry jackals and more.

After they'd been home a few days, Lanlan reentered the Vajravārāhī Cave.

She went to practice the seven-day meditation, keeping body and mind pure for seven days; putting aside every life entanglement, focused on reciting the Vajravārāhī mantra. In the thang-ka illustration, the Vajravārāhī stands with her feet atop the sun and moon on a lotus flower, holding sacred objects in her hands. These images all have symbolic references, lotus for quiet and purity, the moon for compassion, and the sun for wisdom. Every symbol, no matter how arcane, points to being good and kind.

The Cave, being small, could only accommodate seven or eight practitioners for each seven-day meditation. During the period, no one was allowed out (except to relieve oneself), or in (except those delivering food), or to talk (except the one enlightening the disciples), or, especially, to loaf. In any case, there were taboos against many things.

Ying'er's situation grew worse. As Lanlan refused to return to Bai Fu and his family, Ying'er's mother wanted her back home to be remarried. She was expected to leave the baby behind, which they all assumed would be the ideal situation for both families. She felt her mother-in-law's eyes on her back whenever she was out of her room. There were no arguments, but the older woman's solicitous attitude was as disconcerting as it was phony.

The room that had been the core of her existence, where she had lived for a time with a troubled and sickly Hantou, for so long, now felt desolate, filled with a gloomy chill. She heated the kang, but failed to drive away the cold that kept boring into her bones. She was no longer the Ying'er of yesterday, and this was not the same house anymore. She touched her baby's tender face. A warmth rippled inside her, a sensation that had helped her through many lonely nights. A woman must have something to look forward to, sometimes a lover, sometimes a baby, and sometimes other things. Without that something, life is not worth living.

Lingguan had once said that love was just a feeling. The comment had saddened her for a long time. How could sacred love be just a feeling? Now she knew it can be nothing else. The yard was the same, so was the house. The sun had always shone down on the yard, where people talked and laughed, a place infused with peace, plenitude, liveliness. Now it was all gone, as if Lingguan had taken the soul of the place with him, leaving only an old and ugly, stinking shell.

249

And, of course, now that her husband was dead, her status in his family was that of an outsider, despite the presence of her infant son.

As Ying'er lay in bed, the baby beside her, she wondered what life held for her now. She would not be welcome here after her son grew up, and returning to her own home was unthinkable. Maybe Lanlan had the right idea: a religious life provided at least a tangible alternative to despair.

She heard stirrings in the next room. Someone was cautiously shuffling out the door. She knew it must be her mother-in-law, checking to ensure that the lock on the gate had not been disturbed, and that no one had gone through it. Her mother-in-law was afraid she'd run off with the baby.

The footsteps were indeed heading toward the gate, where the lock rang out, followed by more footsteps, and finally all was quiet again.

Tears fell. She tried to hold back, but the disappointing tears always came. No one had ever treated her with such suspicion before. She recalled how she had returned, carrying emotional scars the months away had created, only to be treated as an interloper. Now her mother-in-law guarded against her as if she were a thief.

She discovered that someone had rifled through her chest and walked off with her wedding gift, a bolt of fabric. That was all right with her. She didn't care; she was the daughter-in-law, and it was within her mother-in-law's right to expect something from her. But she ought to have asked first. She could have opened the chest while Ying'er was home; instead she'd waited until Ying'er was away, perhaps thinking she might never return from the desert. Her own mother had crossed the line many times, and now so had her mother-in-law. How could they be so petty, acting so unlike mothers over something so small? They gave "mother" a bad name.

She looked up at the ceiling. It did not appear as if the cover over the cut-out had been disturbed. Beneath it was a chunk of opium, procured when Hantou had been gravely ill. They'd planned to use it when he ran out of painkillers. As with so many women over the centuries who had been abused, demeaned, and discarded, a swallowed chunk of opium offered a way out. She had dreamed about it many times, but each time her baby had brought her back to reality.

Tearing off the cover, she took down the small packet and stashed it inside her undergarment. Maybe it will be of use one day. Love and hope were the reasons for her to stay alive, and for them, she could also die. If she could not live an unsoiled life, she preferred a spotless death.

For a long while she'd felt like a specter drifting in a dream world. The dark nights had seemed to dissolve both her body and her soul. Nighttime had completed a cycle in her life; at first the night was just a night and had nothing to do with her, a separate entity. Later when she met Lingguan, the night had brought her happiness and carnal pleasures. Much later, the night was once again just a night, and so she lingered. It became nearly interminable; she did her best to endure the unending hours, but the eastern sky seemed never to light up.

She was weary, as if she had been traveling down an endless path, with no light to shine on it nor stars to point the way. There was no wind or rain, just silence; not even footsteps. She had heard that after you died, you had to pick up all the footprints you left behind in this world before you could be reborn. She felt like a ghost walking down a winding road at night, searching for footprints buried in the passing of time. Many of her mental pictures had yellowed, like water-logged old paintings. What excited her had ceased to exist; what made her ache no longer caused her pain. It was like flipping through someone else's photo album; few things stirred her heart now, as it was steeped in loneliness.

One thing was clear to her: eventually, she had to leave the room, the yard, and the feeling that was already fading. But it was Panpan's home, and she did not want to leave.

21

Bai Fu came, looking embarrassed and nervous. This was his first visit since the return of Lanlan, his estranged wife, and his sister. The last time he'd been there, he had stormed in with some of his friends and, without so much as a word, grabbed Ying'er and left. It was a drama common among families who exchanged daughters to marry their sons.

Lanlan's mother had managed to keep the baby with her. Bai Fu and his lackeys had not used brute force, as that could have ended badly. Laoshun had stood in the doorway with an angry look and a chopper in his hand.

"You want his mother, we can't argue against it," he said, "but the baby stays. Force the issue, and I'll lop off those bloody gourds on your shoulders, or I'm nothing."

"Sure, the baby can stay," one of his friends had said. "Bai Fu, leave the boy alone. It's fair that they want to continue the family line, but it's also fair that the boy should be with his mother. We'll take her back home and leave it to the court to decide which one is more justified."

Ying'er had stayed with her family only a few days at the time before running away and returning to her in-laws' home on that rainy night. It felt like a lifetime ago and yet nothing much had changed. Bai Fu still needed a wife, and her mother would never relent.

So, he was back. To avoid arousing suspicion, he went first to greet the in-laws and said to Laoshun's wife, "Auntie, my mother isn't feeling well, and she'd like to see my sister. I'll take her home and bring her back in a few days." Laoshun's wife knew he wanted to ease her concern by saying he'd "bring her back," but she decided to go along. "What's the problem?" she asked.

"We don't know. There's a lump in her stomach, but she doesn't want to go for a checkup."

Lanlan's mother sneered. He should have made up a better illness if he wanted to lie; "a lump in her stomach" was meaningless. But she decided to go along,

"Oh, that sounds terrible. My uncle had one of those, and he howled in pain for a month before he died. I hope that's not what your mother has." She silently cursed maliciously: The old witch deserves something like that.

"I don't think so." Bai Fu was too simple-minded to see through her ruse. "She's been too good a person to get a terrible illness like that."

Without meaning to, he'd touched her sore spot. Hantou had died of liver cancer, the terrible illness that had given him a basketball-sized lump. Based on Bai Fu's reasoning, Hantou must not have been a good person, but she could not display anger, so she continued, "With illness it's hard to say. Good people can die of horrible diseases while evil people never get anything bad. It's really hard to say."

Bai Fu could not compete with her brand of social interactions, so he said,

"Auntie, will you let my sister go home for a visit?"

"Of—course." She gave a drawn-out reply. "We can't keep someone else's daughter from visiting her parents, can we? She can stay as long as she wants. We won't stand in her way."

Bai Fu nodded in agreement, either too dense to understand her insinuation about Lanlan or smart enough to see the futility of argument.

Lanlan's mother had been on tenterhooks with Ying'er around since her return from the desert, afraid the young woman would find an opportunity to run back home with her baby. Every time she went out, she had to remind her husband and Mengzi to be on guard, assigning them sentry duty, and still her heart was in her throat the whole time. She hardly slept at night, and when a wind blew or the gate creaked, she thought Ying'er was sneaking out. The baby was her grandson, but his mother was not her daughter, and trying to get the boy back after she'd taken him home would be harder than ascending into the heavens. Sometimes she thought she'd just send her back to her parents. But she couldn't get rid of her like that, not after the formal wedding ceremony. She would damage her reputation if she were to drive away her daughter-in-law, who was well thought of in the neighborhood. She'd tried to scare her into running back home, alone, but Laoshun had given her a tongue-lashing when she brought it up, calling her a cruel, wicked woman. Obviously, there is nothing as inconstant as the human heart—she'd been afraid that Ying'er wanted to go and had done everything she could to keep her, and now she couldn't wait for her daughter-in-law to leave, but without the baby.

Bai Fu was relieved, for he'd thought his sister's in-laws were still angry over the kidnapping, afraid that Mengzi might seek revenge over what his mother had told him to do. But this time, he could not say no to his mother. Besides, there was no one else she could send, for he was still Lanlan's legally married husband, even though she had left home for the Vajravārāhī Cave and refused to even see her parents. He had every right and reason to come. He was surprised by how smoothly it went. "My mother also said for Ying'er to bring the baby with her. She misses him."

"I have no say over her daughter, but she has no say over the baby." Ying'er's mother-in-law smiled coldly. "The baby stays."

"But she really misses him. That's all, nothing more." That put Lanlan's mother on her guard. She sneered. "Pack your things, Ying'er," she said. "Your mother has sent your brother to take you home." She turned to Bai Fu, "No more talk about the baby. That's my final word."

Ying'er had known what was in store for her the moment her brother showed up. She also knew that her mother-in-law had been waiting for this day. It had not taken her long to realize that she was superfluous in this family. Everything had changed so fast, like a magician's sleight-of-hand.

Panpan looked up at his mother with his large, dark pea-sized eyes, as if he sensed something. Separation by death had already occurred and, it was time to be parted from the living. It was clear she could not take Panpan along. Her heart was breaking. She forced back tears, as she cradled her son.

Her mother's illness could be real or not; it was immaterial, just an excuse. Ying'er's family had made up something to get her back home, and her husband's family now had the excuse they needed to send her away. Everyone needed an excuse, almost as if it were a tacit understanding between them. She had to go, she realized. A widow, both a reminder of a dead son and a drain on the family's resources, made her continued stay untenable.

How she wished she could spend the rest of her life in this room. She didn't want to part with the familiar yard, the familiar environment, and the familiar feeling, which had always reminded her of what she had hoped for in life. That wish was pitifully small, and yet fulfilling it was harder than escaping from jackals.

What had brought her happiness and a purpose in life was gone, and what remained was the baby. He had nearly become her whole life, but she knew that separation was inevitable.

Greedily, she feasted her eyes on Panpan, she kissed his face; greedily she watched him look at her with a smile; greedily, she

255

gazed at him, and finally her tears came.

Ying'er took one last lingering look at the room that had brought her bittersweet memories. She would like to take something with her, but she tore her eyes from everything. Her mother-in-law was a petty woman who placed great importance on such trivial things. Ying'er decided to leave it all behind, but then she changed her blouse into the one she'd worn when the fearsome jackals were chasing them in the desert. It was not made of fine material, but was a cherished item.

Bai Fu came in and said in a low voice, "Ma wants you to take whatever is yours. Bring along everything you can."

Ying'er frowned in disgust. The two mothers were the same, placing more importance on objects than on people. What I can? she asked herself. Never in her life had she been able to choose things she wanted, not once. She'd lived a wasted life.

A wasted life. Tears blurred her eyes.

"Ma said to put on all the clothes you can, and wrap the fabric around you too."

She knew her mother was referring to the wedding present and her dowry. Those were what her own mother thought about, and what her mother-in-law cared for. They meant nothing to her, and she meant nothing to either of them.

She brushed her hair hastily. In the mirror, a haggard face looked back. With a sigh, she threw down the brush and mirror and kissed the baby one last time. "Let's go then," she said through clenched teeth.

"What about what Ma said?" Bai Fu asked.

But she was already outside.

Her mother-in-law stood tenaciously guarding the door. She breathed a sigh of relief when she saw Ying'er come out empty-handed.

"I'll be off now, Ma," Ying'er said.

"Yes, you go visit your mother," her mother-in-law responded.

Ying'er brushed wind-blown hair from her face and walked to the gate.

Bai Fu followed from behind, pushing a bicycle, clanging along the way and drawing curious stares. "Going home to see your parents, Ying'er?" one of them asked. "Why aren't you taking the baby along?" She muttered a reply and walked on.

The village and its clay soil looked the same as it had when she first arrived. But she was a different person. She'd been a young virgin when she came, and was now a widow. She'd known nothing when she came, and was time-worn as she left. Tempered by her perilous desert journey and all that had happened at the salt lakes, she knew that the only thing that remained constant was her role as a woman, torn between two families and belonging to neither.

She recalled it had also been an autumn day when the rickety vehicle had brought her here, turning a girl into a woman. It had been a windy day, with dust in the air and above the road ahead. She recalled how it had felt unreal, just like now. The village, the sand, and the date tree were already turning into mere impressions of the past.

Her flight on the stormy night after the kidnapping came to mind. She'd thought she'd managed to escape her fate by going back to the home of her husband, never expecting that she'd have to return. She'd run away on her own and now she had to go back on her own. Are you happy now, Ma? You didn't have to kidnap me this time. I'm coming back willingly, that should make you smile.

"Hop on," her brother said.

She jumped onto the rear rack of the bicycle. Wind sent hair blowing in her face. She ignored it. She must look like what her mother called a scruffy ghost. Why not? I can be anything so long as it makes you happy, Ma. Life has no set form; things come and go in an instant and you can be human one minute and a ghost the next. It doesn't matter, Ma. I could be anything.

It felt good not to have the baby, for there was nothing to tie her down. Her mother-in-law cherished the baby as if he were part of her, so Ying'er needn't worry about him. Her mother had suggested going to court, but she couldn't bring herself to do that. The Chen family had suffered the death of their son, and she could not make them go through the torment of losing their grandson. The law was on her side, she knew, but she couldn't do it. Besides, with the baby being doted on by her mother-in-law, she had nothing to worry about.

Undulating vast desert sand that had given birth to boundless mysteries; mild desert wind that carried all the familiar smells; cramped, squat but pretty village houses; twisted desert date trees with endless vitality, good-bye to you all.

22

Ying'er was to be married.

In preparation for the marriage, her mother went out and bought two satin comforters and a pair of red-lacquered chests. She asked village women to make shoe soles and pillow cases for her. These would be Ying'er's dowry to accompany her to the Zhao family. The engagement ceremony and delivery of betrothal gifts were carried out at the same time; Zhao the butcher sent over ten thousand yuan in cash, and hired a car to bring her to his home.

It was a fine day, with puffy white clouds floating above distance hills, highlighting the clear sky without blotting out the sun. All their relatives came, in high spirits, pleased with the outcome of her "moving forward," which was how the villagers characterized a widow getting remarried. Zhao was, after all, a wealthy man, and the relatives felt they gained plenty of face by association. They arrived at the crack of dawn, and each offered a wedding gift that was usually about a hundred yuan. The gifts alone netted the bride's family several thousands, and the smile on her mother's face all but crowded her eyes shut.

Her eyes dry, Ying'er sat woodenly on the edge of the kang, her face a blank, her heart a void.

She shedded tears only when she was by herself; they belonged to her alone. She swallowed the tears when they flowed into her mouth. In front of people, she had nothing to say, for words were useless, as nothing could express the helplessness and reluctance she felt. She no longer harbored good thoughts about the future.

Her mother was busy running around, mightily pleased, treating her indifference as silent acceptance. But that was just her. Their relatives were surprised by her composure, but that was just them. The chests for her dowry were a dazzling red, but they were just two chests. The world and Ying'er were two entities; they were incompatible. The world could carry her body along, but her heart belonged to her alone.

As they ate, the relatives talked and laughed imprudently. Her family had put out simple dishes to tide them over. When more cars from the Zhao family came, they would all climb in grandly. The groom's family would treat them with respect and put on an impressive array for them to eat to their hearts' content, all thanks to the reluctant bride.

Her father brought her a bowl of vegetable stew, urging her to eat, for once she arrived at the Zhao's house, she'd have no time for herself. There would be the wedding ceremony, then she would be required to toast all the guests, followed by the obligatory antics in the bridal chamber. Ying'er ignored him, so he timidly laid the bowl on a bedside table and quietly walked out. She felt like calling out to him and throwing herself into his arms one last time. But the futility of any action put an end to the urge.

When the sedan arrived, she climbed in impassively. The seat was so soft she sank into it. Villagers came to watch; children ran around, whooping up a storm. Everyone, young and old, was in high spirits. This was a happy event, so naturally, people were smiling. Her mother greeted them joyfully and brought Ying'er a handful of noodles before she left.

Ying'er knew the noodles represented the fortune in her lifetime. They were indispensable, and the woman from the Zhao family who would be there to welcome the bride told her mother she'd make sure Ying'er ate them later. Ying'er would have laughed if she weren't feeling numb. She had eaten the noodles for her first marriage, and see how that had worked out.

The caravan started moving, and villagers parted to let them pass. Columns of dust rose from behind the vehicles and seemingly veiled the village and everyone in it, but not the sun, which continued to scream down at them. They turned onto a main road under the hot sun. The caravan took a different route from the one they'd taken coming over; a bridal sedan must not travel the same route twice, nor can it stop midway. With her marriage to Hantou, the bus had broken down on the road, and later Hantou had gone on before her. That seemed to have happened a lifetime ago, it also seemed to be happening right now. She'd been a mere girl then, and now she was a widow moving forward. How many years had passed in between? She wasn't sure, but it felt like no time at all. It was all a blank, except for the brief dalliance with Lingguan and the grief and pain after Hantou's death. Life was odd; when she thought back, only fragments remained of the long, critical part of her life.

A crowd waiting at the Zhao's door set off firecrackers when they saw the car. There was a large bonfire, something missing in her first marriage. Then there had been only a brazier and a bucket of water. When she'd gotten off the bus Hantou's family had sent, she'd walked over the fire, then through water, and then into the house. That had not worked to avert misfortune, and the fire and water had failed to bring good luck.

The woman welcoming the bride took Ying'er by the hand and made three turns around the fire before walking through the gate. She was barely through when someone sprinkled flour on her head—"being together until the hair turns gray." The flour spotted her red bridal costume. She ignored it.

The yard was packed with people, tables, chairs, voices and eyes. The gazes formed a net through which she entered the bridal chamber, trailed by Bai Fu's voice, "So little money, like sending off a beggar." He hadn't sounded this forceful and self-confident in years.

She knew he was talking about the money he was handed as he sat on the dowry chest. Before the chest was carried into the room, they had to pay him. He would not get up if there wasn't enough; they had to keep giving until he was satisfied with the amount. He'd then get to his feet, a signal for the bride's side of guests to get out of the vehicles.

The bridal chamber was spacious, with far more elaborate furnishings than Hantou's family had supplied. Overhead, the ceiling was draped in gaudy plastic flowers, on the walls were colorful paintings, and on the bed was flowery bedding. There were also fine tables and sofas, lending an air of wealth. A cassette player squawked on one of the tables, deafeningly loud, but on this day, she was too indifferent to care.

The fat man in a blue outfit was Butcher Zhao. With a glance out of the corner of her eye, Ying'er was reminded of the greasy face and bulbous nose she'd seen the time Matchmaker Xu had brought him to the house. That and a booming voice, even louder than Bai Fu's bragging when he won at the gambling table. It was nothing unusual; rich people were all loud. Her mother had abhorred a voice like that, complaining about the aggressiveness, but now she couldn't get enough, because "it sounded just right for a strong man."

Dizziness overwhelmed her, and everything before her seemed hazy.

The ceremony was also more festive than the first time. Fawning guests, joking guests, gawking guests, and cheering guests. Those in charge of the ceremony folded a blanket for the bride and the groom to stand on. She did what she was told, while Zhao acted shy, drawing guffaws from the villagers.

How she wished the show would soon be over. She was exhausted, as if she'd traveled a long road; weariness took over her body, and she wanted to lie down to sleep for a thousand years.

Everything was a blur, all but the chunk of opium she'd swallowed before coming out to formalize the union.

Epilogue

Lanlan came out of her meditation at the Cave and learned that Ying'er was gone. She hadn't expected things to happen so fast they would not have a chance to say good-bye. Her parents thought it was the best outcome for all involved, but not for Ying'er, Lanlan said silently. She went into the room where Ying'er had lived, vainly hoping for a note from her sister-in-law, her desert travel companion. She found nothing in the shabby room, with its peeling walls, looking weather worn, all traces of its former resident gone. She was shocked, but not surprised, that her mother had moved so fast to eliminate Ying'er's presence. It would be converted into a bridal chamber when her younger brother, Mengzi, got married, her mother told her. When she heard about the wedding, Lanlan knew that Ying'er had done it for her, sacrificing her happiness so Lanlan could be free.

She choked up and leaned against the wall.

Everything remained, including the room, the walls, and the desert date tree, but not Ying'er . . . the Ying'er who had worked so cheerfully while singing the tunes she'd learned, the Ying'er who had stood in the wind waiting for the man she loved, the Ying'er who had dug frantically to save her from being buried alive in the sand, the Ying'er who had tried to shoot a rabbit, hoping to surprise her, the Ying'er who had sucked the snake's poison out of her arm . . . weariness from all the tribulations rushed at Lanlan, and she wept silently.

Ying'er was dead, she was told, dying by her own hand before the marriage was formalized. But then rumors began to swirl in Lanlan's village. Someone said that Ying'er had swallowed the opium, but had been saved by her usually henpecked father, who'd put his foot down and demanded that the wedding be canceled. On a dusty afternoon, under a pallid twilight sky, Ying'er, who had gone through so many hardships in life, they said, walked out of the small village tucked in the crease of the desert. It was everyone's favorite version, the happiest possible ending. They were convinced she'd defied her fate and had gone in search of what she'd been looking for. They refused to believe that if she searched the wide world, she would not find Lingguan. But some were worried, for even if she found him, would it still be the same Lingguan, the one she'd longed to see for so long?

The night after Lanlan heard the rumors, she strolled alone down the path to the desert, recalling the autumn of their trek and all that she and Ying'er had gone through. She considered asking people from Bai Fu's village, but the thought of running into anyone from that family stopped her. Ying'er would be gone if she was still alive, and if not, she would still be gone. What was the point of finding out?

Wherever you are, my dear sister, I hope you're happy.

Afterword

The novel you've just finished is set in the late twentieth century, when residents of China's major cities and the coastal provinces were already enjoying newfound prosperity after a decade of economic growth. But not the impoverished villagers of Liangzhou, Gansu. They were forced to eke out a living on largely barren, sandy soul. Still bound by tradition, the villagers considered having a son to continue the family line an inviolate obligation to their ancestors. Those with means spent a large sum for their sons to marry; those who could not still found ways, one of which was to exchange daughters, like Ying'er and Lanlan in this novel. They fare differently with each other's brother, but their fates are similar. To break away so that one of them can live without spousal abuse and the other to be free of maternal pressure to remarry, they go into the desert to seek their fortune and change their lives. The journey, like their lives, is fraught with danger and hardships, and yet, with keen intelligence and dogged perseverance, they survive and make their way back home to the village. It is not a particularly successful trip, which is emblematic of daily realities in this part of the world, though both Ying'er and Lanlan learn something about themselves and about each other; they grow stronger and more resolute. Through their travails, we witness the powerful bond of sisterhood and, even in extreme poverty, the indomitability of the human spirit.

Xuemo has recreated a bygone village in Liangzhou, a place

265

where camels are as common as automobiles and potatoes replace rice. With his discerning eye for desert landscape, a fine ear for colorful local expressions, and an acute sensitivity to the inner world of his characters, the final result was a trilogy of more than a million words and dozens of characters involved in gripping incidents. Surely, we knew, it would be virtually impossible to publish all three volumes to share with the English reading world. But, we believed, the story of Ying'er and Lanlan is so captivating that it would have been a shame not to make it available.

In late 2020, as we entered our first winter of pandemic-imposed isolation, we realized how indispensable reading a good book was to our life. Not being able to travel, reading was our only means of leaving our confinement and being transported to a different world. We thought we would do the same for English readers, and contacted Xuemo, asking about excerpting sections of his trilogy to create a new, smaller, but equally powerful narrative. We are grateful to the author for giving us permission and his full support to edit and make necessary adjustments to ensure the narrative flow. What you have read derives from two volumes of his *Desert Trilogy*: from *White Tiger Pass* came the two women's journey into the desert, their adventures at the salt lakes, and their return home; *Desert Rites* provided us with their background stories, including Lanlan's abuse by her husband and the death of her daughter, as well as Ying'er's affair with her brother-in-law and her husband's death from liver cancer.

Xuemo writes with compassion and presents an evocative picture of life in the desert, and we hope the present volume has given you a vivid glimpse into his world. Once again, we extend our gratitude to him for his confidence in us and his unwavering support over the years of translating his novels (six to date). Our friend George Sidney read an early version and offered his astute comments and suggestions. He is a reader any writer/translator could hope for. And to Chris Robyn, our publisher, our thanks for always being interested in our work and for taking on this hybrid project. A less courageous publisher would have said no to such an unconventional work.

As the pandemic continues to shut us in, we are planning a similar volume, this time focusing on two male characters from the novels, in which hunting down poachers, panning and digging for gold, murder and suicide, and more provide a compelling read. So, until next time, when we go into the desert again!

S. L.
H. G.